∽

*Prepare yourself for combat, came
the nerve-shaking reply. You asked for
something you can fight. I will oblige you.*

The air in the cave was cool, but not cold. She
began to strip, preparing herself mentally. She
peeled everything down to her woolen layer, leaving the clothing in a pile on the cave floor. Her
mind took careful inventory of her physical condition, and she was unhappy with what she found.
She'd never taken on a fight in worse shape.

Nothing to it, she thought as she unsheathed
Lightning and loosened her arms. *Next time I go
after something, I hope it's in a dusty corner where no
one sees or cares if I take it. I did ask for this.*

Something padded toward her in the tunnel.
Moving into the center of the cave, Alanna set
herself.

When it came into the light, she understood
instantly that Chitral had assumed this form—she
couldn't say how she knew it, but she did. He'd
come as one of the great rock-apes that inhabited
the Roof of the World. Incredibly shy of people,
they were seldom seen, and they never carried short
swords as this one did. The blade was black iron
and very primitive, but Alanna had no doubt it
would do the job intended for it. *Oh, gods*, she
thought as the ape squared off against her, its deep-
set eyes bright with intelligence. *I'm in for it now.*

Lioness Rampant

Song of the Lioness
Book Four

TAMORA PIERCE

Random House ⌂ New York

Library of Congress Catalog Card Number: 88-6213
ISBN: 0-679-80113-8
RL: 6.3

Printed in the United States of America
OPM 20 19 18 17 16 15 14

To my husband, Tim, who is teaching me
that "the M word" can be a good word.
And to my editor, Jean Karl,
who changed her initial "no" to "yes."

❧

Acknowledgments

Now that Alanna's story winds down to a close (as far as I am concerned), I'd like to thank some of the people who helped and supported me during the telling: Claire M. Smith and my friends at Harold Ober; my family, Ma, Pa, and the Cap'n, and my spouse, Tim; the crazy guys of ZPPR Productions, with a special mention to George Zarr, who mapped Alanna's world, and to Pam Peterson, who served as my own patron of the arts through some hard times; to Pat, Ev, Rosy, Dawn, and the other bushi and samurai of the Investment Leasing Division; to Steve McConnell and Vic Doria, whose "attack secretary" came with an extra string to her bow; to Peter and James Thomas of Books of Wonder, the best bookstore in the universe; to David Fickling across the Big Pond; to the girls of the McAuley Home, who taught me the basics of storytelling for teenagers; and to David Bradley, a most unusual Obi-Wan Kenobi.

Contents

Lioness Rampant

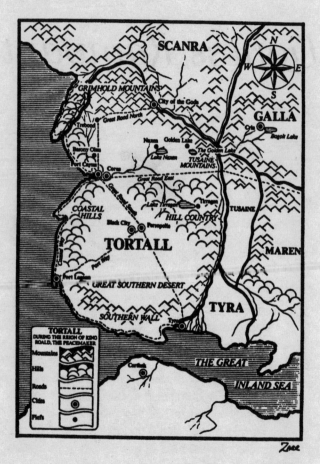

SCANRA

GRIMHOLD MOUNTAINS

City of the Gods

GALLA

Orts

Bagok Lake

Trebond

Great Road North

Barony Olau

Port Caynn

Corus

Nazen

Golden Lake

Lake Naxen

The Golden Lake

TUSAINE MOUNTAINS

Great Road East

COASTAL HILLS

Lake Tirragen

Tirragen

TUSAINE

Black City

Persopolis

HILL COUNTRY

TORTALL

MAREN

Port Legann

Port Roy

GREAT SOUTHERN DESERT

TYRA

SOUTHERN WALL

Tyra

Carthak

THE GREAT

INLAND SEA

TORTALL
DURING THE REIGN OF KING
ROALD, THE PEACEMAKER.

Mountains

Hills

Roads

Cities

Fiefs

Zace

one

Lioness from Tortall

On a March afternoon a knight and a man-at-arms reached the gates of the Marenite city of Berat. The guards hid their smiles as they looked the noble over—in size the beardless youth could as well have been a squire, with only a shield to reveal his higher rank. They wondered aloud if the youngster could *hold* his lance, let alone unseat an opponent with it. Hearing them, the knight favored them with a broad grin. The guards, liking his reaction, fell silent. The man-at-arms gave a tug on their packhorse's lead rein, and the small party moved through the gates into the city.

Most nobles dressed richly, but this knight wore well-traveled leather, covered with a white burnoose like those worn by the Bazhir of the Tortallan desert. With the burnoose's hood pushed back, everyone could see that the knight's hair was copper, cut so it brushed his shoulders. His eyes were an odd purple shade that drew stares; his face determined. Before him, in a cup fixed to his mare's saddle, rode a black cat.

The man-at-arms was dressed like the knight.

There were no grins for him—he was a burly, dark-haired commoner with no-nonsense eyes. It was he who asked directions to the inn called the Wandering Bard while the knight looked with interest at the streets around them. They set off in the direction of the inn, picking their way through the crowds with ease.

The cat swiveled his head, looking up at the knight. *They think you're a boy.* To most, his utterances sounded like those of any cat; to the few he chose, he spoke as plainly as a human.

"Good," the knight replied. "That's less fuss over me."

Is that why you left your shield covered?

"Be sensible, Faithful," was the tart reply. "The shield's covered because I don't want it to get all over dust. It takes forever to clean it. This far south, who'd've heard of *me*?"

The man-at-arms, who'd drawn level with them, grinned. "Ye'd be surprised. News has a way of travelin'."

∾

The common room of the Wandering Bard was deserted except for the innkeeper, Windfeld, who was resting after the noon rush. He'd just begun his own meal when a stable boy charged in.

"Y'want t'hurry, master," the boy puffed, excited. "They's a knight in th'yards—a Tortall knight!"

"What of that?" Windfeld replied. "We've had knights at the Bard afore."

"Not a knight like this'un," the boy announced. "This'un be a *girl!*"

"Don't joke with me, lad," Windfeld began. Then he remembered. "That's right. Sir Myles wrote me of the lass he adopted a year past. Said she went as a lad for years, as page and squire, 'till she was knighted. That was when our stables almost burned, and I didn't pay his letter the attention I ought. What's her shield?"

"Shield's a-covered," was the reply. "But her man wears a pin like one. It's red, with a gold cat a-rearin' on it."

"That's her—Alanna of Trebond and Olau, Sir Myles's heir." Windfeld got up, removing his apron to throw it on the table. "And with the Shang Dragon here already! It's bound to be a good week. The stableyard, you said?"

∾

*A*lanna of Trebond and Olau, sometimes called "the Lioness" for the cat on her shield, was surprised to be greeted by the innkeeper. The host of such a prosperous house did not meet his guests unless they were wealthy or famous. Since she had lived in Tortall's Great Southern Desert for over a year, Alanna did not realize *she* had become famous.

Afoot, her cat cradled in her arms, she was

short and stocky—sturdy rather than muscular. She did not look as if she could have disguised her sex for years to undergo a knight's harsh training. And she certainly did not look as if she would excel at her training to the point where some—men who were qualified to judge such matters—would call her "the finest squire in Tortall."

She also did not look like the adopted heir of one of her realm's wealthiest noblemen. "I don't know if Sir Myles told you," Windfeld explained, "but I'm honored to serve his interests here in Berat. I bid you and your man welcome to the Wanderin' Bard." He nodded to the man-at-arms, who supervised the stabling of the horses. "Whatever you wish, just let my folk know. Would the two of you like a cool drink, to lay the dust?"

"I'll see to the packs and the rooms," the man told them. "I know," he said quickly as his knight-mistress opened her mouth. "Ye're wantin' a bath; hot water, soap, and soon." He grinned at Windfeld. "She's that finicky, for a lass who's livin' on the road."

Alanna shrugged. "What can I say? I like to be clean. Thanks, Coram."

"He's been with you long?" Windfeld asked, as he showed her into the common room, indicated a seat, and sat down facing her.

"Forever," Alanna replied. "Coram changed my diapers, and he never lets me forget it. He helped raise my twin brother and me." To a maid who'd come to ask what she'd like, Alanna said, "Fruit juice would be wonderful, if you have it."

The innkeeper smiled as the servant girl left. "The Wanderin' Bard has whatever may hit your fancy, Lady Alanna. How is your honored father, if you don't mind my askin'?"

The maid returned with a pitcher and a tankard on a tray, presenting them to Alanna. Taking a swallow from her tankard, the knight sat back with a sigh. "He was fine when last I heard from him two months ago. Coram and I've been on the road for weeks. I've never been out of Tortall before, so we took our time. Maren doesn't seem much different."

Windfeld grinned. "Nor should it, Tortall and Tusaine and Maren bein' cut from the same cloth. Things change, east of here."

Alanna saw a shadow cross her host's face. "Trouble?"

"Just the sickness that comes on a land now and then," was the reply. "There's war in Sarain the last eighteen months or so. Only a Saren could tell you what started it, or what'll finish it. But there," Windfeld added, seeing a chambermaid at the door. "Your rooms be ready, along with your bath."

The knight picked up her cat, who was playing with Windfeld's apron. "Come on, Faithful," she groaned, settling him over her shoulder. "Let's get clean."

A chill went through the innkeeper as he

watched them go. Only now had he seen that the cat's eyes were not a proper shade of amber, green, or grey; they were as purple as Alanna's. Instinctively he made the Sign against Evil.

～

*T*he bath was everything a worn and dirty knight could wish: large enough to fit all of her and filled with hot water. She splashed contentedly, rinsing a week's grit from her hair.

Tongue and paws are all I need, Faithful commented.

"Is that why you smell after a night in the woods?" demanded Alanna.

Faithful ignored her, curling up on the bed. Alanna made a face at him and reached for the copper pitcher filled with rinse water. Sunlight hit its side, dazzling her. Her blinded vision held an image: *A gem, blue-violet, the size of a silver noble piece, set into a disc of gold, its facets absorbing light, not reflecting it. Beyond it was snow, a blizzard's worth.*

The picture faded when she blinked. She knew there was no sense in worrying about it. Sooner or later she would find out what it meant—she'd had the vision before. In the meantime, her bath was getting cold.

Coram knocked as she combed her hair. "I've eaten," he called through the door. "I'll find out where your scholar lives, then have a bit of enjoyment. Do us both a favor and stay out of trouble."

"I can take care of myself," she reminded him.

"That's what worries me."

"Have fun," Alanna called as his footsteps retreated, thinking, *Why is he worried?* She rarely sought trouble. Tonight she planned to avoid it entirely.

Downstairs, Faithful abandoned her for the kitchen. Alanna found a corner where she would have a good view of the rest of the common room. While the Wandering Bard seemed respectable, she'd been traveling long enough to know she could never be *too* prepared. Adjusting her sword—so she'd have room to draw it if necessary—she settled back to enjoy the meal.

Windfeld came over after she finished. "If there's anything you want, anything at all, you've only to ask," he assured her, taking a chair at her invitation. "No service is too great for Myles of Olau's heir, not in a house of mine. He pays us well as his agents—a generous man, your father."

Alanna smiled. "He's generous with everything." Remembering what Windfeld had said earlier, she asked, "What's going on in Sarain?"

The innkeeper looked away. "She rips herself apart. The K'miri tribes hunt lowlanders through the mountains, sometimes on the Southern Plain itself. The mountain-born come west in flocks, runnin' from the fightin'. The lowlanders are so busy slayin' K'mir that they let all else go, even the harvest. Only when their belts could be tightened no more did the Warlord bring in paid soldiers and send the lowlanders back to their farms. The refugees talk of little but hunger and killin'. My wife's Saren—it breaks her heart, and no end in sight." He forced a smile and added, "Enough of such doom-talk. What brings you here, my lady—if I can be so bold as to ask?"

"We're looking for a scholar," Alanna explained. "Nahom Jendrai."

"Another friend of your father's. He's well thought of, is Master Jendrai."

"I need him to translate something." Alanna reached inside her tunic to draw out a leather envelope. Carefully she opened it and unfolded its contents: a map of the Eastern Lands and the Inland Sea, charred at the left and top edges. Only natural landmarks—rivers and mountain ranges—were shown. A tiny star marked a spot in the Roof of the World, the great mountain range that cuts off the Eastern Lands from the rest of their world. Silvery runes—the writing that brought her to Maren for a translation—formed a column on the right side. "This looks like the Old Ones' writing," she explained. "Myles says the best translator is Nahom Jendrai of Berat."

Windfeld touched the charred edges. "How did this happen, my lady? Do you know?"

Alanna ran her fingers over the map. "You know Coram and I've been living with the Bazhir?"

Windfeld nodded. "Our headman, Halef Seif, was worried about a friend of his, a shaman living near Lake Tirragen. Coram and I went to see her." She drew a breath. "Her village was having a bad winter, what with famine and cold. A wandering priest had convinced the people that if they 'purified' themselves—if they killed their sorceress—his god would put food in their storehouses."

"I've seen things like it. Folk aren't sensible when they're hungry."

"Coram and I got there as they started to burn her. We stopped it and got her away, but…She was hurt too badly for me to fix." In answer to his questioning look, she explained, "I know some healing magic. Anyway, she died. The map was all she had. She asked us to take it back to Halef Seif."

"And he sent it to Master Jendrai for readin'?" Windfeld asked.

Alanna shook her head. "He didn't want it. He gave it to me—said it was for me, not him." She smiled wryly. "Halef Seif can be determined when he likes. He says he's happy with the Bloody Hawk—that's our tribe. Some of it didn't make sense, what he said, about destiny and quests. So here I am."

Windfeld rose in answer to a yell for service. "You've come a long way for curiosity, my lady."

Alanna grinned at him. "I didn't have anything more important to do."

There was another yell; with a voice that shook

the rafters, Windfeld bellowed, "Just hold on, Joss, you'll be served afore you go home!" He bowed to Alanna and went to help the barkeep.

A maid placed a glass of wine in front of Alanna. "*He* sent it t'you, my lady," the girl explained, pointing to a man by the hearth. "He said I was t'tell you redheads must sit together for safety's sake, and he wonders if you might join him when this glass is done." Leaning down, she whispered, "Not meanin' any disrespect, but if you don't want 'im, *I* do!"

Alanna looked at the man; he was toasting her. His eyes were blue-green in a tan, pockmarked face. His hair was as copper as hers, clipped short. His nose had met several hard objects. A mustache framed his sensual mouth; his jaw was heavy. He was in excellent fighting condition: broad shoulders, powerful chest, hard waist, heavily muscled limbs. He dressed as she did, in shirt and breeches. She also saw he carried no weapons, not even a dagger. To a knight this was important: the only men who went weaponless were sorcerers, priests, fools—or those who didn't need them. In a violent world, few did *not* need to carry some kind of weapon.

He shouldn't be attractive, not with a broken nose and his face all scarred. From what, I wonder? Bad skin as a boy, perhaps. But he is attractive! she thought nervously. *Why* is *he interested in me? I'm not as pretty as some of the other women here.*

She raised her glass and drank, her eyes not leaving his.

From her arrival at court until she'd won her shield, few had known she was female. Although Prince Jonathan had been her lover, he was also her friend and her knight-master; they hadn't needed the courting rituals Jon used with noble ladies. George Cooper, who also loved her, had flirted with Alanna sometimes; when he did it to the point of flustering her, she'd simply ordered him to stop. Of the other men she knew, most couldn't forget her knighthood enough to indicate a romantic interest in her. Since the revelation of her real identity and sex, the young knight had lived among the Bazhir. To them she was the Woman Who Rides Like a Man, and sexless.

So, though she wanted to join this man, or to indicate she was interested, Alanna didn't know how. How did a lady knight flirt with a total stranger? Noblewomen showed interest with fluttered fan or dropped handkerchief. Bazhir women used their eyes over their veils. She had no fan or veil. Her handkerchief wouldn't be noticed if she dropped it here. And she didn't have the courage to walk over to his table and sit down.

She didn't know pleading filled her eyes. He grinned—a slow, white-toothed smile that made her insides turn over—and came to her.

"Liam," he introduced himself, holding out a massive hand. "And you're Alanna the Lioness, from Tortall." She returned his firm grip; Liam's palm was warm and callused, like her own. "May I join you?" he asked, his eyes dancing. Alanna nodded, and Liam sat. "In Berat long?" he wanted to know, as the maid brought more wine and fruit.

Alanna shook her head. "Not for longer than I can help." She filled his glass. "I'd forgotten how noisy cities are. I've been with the Bazhir."

"So I heard. It took some asking to find out what happened after you killed the Conté Duke." He spoke with a peasant's broad vowels and nearly skipped r's.

She frowned. "You make it a habit to follow my doings?" She wasn't sure she liked the idea.

He nodded. "People like you change the world; a smart man keeps track of such folk. It was a great thing, killing your King's nephew and proving him a traitor. Duke Roger was a powerful man."

Alanna looked away, feeling cold. "He deserved to die. He tried to murder the Queen."

"It bothers you still?"

Looking at him, Alanna saw understanding. *He knows,* she thought. *He knows about things like betrayal, and being afraid, and the looks on people's faces when they know you did something they thought impossible.* "Sometimes. Everyone admired him. It all happened at once: me finding what he planned; him revealing that I'm a girl in front of the court. I wanted to have time for people to get used to who I really am!

"Then I killed him. I don't even *like* killing. So I wonder, sometimes."

"Don't fret." He took her hand and gave it a squeeze. "He was rotten clean through—take my word for it."

"You *knew* him?"

He nodded, his eyes a distant green. "We met— a long time ago."

"How? Why did you hate him? I mean, it seems as if you hated him. Everyone *I* knew liked him, nearly everyone." She sat up eagerly. "It isn't fair. You know everything about *me*."

He chuckled, his eyes warming. "I'll tell you someday, kitten—if you're *very* good." He smoothed his mustache.

She blushed. A cautious thought warned, *You'll be in trouble if you don't watch out! You don't know anything about him, and he's got you half into his arms!* She drew back. "You're flirting with me," she told him sternly.

"Fun, isn't it?" he grinned.

"Who *are* you? What do you do?" Alanna wanted to know. "Fair's fair!"

She stopped, hearing a commotion at the door. A familiar voice caroled, "Such sights the Princes never did see/And they honor the Beggar to this very day!" She winced.

"That's my friend Coram," she told Liam, rising. "If I don't stop him, he'll sing the verse with the merchants and the fishwives, and we'll all be in for it."

Liam's grin flashed. "I know the song." He kissed her hand. "You'll see me again—my word on it."

ᴄᴠ

*W*ith persuasion and bullying she got her boisterous man-at-arms to his chamber, where he collapsed on the bed. "Jendrai is back from his country house today," he yawned. "He'll see us tomorrow evenin'." Within seconds he was snoring.

Alanna let herself out of his room, planning to go to bed rather than look for the unsettling Liam again. She had unlocked her door when the innkeeper came up the stairs, rubbing his hands delightedly. Seeing her, he asked, "Be there anything else you need?"

"I'm fine," she reassured him. Nodding toward the noisy common room downstairs, she added, "It sounds like you have more than enough to do."

Windfeld beamed. "It's a good house tonight— a very good house. No surprise, with you and the Shang Dragon here."

"The Shang Dragon?" She'd never had a chance to talk with one of the fabled Shang warriors. She'd always wanted to; now the gods had put her in the same inn with the best of them. "He's here? Will you introduce me?"

Windfeld looked at her strangely. "I didn't think you needed introducin', not with you and him talkin' like you were."

"Liam?"

"Liam Ironarm, the Dragon of Shang. He didn't tell you?" Alanna shook her head. "And you didn't know? He knows of you—he told me so this mornin.'"

"I don't know anyone in the Order of Shang," she informed him. "They don't associate much with nobles or with the Bazhir."

"Well, you seem to be on good enough terms with the Dragon," the man said slyly. Alanna blushed a beet red and went into her room with a hasty "Good night."

To give Windfeld and the Wandering Bard credit, it was not her bed or her room that kept her awake. The bed was comfortable; the walls were thick enough to muffle the common room's noise. At first it seemed as if little things kept her awake. First it was her cat, scratching on the door for admittance. Then it was the light of the full moon falling across her eyes, until she got up and drew the curtain across her window. Then she found the room stuffy. With a sigh she rose again to open the window only a crack, because the weather was still raw.

She couldn't clear her mind of thought. Partly it was the excitement of having a chance at last to talk with a Shang warrior. What she knew of the legendary order of warriors she'd learned piece-meal. Warriors named after mythical beasts—unicorn, griffin, phoenix—were the best of their order:

the Dragon was the best of the best. Each Shang warrior received an animal's name after passing an ordeal and then living in the world a year. She knew that Shang accepted boy and girl children, no older than seven years of age and as young as four, to study their hard way of life. The were required to master many kinds of weapons and, more interestingly, a number of barehand techniques of fighting.

So Liam was the Shang Dragon. That explained why he was bold enough—or uncaring enough—to go weaponless. He had little to fear from human predators. *He has dragon's eyes,* she thought, remembering how they changed color. *Pale green when he doesn't want to share anything with you, and*—she grinned—*blue-green when he's flirting.*

She finally gave up on sleep and dressed, thinking maybe a ride would settle her. Within moments she, Faithful, and her gold-colored horse Moonlight were galloping out of Berat. They rode on and on while Alanna remained deep in her thoughts, not noticing how much ground they covered. She paid little attention to the road or the fog that closed in. She was too preoccupied.

All her life she'd planned to be a knight-errant, roving the world to do great deeds. But now she was learning that such a life included periods of boredom, riding through countryside that seldom changed. Not every village had a cruel overlord; few crossroads were held by evil knights.

At home, if the King wished it, he could put her

on border patrols like the other knights she knew, hunting bandits and raiders. But she didn't think the King *would* give her such work. Roald was most displeased that she had lied about who she truly was. A quiet man who preferred harmony at his court, the King said little, but he left Alanna no doubt that he disapproved of her.

In any case, she *knew* Tortall. She wanted to go places she *didn't* know. She wanted to see places left off most Tortallan maps—the lands south of Carthak; the Roof of the World and what lay beyond it. Surely there would be things for her to do once she'd left the more civilized areas behind.

Moonlight stopped, tossing her head nervously, and Alanna had to take notice. By then the fog was so thick she couldn't see the road beneath the mare's feet. The knight dismounted, taking the reins to lead her mare, but they had plodded only a few yards when Moonlight halted, ears flat with alarm. No amount of urging would make her go forward, which worried her mistress. Moonlight was careful, but not timid. If she thought something was wrong, Alanna paid attention. She looked at Faithful. The cat sat calmly in his saddle-cup, ears pricked forward. Fog held them; it muffled even the clink of the harness.

Now Alanna felt something odd. She sneezed. The emberlike stone she wore at her throat burst into fiery light, growing warm against her skin. In front of them the fog wove and braided itself to form a tall woman. She was green-eyed and black-haired, shining in her own magic light. The fog was her dress, glittering with drops of water.

Alanna had only seen her once before, when the woman had given her the emberstone. Now she released the reins and dropped to her knees, bowing her head. "Goddess," she whispered.

"Where do you ride, my Daughter?" The immortal's voice was beautiful and terrible, carrying echoes of the wind and of hounds in a pack. "Is it not late for a ride for pleasure?"

"I couldn't sleep, my Mother."

A cool hand cupped Alanna's chin, making her look up. She met the Great Goddess's eyes without flinching, even though her body was quivering. "You have achieved all you desired, have you not? A shield is yours, rightfully won. You have slain your greatest enemy. What do you seek now, Alanna?"

Alanna shrugged. "I don't know. I feel there's something *important* I should be doing, but I have no idea what it is. I'm just—drifting. That's why I brought the map here to be translated. Maybe it'll point me toward— Unless you need me for something?" she asked, hopeful.

The Goddess smiled. "I do not plan mortals' lives for them, Alanna. *You* must do that for yourself. However, if you follow the map, you will find its path interesting. But think as you ride." She picked up Faithful, who'd been waiting at her feet. "What will become of you? Will you drift all your days?"

Faithful chirped to the Goddess, his tail waving, and she smiled at him. Now that he had the Mother's attention, he addressed her at length. Try though she might, Alanna couldn't tell what he said.

Finally the Goddess put him down. The edges of her form grew indistinct, blending with the fog once again. "For a while longer, my friend," she told the cat. "Do not disappoint me." Faithful returned to Alanna, who held him close. The immortal was now a shadow, her voice distant. "Who will you be, Alanna?" She was gone.

For the first time since she'd saddled Moonlight, Alanna paid attention to her surroundings. She was in a forest, and that was baffling. This was the same road she and Coram had taken on their way to Berat. That morning they'd left the woods just after dawn, entering farm country. How could she have done a day's ride in a few hours?

The fog was still too thick for safe riding. Finding a rock, the knight sat to await the dawn, feeling cold, damp, and tired. She was beginning to nod off when the breezes came to scatter the mist, unveiling the road. Yawning, she mounted up and urged Moonlight into a trot. Faithful went to sleep without a word. Alanna envied him. Her jaws cracked every time she yawned, and her eyelids felt heavy. At last she dozed.

A jolt—then a burst of pain as she struck the road—woke her. Like the stablemen and troopers who'd taught her, she filled the air with curses.

There were words for people who fell asleep and dropped from their saddles!

Moonlight stared at her mistress, wondering why Alanna had chosen to dismount and sit in the mud.

Swearing doesn't help, Faithful remarked. *Besides, you woke me up.*

"Does your worship want me to pull the curtains so the light won't hurt your eyes?" Alanna yelled, beet red with embarrassment. "Shall I call you for the noon meal, or will you sleep the day out?"

There's no talking to you when you're like this, was the cat's smug reply. He went back to sleep.

Moonlight nudged her. With a groan, Alanna rose. "I can only blame myself," she growled. "I could've gone to a convent, never learned to wrestle and be dumped on my head, never have broken any bones or fallen in the dirt. I'd be clean and wear pretty dresses. By now I'd be married to a buffle-brained nobleman with a small fief. I'd probably even have clean, pretty, buffle-brained children." Trying to wipe her hands before taking the reins, she found her breeches were as muddy as her hands. "Don't remind me *I* picked this life. I've no one to blame but myself." Moonlight shook her head as if to say she wouldn't. "I always knew there was insanity in my family."

Alanna heard hoofbeats and froze. She didn't want a passerby to see her in this fix! Determinedly, she looked away as the other horse came closer. Her hands tightened on Moonlight's reins as her face went a darker red. *If a stranger sees me, that's bad, she told herself. The worst that can happen is for this to be Liam Ironarm, and me falling off my horse like an incompetent.* She turned.

It *was* Liam. He was not trying to hide his grin. "Nice morning for a ride," he greeted her. "A little wet, though."

Alanna swallowed, fighting her temper. "I don't normally *do* this, you know!"

"Not for a moment did I think it."

"Why are you here, anyway?" she demanded, too embarrassed to be polite. "It's a long way for a morning ride!"

"I saw you go out. When you didn't come back, I thought I'd check." Too kindly, he added, "Oh, don't think I figured you'd run out on Windfeld's bill. You left your man and your bags, so I *knew* it wouldn't be that."

Alanna gasped with fury. "How *dare*—"

"Don't like to be teased, is that it?" Relenting, he said, "Hitch the mare to a lead and ride double with me. I'll keep you a-horse."

"I'll be fine!"

With a sigh the redheaded man dismounted. "Didn't your mamma teach you to speak polite to strangers on the road?" He put Moonlight on a lead with his big-boned grey. "I could be a sorcerer and turn you into a mouse."

"You're the Shang Dragon. You won't turn me into *anything*."

"Don't worry about it," he said cheerfully. "I pull on my breeches one leg at a time, same as you." Unstrapping a blanket from his saddle, he wrapped it around her. "There now. You're tired and wet and grumpy—in no condition to ride. I fell asleep once, Alanna the Lioness. A tree knocked me from the saddle into a ditch, right in front of the men I was to command. Bless their hearts, they didn't tease me about it—not much. Up with you." He threw her into the saddle as easily as if she were a child, mounting behind her and settling her in the circle of his arms.

"Go to sleep, kitten," he murmured. His voice rumbled in his deep chest. "You're all right now."

⮔

Coram awoke late, with a head he would not wish on his worst enemy. For a long time he waited for his knight-mistress to arrive with her hangover cure. When she did not appear, he went in search of her. It hurt even to dress. It would be worth her heartless quips to rid himself of the headache and nausea.

After the pain of dressing, he was in no humor to find a stranger letting himself out of Alanna's room. Hadn't she been talking to this redheaded fellow in the common room the night before? Coram couldn't remember.

He barred Liam's path. "I suppose ye've excellent reasons for bein' in there, all of which ye'll tell me without delay." Alanna had friends to protect her name and person, as this man was about to learn!

The Dragon grinned, recognizing the older man. "You must be Coram."

"I am. That tells me nothin' about ye."

Liam eyed the burly man-at-arms. "It seems to me the young lady takes care of herself."

"I suppose ye had that from her," snapped Coram. "She's wrong. Is there someone in the city who'll speak for ye?" His hand shifted warningly to his dagger hilt.

"The Shang Dragon needs nobody to speak for him." Liam's eyes went a pale green. "I understand your wanting to protect her, but I don't like threats."

Coram frowned. "I'm t'*believe* ye're Liam Ironarm?"

"Come downstairs, before she hears you," Liam sighed. "Windfeld knows me."

The host's verification of the Dragon's identity told Coram it was time to change tactics. So he invited Liam to share his morning meal, and the food eased his hangover. He could concentrate better on quizzing the redheaded man.

"Does she know?" he asked. "Lady Alanna?"

A slow grin spread across Liam's face. "She knows."

"No doubt she's in a dither tryin' to decide what she wants to ask ye first." Coram thought for a moment, then met the Dragon's now-grey eyes. "What's the likes of ye want with Alanna of Trebond?"

The big man shrugged. "She's a pretty thing— different, and full of fight. I never heard that she avoids men."

Remembering Prince Jonathan and the thief, George, Coram flushed. "She's *still* not a woman without all virtue."

Liam chuckled. "She's too good a warrior to have a bad reputation as a woman. At least, no one will call her bad when she might hear."

"I'd think the Shang Dragon had his pick of pretty ladies," growled Coram.

Liam rose. "Maybe. But she's not just that, is she? She's as known in her way as I am in mine." He put a massive hand on Coram's arm. "I'm not a village lad wanting to boast of having the Lioness's pelt in my hut, Master Smythesson. I like her. I'd probably like *you*, if you stopped glumping about my being in her room."

He left a coin for his food and strolled out as Coram sank his face into his hands. "Life used to be simple," he told his palms.

Faithful jumped up to sniff at Liam's plate. *Probably more boring, too.*

～

*A*fter running errands until noon, Coram returned to find Alanna dressed and cleaning her weapons. "Don't scowl," she told him. "I'm not awake."

"The chambermaid says yer clothes were all over mud. What kind of larks were ye kickin' up last night without me to keep an eye on ye?"

"I wasn't 'kicking up any larks,'" she yawned. "I couldn't sleep, so I went for a ride out of the city."

"Were ye ridin' under the horse's belly, then?"

Alanna could feel a blush creeping up her cheeks. "It's too embarrassing to talk about."

Coram wasn't to be so lightly dismissed. "Does this have anythin' to do with that Liam bein' in your room this mornin'?"

"I got tired and fell off my horse," Alanna said grumpily. "I met Liam on the road. He just made sure I got back all right. He never touched me."

"Maybe he didn't," Coram rumbled, as red as she was. "And maybe he's plannin' to."

Closing the door, he heard Alanna murmur, "Nothing wrong with that."

⟶

*T*hey reached House Jendrai as the sun touched the horizon, to be greeted by Nahom Jendrai in person. Alanna had expected him to resemble Myles of Olau—quiet, unkempt, and absent-minded. Instead, she and Coram found a trim man in his early thirties, surrounded by children, servants, pack animals, dogs, and baggage. He waved to Coram and waded out of the mess.

"My wife would greet you properly, Lady Alanna, Master Smythesson, but she has only recently come from childbed, and she is resting. Our sixth," he explained with a smile. "A girl." He accepted their congratulations with a bow, adding, "Excuse the bustle—our bags didn't come until this afternoon."

He led them into the house. "I'm happy to assist Myles's daughter. If it weren't for him, I'd be just another nobleman, administering my estates, worrying about how I stood with the King, and scheming to get into power at court. My wife handles the fief—better than I ever could—and the only kings I bother with are hundreds of years gone. I owe that to Myles. He was the best teacher I had. What an incredible mind!"

Alanna picked up Faithful, who was trading sharp words with a dog in the hall. "You were one of Myles's students?"

"For six years." He showed them into a room that was lit only by the dying sun. "I suppose it's too dark." He began a futile search for flint and steel. "I tell the maids I keep demons in here so they won't disturb anything. Unfortunately, I don't get my candles lit."

Alanna laughed. *Now* he reminded her of Myles. Pointing at the hearth logs, she sent her Gift out in a burst of violet until they caught flame. With quick gestures she shooed flames to the branches of candles.

Show-off, Faithful grumbled.

Alanna looked at him in surprise. "I am not. This is handier."

A year ago you would have taken forever to do it the hard way, the cat pointed out.

Alanna blushed. "A year ago I was different."

"Do they always chat like this?" Nahom Jendrai asked Coram.

"Often enough." The older man gave him the map.

Jendrai stretched the parchment out on a table, studying it for several minutes. Finally Alanna said, "Should we go and come back when you've had a chance to work on it?"

He glanced up, startled—clearly he'd forgotten they were there. "No, of course not. I can tell you what it says. Please, come closer." Alanna and Coram gathered around the desk, Faithful perched on the knight's shoulder.

Jendrai's finger traveled over the map's surface. "Here are the Eastern Lands, the Inland Sea, a bit of the Southern Lands. That's to locate the reader— this map isn't for everyday geography. Much is left out. There are cities, nations, roads—a hundred things not shown. Only the points of interest are here, at the eastern end of the Great Inland Sea.

"The mountains—these jagged lines—show the Roof of the World, east of Sarain. This valley lies inside the Roof's western edge, north of where Port Udayapur is now. At the valley's northern end are two passes, Lumuhu and Chitral. This star marks Chitral Pass." He tapped the silvery star embossed into the map. "Translated, the writing says, 'In Chitral's hidden chamber, guarded by the being whose essence is Time, the Dominion Jewel is kept for those with the will to strive. Take it at your risk, for the saving of a troubled land.'"

"The Dominion Jewel," Coram whispered.

Alanna shivered. "Fairy stories," she scoffed.

"Ye were impressed by those stories in yer day, Miss," retorted Coram. "Yer brother always wanted the tale of Giamo the Tyrant. *Ye* liked t'hear about Norrin and Anj'la." He looked at Nahom. "The Jewel is *real?*"

"Very real," the scholar replied. "In Maren we remember the changes made by King Norrin and Queen Anj'la, two centuries ago. Our wealth and peace are their legacy. We have had no wars or famines or plagues since their day." He rapped the table to ward off the evils he'd mentioned. "If you have a chance to visit the capital city, you might examine the stonework on the Great Temple of Mithros and on the ceremonial doors of the palace. The same motif is repeated over and over: Norrin's symbol, a snow-capped mountain, Anj'la's, a willow branch, and the Dominion Jewel between them. Marenites know what we owe to them and the Jewel."

"But it's been used for evil, too," Coram reminded Jendrai softly.

"Indeed." The younger man's face darkened. "Giamo stole the Jewel to build his Gallan Empire. With it he conquered parts of Tusaine, Tortall, and Scanra." Alanna saw Tusaine armies camped along the Drell River, as they had when she was a squire. She swallowed; her memories of the Tusaine War were unpleasant. "Someone stole it from Giamo's heir. His empire devoured itself, four hundred years ago.

"Fairy stories are important," Jendrai told Alanna. "Legends teach us and guide scholars in searching out the truth of history." He smoothed the map before folding it. "It would be the adventure of a lifetime to find the Dominion Jewel."

Faithful and Alanna looked at each other. The cat's ears had pricked forward at *adventure*. The knight thought it over. *If I win it and return home bringing the Dominion Jewel for the glory of Tortall, no one can suggest that I got my shield with magic and trickery. Instead of being his Majesty's most talked-of knight, I'll be the honored vassal who brought a prize to honor his reign.* Another voice in her mind whispered, *The Roof of the World! Did I ever meet anyone who'd been that far in his lifetime? It's a place to go. Someplace new. The Goddess said my path would be interesting.*

Nahom sighed and put the map away. "Seldom do I regret my family and my duty to them. This is one of those times. I would love to go seeking such a thing. What land wouldn't prosper with the Jewel in its ruler's hands?" He gave the map to Alanna.

"How does it work?" Alanna asked. She fingered the emberstone at her neck. "Do you have to be a sorcerer to wield it?"

"Giamo was no sorcerer," Coram pointed out. "Look at the damage *he* did."

"Norrin wasn't Gifted, either, although Anj'la knew herb-lore and healing magic," added Jendrai, scanning a scroll rack. "Here." He pulled out one, blew the dust from it (making Faithful sneeze), and unrolled it on the table. "This is in High Gaulish— do you read it?" Alanna and Coram shook their heads. "Here's the section I want. A rough translation is, 'Said Jewel worketh its power in two fashions. In the hands of the un-Gifted, it exerteth natural benefices, knitting its power with the Earth's own for as far as its ruler's holdeth sway.'" Stopping, he explained. "The Jewel only works for those who are rulers or conquerors *by nature*. It also explains why the Jewel was often better used by a commoner than by someone royal-born. Just because you're born to be a king doesn't mean you have the will for it.

"Where was I...? 'In the hand of one Gifted, one who understandeth the devices of sorcery, the Jewel may be more directly used, in healing and war, for fertility or death. A knowledgeable ruler, knowing fully the creation of magical formulae, may create new land from ocean deeps, or return the breath of a dead child. With its wielder's knowledge and the will to rule, the Jewel maketh possible all things.'"

"That's scary," Alanna whispered. "What could Roger have done with the Dominion Jewel?"

Coram said, "Thank the gods we'll never learn."

∾

Outside the air was raw, a reminder that winter was not done. Alanna shivered, walking briskly to keep up with Coram. Faithful trotted in front, sniffing the night wind. Alanna thought wistfully about the Bazhir lands—winter came to them as chilly rains, not snow and ice. She preferred the desert winter; she was afraid of cold weather, in a way she couldn't understand.

They weren't far from the inn when Coram spoke. "What will ye do?" Realizing she'd been thinking of something else, he explained, "The Jewel, my lady."

"I think we should find it."

"Knowin' how ye like the cold, I didn't think ye'd fancy the Roof."

Alanna made a face. "You're right. Still, if that's where the Jewel is—"

Faithful hissed, *We have company.*

Coram glanced around. "Rogues." His voice was loud enough for Alanna to hear, no louder. "Wantin' to take our purses, doubtless."

Alanna glanced to the corner ahead, where five men in dark clothing blocked their escape. She drew Lightning: it shimmered faintly. "Why so many of them for two of us?"

"Four more on yer right," Coram hissed. "Because they've little else to do?" Out came his broadsword.

Of the thieves, two held swords, two more carried short axes, three had iron-shod staffs. Alanna guessed that the others had knives. "Let us by," she ordered. "You don't want the trouble it'll take to get our money." She made the sign George taught her, the one to give her safe passage among rogues.

One of them stepped forward, his sword up. "Be ye Alanna of Trebond in Tortall? Her as claims she's a true knight?"

Coram bristled. "Ye'll find she's knight enough if ye step just a bit closer."

"Our business ain't with ye, master," someone else barked. "Leave now, else ye be hurt."

"I'll leave if ye do the same—or when ye're dead. It's all the same to me." Coram shifted his stance, planting himself firmly.

Alanna looked at the one who'd spoken first. "I'm Alanna of Trebond and Olau."

"We bring ye regards from him known as Claw, back in Tortall. He bids us tell ye mourn for yer lover now, whilst ye have breath. George Cooper will be dead afore summer, but we're to send *ye* t'the Black God first!"

He threw himself at Alanna, the swordsmen and staffmen following with a yell. Alanna moved until she and Coram were back to back, meeting the speaker's charge and knocking his weapon aside. He came at her again with a backhand chop, and she knew he'd had a little training. It wasn't enough compared to hers. She brought Lightning down across his chest, cutting deeply. He fell, and she looked for her next foe.

There was little room to maneuver, little chance to counter single opponents. The thieves understood simultaneous attack. Alanna and Coram blocked automatically, searching for anything that could be turned to their advantage. Hesitation now would mean death.

One of the staffmen swung and missed—she ran him through. Coram shouted fiercely, and someone screamed. When a swordsman looked to see the screamer's fate, Alanna slashed his leg. He dropped with a cry. A knife fighter rushed to pick up the fallen sword.

A black lump dropped from a roof, clinging to one man's scalp. Trying to dislodge Faithful, the thief fell into an axe's downswing. He lost his life. A second later the axeman was down, a victim of Alanna's rapid side-cut. She could hear Coram gasping. Sweat dripped into her eyes.

Alanna's left arm stung. She reversed Lightning in a crescent, killing the man who'd wounded her. She was bleeding, but she didn't dare stop to bind the cut.

Faithful launched himself again, yowling

fiercely. Coram shouted and was down, bleeding from the thigh. Alanna swung to stand over him, her brain coldly taking charge. Later she'd remember that sweat stung in her eyes, that her arm hurt, that she was scared for Coram. Now she blocked and cut like a machine, looking everywhere at once.

For a moment Lightning was caught under an axe blade. Trying to free her sword, Alanna was knocked down by a staff. Cursing, she rolled to her feet. Before she had her balance, two thieves leaped on her, forcing her down.

One gripped her arms, yanking them behind her back. Alanna bit her lip to keep from screaming. She'd always been afraid this would happen. Disarmed, in the clutch of a stronger opponent, she was trapped. The second rogue grinned at her, reaching for her tunic.

The street echoed with an animal roar. Something shot into the man in front of Alanna: he rammed into a nearby wall and was still. Liam hit the ground on both feet, spun and kicked back into an attacker. The man seemed to leap backward, sprawling yards away. The Dragon shifted, his leg furling up and out, streaking toward Alanna. She froze, and Liam's kick struck the man gripping her. She was free.

Liam grinned, then whirled to face the last killers. They fought and died, the street echoing with the Dragon's cry. Alanna's hands worked as she watched, cutting up her tunic for a bandage.

Kneeling by Coram, she examined his bleeding thigh.

"It's not bad," Coram assured her through clenched teeth. "I've had worse. He's a sight, isn't he?"

Alanna nodded as she tied the bandage over the wound, pressing to stop the bleeding. The stories she'd heard about Shang came nowhere near the truth. The Dragon went from blow to kick in a blur. When he struck a man, that man went down and stayed down.

"Ye're bleedin'," Coram rasped, holding her arm. "Ye must have it seen to."

Alanna barely heard him. Awed by Liam, she whispered, "I'll never be that good."

Coram snorted. "I've news for your ladyship." He sat up, replacing her hands on the bandage with one of his own. "Ye're just as quick, with a sword in yer hand."

Silence returned. Those of their attackers who were able had fled. The ones who remained were either too badly hurt to run or were dead.

The Dragon came to Alanna and Coram, examining a tear in his sleeve. "You're all right?" He looked worriedly at Alanna, who was beginning to feel dizzy and a little sick. Coram reached up, and Liam helped him to his feet. "I was coming back from the home of a friend, and I heard the noise. Don't you know enough to stay out of trouble?"

Faithful came out of the shadows, his tail

switching irritably. *We do, the man and I. She doesn't.*

Liam glanced down at the cat, frowning. "Did…? No." He caught Alanna as she faltered and dropped in a faint.

"It didn't look like a bad wound," Coram said, taking Alanna's left hand and examining the cut running across her forearm. Then he swore, seeing the wound reached up the back of her arm to the shoulder. Alanna's shirtsleeve was thick with blood. "I'll tear a bandage," he ordered Liam, pulling off his tunic. "We'd best take her to the inn fast—Windfeld can fetch a healer." Quickly he reduced the garment to strips and formed a bandage for the knight's arm. Once it was in place, he set off down the street.

"Does she often do this?" the Dragon asked, following with Alanna.

"She's worn herself out other ways before this, silly lass. She's quick t'tell ye when to stop, but she never thinks maybe she should listen to her own advice."

When they reached the Wandering Bard, Windfeld took over. In the space of a few minutes a healer was seeing to Alanna while another stitched Coram's thigh. Liam went to the kitchen and returned with a mug of tea for Coram. The man-at-arms took one sniff and coughed.

"What've I ever done to ye?" he demanded.

Liam grinned. "It smells better than it tastes.

Drink it—I've had to myself. Shang taught us all manner of herb-lore, in case we get caught with no healer near."

Coram shrugged and obeyed, choking as the stuff went down. He felt better almost immediately. "Whatever it is, it works. I don't *want* t'know what it is," he said quickly when Liam opened his mouth.

"It's only herbs. Your lady gets the same, when she wakes up. Now—who were those men?"

"Messengers, of a kind. From an enemy of—of a friend of hers." Coram blushed. Liam raised an eyebrow, but the older man shook his head. He was *not* going to tell an almost-stranger, not even this one, the whole truth. "Someone who knew that if she was killed, it'd hurt Cooper—her friend."

Liam yawned and stretched. Coram was envious. The redheaded man looked as if he'd been exercising hard, not fighting. "Well, this Cooper's unhurt, and the two of you will heal."

Coram got up stiffly and offered Liam his hand. "We owe ye our lives. We won't forget."

Liam returned his grip. "You'd've managed, I think. I just speeded things along."

two

The Road East

She supposed she was sleeping. Her twin brother, the sorcerer Thom, stood before a tomb with his hands upraised. His Gift, violet-colored like her own, glittered around him. Thom was pale, sick-looking. The door to the tomb began to open.

Thom looked at her. "I don't have enough power to shut it. I need your Gift. And I need that." He reached for the emberstone at her throat. She clung to it. "No, Thom! The Goddess gave it to me. I'll never take it off!"

"Calm down." The voice was male, warm. "Keep your trinket."

She dreamed again. George Cooper sat at Myles's desk, staring moodily at a painting. With surprise she saw it was a miniature of her in gold-washed chain mail, her lioness shield at her feet. Did he have it painted from his description of her?

There were silver threads in his dark hair. "But you aren't even thirty!" she protested.

He didn't hear. "Who will you be, my darlin'?" he asked the painting.

The door flew open. Jonathan entered, looking as

if he'd been in a fight. "I hear the Earth cracking," he
whispered.

Her eyes flew open. "Coram!" she yelled, scared
because she felt so weak. She was in bed.

"He's sleeping." Liam stood beside her, a steam-
ing mug in his hands. "He didn't lose as much
blood as you, but he still tires fast."

Alanna sat up. Outside rain fell; somewhere
closer a fire crackled. If only her head would stop
spinning! "How'd you get to be assistant nurse?"

He winked at her. "Coram trusts me. Don't
you?"

In spite of herself, Alanna smiled. "Not a bit."

Liam shook his head. "So young, and so cyni-
cal. Drink this."

Coram would have warned her about the brew,
had he been there. As it was, she took a good swallow before she even noticed the smell. It was nasty,
bitter stuff with herbs in it. Her stomach tried to
heave. With an act of will Alanna made it stay put.
Closing her eyes, she went back to sleep.

∽

*L*iam was by the fire when she woke again.
Faithful curled beside him, purring—the big man
plainly had the cat's approval. The scent of meat
cooking rose from downstairs, making Alanna's
mouth water. She was hungry!

Liam smiled. "About time." He gave her another
mug of tea, one that smelled far better than the

last. "Sit up and try this. If it stays down, you can eat."

Alanna obeyed, still amazed that the Shang Dragon should have an interest in her. His tea tasted of cinnamon and oranges.

His eyes held hers until she blushed. Lifting her hand, he kissed it—his lips were warm. *This gets more interesting all the time!* she thought.

"Enough of that." It was Coram, bearing a heavily laden tray. "If ye're not embarrassin' each other, ye might think of *my* tender feelin's."

Liam helped with the tray. "*Your* tender feelings?" he joked. "You haven't any."

Alanna watched as they set out the food. Clearly they'd become friends, which was good if Liam pursued her (as he clearly meant to). Coram was difficult if he didn't approve of her romances. His feelings had made for an uncomfortable week in George's Port Caynn house, until the two men came to a truce (it helped that Coram had fallen in love with George's cousin Rispah).

She watched the Dragon, remembering what she'd seen of his fighting. *What was he like with sword or axe? If he was as fast with weapons as he was unarmed, he'd be almost unstoppable. She was good with sword and axe and bow, but take away her weapons and she was in trouble.*

How can he want me? she asked herself, puzzled. *He could have any woman—why pick one who's not even very feminine?* She took the tray he gave her, blushing when their hands touched. *Well, that's part of it*, she thought as she spooned up soup. *Sheer physical attraction.*

Once the servants cleared the dishes, the three settled back to talk. "Coram showed me your map," Liam informed her. "He tells me you're bound for the Roof of the World."

"Coram's been very talkative," she said dryly.

The older man flushed. "Liam's been about these parts a bit, Miss. If he can advise us on the road to take, so much the better!"

Alanna turned to Liam. "Well?"

"You should avoid Sarain."

"Is their civil war so bad?"

Peeling an orange, he nodded. "Do you know *anything* about the Saren?"

"Some," she replied, bristling at the hint she was ignorant. "I had an *excellent* education."

He looked doubtful. "Nobles rarely know as much as they think they do—not about the real world. Who rules Sarain?"

Alanna scowled. She had not thought Liam might have a side she *didn't* like, but this older-and-wiser-head approach got under her skin. "The *jin* Wilima—their title is warlord, not king. The current one is—uhm—Adigun, the third *jin* Wilima ruler. Two years ago rebels tried to overthrow him and crown Dusan *zhir* Anduo in his place. *Zhir* Anduo's descended from their former kings, the *zhirit* Kaufain."

Coram gave the Dragon an elbow in the ribs. "So there."

"You *are* educated," chuckled Liam.

Alanna glared at both men. "My adoptive father keeps up with things. He says *zhir* Anduo's rebels won't unseat their Warlord."

"That was true once." Liam poked the fire and added another log. "*Jin* Wilima bought mercenaries last spring. They destroyed towns, crops—people." His eyes turned icy green. "The K'mir rebelled against both sides."

"The K'mir are tribesmen, like our Bazhir," explained Coram.

"*Jin* Wilima married one—her name was Kalasin." Liam scratched Faithful's upturned chin. "The most beautiful woman in the world."

"What happened to her?" Alanna sat up, hugging her knees, intrigued by this glimpse of an alien society.

Liam shook his head. It was Coram who answered quietly, "Killed herself last summer. Her daughter Thayet's as lovely as she was, they say."

"But Thayet isn't the heir," Liam said. "The throne's up for whoever can take it, and the K'mir promise to fight the winner."

Alanna thought it over. "Can we avoid passing through Sarain?"

"Get a boat out of Fortress Jirokan at the border," Liam told her. "Take it down the Shappa, then a coastal runner to Udayapur—"

Alanna blanched. "No boats!" The handful of times she'd been in one, she had been disgracefully sick.

Coram grinned. "I told ye, lad."

The Dragon smoothed his mustache. "Then take the Shappa Road to the Inland Sea, and the Coast Road east. The war's in the mountains and highlands, not down by their coast."

Alanna struggled with a yawn. Liam rose. "Past your bedtime, little girl. I'll ride with you as far as the Saren border, whichever way you choose."

Alanna consulted Coram with a look; he nodded his approval. "We'll be glad to have your company." She added, "I always wanted to learn Shang fighting—the unarmed kind."

Liam shook his head. "You're too old."

Alanna glared at him. "First you call me 'little girl' and then you say I'm too old. Make up your mind."

"And *then* she'll go to a great deal of effort t'prove ye wrong," Coram joked as the opened he door for Liam. Returning to his knight-mistress, he drew his chair over to the bed. "I like him. *He* won't let ye run him ragged."

Alanna fidgeted with her blankets. "You don't look ragged to me."

"I put on a brave front," he teased. More seriously, he went on, "Have ye decided which road we'll take?"

"I like going straight through Sarain. We can

deal with bandits, one way or another."

Startled, Coram asked, "Ye'll use yer Gift?"

"What's wrong with that?"

The man shrugged. "I don't know. I had the thought ye didn't care to mix fightin' and magic."

"I don't care to get either of us killed, if it comes to that. We can avoid the armies, if any of them are in the highlands this time of year. That way, we come to the Roof just five days' ride from Chitral Pass. If we take the Coast Road, we'll be two weeks riding north from Udayapur. That's an extra nine days in those mountains in May or June." Alanna shivered.

Coram thought it over, then met her eyes. "Not t'mention ye think a ride through the Saren highlands will be more interestin'."

Alanna grinned. "There's that." She smothered a yawn. "Do me a favor, Coram?"

"It depends." Long experience with her had made him wary.

"Tell me a story of the Dominion Jewel, please," she suggested. "I've forgotten most of them."

He sat back. "A tale, then? Ye haven't asked me for one of them in years. Which one? Ah. Miache was a Carthaki waterfront thief, three hundred years ago. The Gallans hired her t'steal the Jewel from their own king, that was descended from Giamo—a great-great grandson, he was. Them that hired Miache wanted t'rule in his place.

"Miache stole the Jewel, right enough—and she

kept it. She ran for the River Drell, the same that's our border with Galla and Tusaine and Maren. She might've borne it home to Carthak, too, but for Zefrem the Bear. He was a mercenary, and a good one, headin' south on the river when he pulled Miache out of it. Before long they were lovers. She was a pretty thing, with hair like moonglow and a heart of pure ice. Zefrem cracked that heart some, though.

"When they came t'the city of Tyra, the Carthaki navy was attackin'. The local folk were starvin'. Their nobles had run; their rulin' duke was crazy. The only thing keepin' Carthak out was the walls, and they couldn't hold against Carthaki siege engines." Faithful jumped up on the bed and curled up beside Alanna while Coram poured himself a tankard of ale. He took a good swallow and continued.

"Zefrem, now, was never a man for a losin' fight, let alone one already lost. And Miache—she'd watch her own mother starve unless there was somethin' in it for her. All who knew them said it had t'be the Dominion Jewel that brought them t'stay in Tyra. They didn't even know how to use it, but it seems the Jewel used them.

"Zefrem took command, trainin' the men who were left and buildin' catapults to throw fireballs at the ships. Miache and the city's swimmers, some of them younglings, they'd swim out t'harry the Carthaki navy. They even sank some of the barges full of men and catapults. Miracles started happenin'—birds found nestin', when the city had none. Schools of fish appearin' in canals under the city, where no fish'd been before. Men and their families began to move into the city even durin' the war, t'make their homes and t'fight for Tyra. *They* didn't know why they came. It was the Jewel, callin' them.

"They saved Tyra, Miache and Zefrem and the Dominion Jewel. The city was a pirate's nest when they came, a sinkhole fit only for cutthroats and thieves. They made it a lawful tradin' city where a man's word was a bindin' contract. The man and woman vanished, and the Jewel came next to Norrin, but Tyra still prospers. That was three hundred years gone."

Alanna sighed when Coram finished, moved by his tale and the matter-of-fact way he'd told it.

He got up and stretched. "Anything else?"

"Coram, thank you. For everything—for bringing me up, and helping me…"

"There, now," he scolded gently. "Don't go all sentimental. Ye'll embarrass us both." Surprisingly, he bent and kissed her forehead. "Good night, yer ladyship."

～

*E*xperience had taught Alanna how long injuries took to heal and how far she could push herself during the recovery process. She hated to stay in bed any longer than necessary. Each hour there meant more work to return to peak condition. The day after she awoke, she was outside, going through sword exercises using Coram's broadsword. She was careful not to overdo or to rush, but she was persistent.

To the boys who loitered in the courtyard, she was a godsend. They jeered, at first. But once they saw that the lady knew how to use a sword, they grabbed sticks and imitated her. She paid them no attention. If she did, they would turn shy and run, afraid other boys would laugh. Instead, she pretended to be absorbed, and her imitators grew bolder. Their number increased. By her third day's exercise, ten of them followed her movements. So preoccupied were the boys that they didn't notice right away when Alanna began to correct a stance or a grip.

Liam watched. So did Coram. "She did the same for the Bazhir lads," he told the Dragon with pride. "She even taught our tribe's shamans, and her learnin' to be a shaman alongside them. Not bad for a noble, is it?"

Liam smoothed his mustache as he watched. "She's serious about learning Shang fighting?"

Coram nodded. "Perhaps I should've brought her to Shang when I saw how it was with her. But she was *Trebond*. I never heard of a noble comin' to ye without bein' thrown off by their families—and none of them were lasses."

"You did right," Liam said. "She's happy as the one lady knight in the Eastern Lands, your Lioness."

Coram made a face. "She's not *my* Lioness. Cooper's, perhaps, or Prince Jonathan's, but not mine."

"Yours," repeated Liam. "Yours, and Myles of Olau's, and her brother's. Cooper's, too. The Prince's certainly." He grinned. "Maybe even mine. Who knows?"

∾

*F*ive days after she began working out, Alanna put down Coram's sword with a grin. The boys couldn't understand why she was so glad to finish an *exercise;* for them the glory of fencing lay in the defeat of an opponent. Alanna knew she'd finished the hardest of her exercises with no mistakes, using a heavier sword than Lightning. Her body had complained only a few times, not very loudly. She was healed, and they could be on the road again!

Someone put Lightning's jewel-studded hilt into her hand. Puzzled, she looked up to see Liam.

"Now you're warmed up, let's see what you can do," he said.

It didn't sink in right away. "What?"

"A match," he explained patiently. "Swords alone. No kicks or punches. No tricks. I want to see how good you are."

Alanna shrugged. Moving into the center of the yard, she took a sideways "guard" stance. She fixed on the Dragon as he took a similar position. *He's bigger and faster, she calculated. He's more experienced, and his blade's heavier. If the stories are true, he's trained to be as good with either hand. Great Merciful Mother, what have I gotten myself into!*

She moved to the side just a bit. Liam's blade arced up and down with blinding speed.

Alanna swung Lightning up, blocked Liam's sword, then broke away. The Dragon came in with a side cut; she parried and darted back, circling warily. He spun and hacked: blocking his powerful swing made her shoulder ache. Stepping back, she assumed the two-handed guard position. He cut down and in; she responded, Lightning moving as rapidly as his blade.

By now they had an audience. Word had spread through the inn; Alanna's boys were joined by servants, guests, hostlers, and passersby. The boys had the best seats; they watched their heroes intently. Faithful sat by Coram's feet, his eyes slitted against the sun's glare. He'd fetched Alanna's companion, knowing Coram would want to see this.

The exchange stretched out in strikes, blocks, and parries, neither opponent gaining an advantage. Since Liam had ruled out the unarmed tactics that would give him the victory, Alanna could show him the full range of her skill. Coram beamed in pride: with sword—or, he would bet, with axe or longbow—Alanna matched the Shang Dragon. How many knights could make that claim?

Both Liam and Alanna were sweating heavily; her wound began to ache. Throughout the exchange she had studied the Dragon's style as she knew he had studied hers, searching for any flaw. Now she blocked swiftly, parried his return cut, blocked him again—and came up into a split-second opening, barring his sword arm with her shoulder as Lightning snaked up to kiss his throat.

They froze in place for a moment. Then Liam grinned. "You're good." He lowered his blade as Alanna stepped back. "I haven't lost to a swordsman in years."

The boys circled them to offer water and towels. Alanna drank deeply from a waterskin, pouring some onto her face. "Why didn't you hit me, or kick me?" she panted. "You'd've won."

"That wasn't the point." The Dragon dumped a waterskin over his head with a grateful sigh. "Are you the best in Tortall?"

"I don't know." She smiled gratefully at the boy who'd given her the water. "There may be some commoners better than me—I only fought knights." Alanna wiped her face with a sigh. "Against Duke Gareth of Naxen—Gareth the Elder, not the Younger—I can win one out of three bouts. He's the best. Alex—Alexander of Tirragen. He beat me once." That memory hurt: Alex had nearly killed her. Her recent scar pulled as she dried her arms, and she bit back a yelp. "Thank you—I *think*."

∾

*T*hey left Berat the next day, Alanna and Faithful on Moonlight, Coram on his bay Anvil, their pack-horse Bother, and Liam astride a big-boned grey he called Drifter. The weather was sunny, and the breezes hinted that spring was on its way. They spent the night in a sheltered hollow, out of the wind. Settling into her bedroll, Alanna thought she could hear the forest waking up after the winter rains. Spring was her favorite time of year. She wondered when it came to the Roof of the World.

She rose an hour before dawn to exercise. Liam was already awake, preparing to do the same thing. They came to a silent agreement and found a clearing a little distance away, where they wouldn't disturb Coram. Faithful trotted after them, to perch on a rock where he could see everything.

She'd exercised for so long that her body knew what was expected. Habit took over, so she could keep an eye on Liam. The Dragon went through intricate routines, slow the first time, fast the second. He punched and blocked with his arms. He kicked from standing positions. Then while leaping, he flipped back and forth with a tumbler's ease that looked odd on his heavily muscled frame. By the time he finished, he'd exercised every part of his body.

Once that was done, he wiped his face on his arm and looked at Alanna. "Come here."

Warily she obeyed. Taking Alanna's hand, Liam

shaped it into a thumb-over-fingers fist. "Always hit with the first two knuckles," he explained. "It'll get easier if you practice on every flat surface you find—dirt, rock, a wall, whatever. That's how you build enough callus to protect those two knuckles." He held up his hands, showing her what he meant.

Liam then guided Alanna through a different punch from the one she'd learned as a page. Her fist started palm up at her waist, turning as she punched until it hit the target palm down. She punched until her right arm was sore, then switched hands. •

The man circled, watching. Often he adjusted her feet or repositioned her shoulders. Once he rapped her stomach hard: "Keep those muscles tight!" Alanna blushed: he'd caught her forgetting something she already knew.

"Picture an opponent right where your punch ends—aim for the bottom of his rib cage," Liam explained. "On me that's the same as where *my* ribs end, but *you* aim higher. Otherwise you'll hit most folk on the knees." Alanna glared at him, then tried again. Later he added high and low punches, then arm blocks. "Practice till it hurts," he said when they were finished. "You know that from fencing. You do it so much that by the time you need it, you don't have to think. The punch or the block just happens."

Alanna nodded, exhausted.

This was your idea, Faithful reminded her as she trudged to the stream to wash. As she rolled up her sleeves—nothing could make her take an outdoor bath at this time of year!—the cat added, *When will you learn to leave well enough alone?*

Alanna sighed. "When I want to stop learning, I guess."

∾

Coram was awake when she returned. "It's your turn to fix breakfast," he reminded Alanna, adding softly, "Gods help us." Picking up his gear, he joined Liam at the stream.

Alanna ignored his comment and started to work. Liam was the first to return from the stream. He sat by the fire, watching her movements with suspicion.

"Do you put yourself through this often?" Alanna filled Liam's bowl with porridge and handed it to him.

The Dragon sorted through his breakfast with a spoon. "Every morning, plus whatever else I fit in later. You clean your armor and weapons regularly, and you do your own exercises."

"I don't half kill myself. It isn't burnt or anything," she snapped, meaning the porridge. "I know how to cook!"

"Shang discipline is stricter than a knight's." He tasted his food, shuddered, and continued to eat.

"Is it worth it?" she demanded. She was stung by his attitude toward her cooking and by the idea that anyone might think themselves better than a proven knight.

He looked at her. "If something happens to my

weapons, I can still protect myself and anyone else who comes along."

Alanna shut up.

Her curiosity didn't desert her for long. "How long have you been doing this?" she asked when they'd been riding for several hours.

Liam had to think a moment. "Thirty years, give or take a month."

"Thirty *years!*"

He nodded. "I was four when the Shang Bear came to our village and looked us young ones over. Of us all, he said I 'might do.' I wouldn't let my dadda alone until he sent me. Lucky I wasn't the oldest, or I'd be a farmer now." He looked at her and smiled. "Then I wouldn't have met you."

Alanna looked away. When he turned all of his charm on her, she could feel her insides melt.

Think about what you're getting into, Faithful advised.

Alanna glared at him. "I'm not 'getting into' anything, and I'll thank you to keep your opinions to yourself!" she snapped. Seeing Liam's stare, she turned red.

"Is that a cute habit of yours, or did he really speak?" His face had an odd, tight look; his eyes were pale crystal in color.

"He talks. Sometimes other people understand him. Most of the time they don't. Faithful is the one who decides."

"Magic." Liam frowned. "That's right—you have it."

"You have something against people with the Gift?" She suddenly felt defensive.

Their eyes met and held, until he grinned and pinched her nose. Crystal was replaced by blue-green. "Since it's *you*, kitten, I'll make an exception."

Alanna decided it was time Moonlight had a gallop. Kicking the mare lightly, they leaped ahead, leaving the Dragon behind—for a little while.

～

There's so much we don't know about each other, she reflected as she watched Liam cook their night's meal. *I know he's the Dragon, which means he's brave and adventurous and probably has a temper—dragons are supposed to be fierce and protective. It means he's a hero if ever there are real heroes.*

She sighed. *Will he come to the Roof with us? I'd feel a lot easier if I knew I had a Dragon at my back up there.*

"Do you plan to marry?" Liam asked suddenly.

"What?" she cried, startled.

"You heard me. Your plans for the future—do they include a husband? Children?"

She fingered her emberstone. "Give up my shield after working so hard? Spend my time at court or on my husband's lands? I have no patience for that kind of life. Besides—I don't know anything about children younger than ten."

"Have you ever tried to learn?"

"When did I have a chance?" she wanted to know. "Child care is one of the *few* duties a squire isn't expected to perform, Ironarm! The Bazhir never asked me to, unless a child was sick. Then I was a healer, not a nanny." *Why was he asking such uncomfortable questions?*

"I just wondered why you feel you have to be all warrior or all woman. Can't you be both?"

Coram came back from washing, sparing Alanna the need to answer Liam's question. It was just as well—she had no answer.

How did Liam unsettle her in so many different ways? Neither Jonathan nor George had laid siege to her as he did. *I wish he'd stop putting me off balance, but he doesn't seem to want to do that, either.* Liam glanced up; their eyes met and held.

Coram broke the silence, kicking the Dragon gently. "Kindly wait t'romance her 'til I'm not here," he advised. "I've a father's interest in my lady still. And go easy on her. She's not used to the game ye're playin.'"

Liam grinned; Alanna blushed. "I can speak for myself," she protested.

If you wanted to, Faithful put in. Coram guffawed, and Alanna decided to go for a walk rather than stay to be teased.

When she returned, Coram looked up hopefully. She'd been too tired the preceding night to show him Rispah in the fire. Now she crouched and held her palms out to the flames, reaching for her Gift. Her fingers glowed with purple fire: she sent it into the flames, until they matched the color of her

Gift. Rispah's image took shape, and Coram drew close, his eyes riveted on her.

She walked away, leaving Coram in private. Where was Liam? Why had he left—because he didn't want to intrude? Or did it have something to do with her Gift? He'd sounded very odd when he mentioned it that morning.

She checked the horses and the spring, with no luck. At last she found him in a clearing near the stream, lying under a willow.

"You use your magic a lot," he said flatly as she drew near.

"I've had it all my life. I'm used to it by now." She sat beside him, puzzled by the odd tone of his voice. "You must have seen plenty of sorcery, roaming the way you do."

His smoky voice was quiet. "No one is Gifted in Shang."

Reaching to pluck a stalk of wildgrass, she stopped. She couldn't have heard correctly. "You keep us out *on purpose? Why?*"

He wouldn't look at her. "The Gifted use magic for a crutch. They won't surrender to Shang study, because they know the Gift can always win them an escape."

"We *cheat*, you mean." She bit back other angry words.

"You'd be helpless, if your Gift was taken," he challenged.

"Of course not!"

"How do you *know?*"

That silenced her. She *didn't* know. All her life she'd had magic, even when she'd tried to ignore it. "I can't *help* being Gifted," she replied at last. "I tried to fight it, when I was a page. Then the Sweating Sickness came and a lot of people died. Prince Jonathan would have died, too, if I hadn't used my Gift."

"I just told you what we're taught."

She wished she could see his face. "Tell me— where would your great Shang masters be without healers and their magic? Where would *you* be?" He didn't answer, so she went on. "My Gift brings Coram pleasure—how else could he see Rispah?"

"Maybe the lady doesn't want to be spied on." There was a dangerous rumble in his voice.

"Nonsense! She agreed to it. Would you like to see the letter?" Alanna demanded sharply, her temper rising. "My tribe would've fallen to hillmen, without my Gift and the Gifts of my students. I use my magic to heal, to pay back for some of the lives I take. What do *you* do to repay?"

"Whatever it is I do, Lady Pry, I do it with my own two hands!" She started to get up, and Liam held her back. "Alanna, wait! I didn't mean—I have a temper."

"So do I," she snapped. She let him pull her down beside him again.

"Shang allows healers to work on us, it's true. The students are Giftless. Not so much because the masters think people use it for a crutch as because they know training a Gift takes the student's attention away from other things. When you follow Shang, you follow *only* Shang—if you're to succeed." He stroked Alanna's hair. "Don't scowl so, kitten. You've got me shaking in my boots."

"I can't change what I am," she told him, cooling off. "I never *asked* to be half witch and half warrior."

"I know." The Dragon sighed. "Listen. I got heated up because I'm—because I'm afraid of magic."

Was he teasing? She was in no mood for it! "You aren't afraid of anything."

"Everyone's afraid of *something*." He had a point, and she knew it. "I fear dying for nothing. I fear being sick—my grandda took a wound and rotted to death." She patted his arm in sympathy but didn't interrupt. "I hate being helpless. Then what's the good of being a Dragon?"

"Or a Lioness," she whispered.

He nodded. "But I'm also afraid of the Gift—I don't even let healers use magic on me. Some folk are afraid of spiders—with me, it's that."

Alanna shuddered; she hated spiders with a passion! "I never heard of someone *fearing* magic, not like that. Disliking it, yes."

"Well, I'm afraid of it."

She fingered the stone at her throat. "Liam?"

"What?"

"How…" She felt herself blush and was grateful for the dark. "How can we be—well, *anything*—if you fear my Gift?"

He put his arms around her, gathering her close. "I want to try anyway. What about you?"

"I don't know you very well at all," she whispered, half complaining. "You don't know *me*."

He was smiling. "That's the fun of it, kitten." He kissed her gently, then passionately, and Alanna surrendered. Any misgivings she had were put away for thought at another, less interesting, time.

∽

*L*iam was shaking her gently. From the other side of their banked campfire she heard Coram's snore. "Let's go," the Dragon whispered.

"Go where?" she yawned.

"You won't learn Shang fighting in bed."

She started to protest, and thought the better of it. Even at this hour she wanted his good opinion. Never mind that her arms felt as if they weighed triple what they usually did. He'd probably felt worse and *still* had gone about his morning routine. *This was my idea*, she prodded herself. Stifling a moan—Coram at least would have his sleep!— she obeyed.

∽

*F*ortress Jirokan was a well-fortified town, with a tent city outside its walls. Coram pointed at the river where a barge filled with people made its way downstream. "They're fleein' the Saren War," he explained to Alanna as they rode toward the town gates. "Like as not their farms were burned or looted. Now they hope Maren'll grant a place for them to start again.

"The boats take them south. The King's too smart to keep all these rootless folk in one spot." The Dragon nodded in the direction of the tent city. Now that she was closer, Alanna saw furniture piled in the mud and a wide variety of animals: cows, dogs, goats, horses, pigs, and chickens. People dressed in tattered, dirty clothes stared at the travelers on the road. "These camps are trouble. They breed thieves and killers. South Maren has room to feed them and land for new farms."

Alanna was silent as they entered the city and made for the inn Liam recommended. There was nothing she or Liam could do for the Saren refugees. Poverty was an illness she couldn't cure; a civil war could not be stopped by just one knight. *That's something Liam and I have in common,* she told herself. *I don't like feeling helpless, either.*

The inn was the Mongrel Cur; it lived up to Liam's recommendation. She spent the afternoon bathing, washing her hair, mending her clothes— simply relaxing. She wrote to Myles, Halef Seif, and Thom, although it would be weeks before she could hear from them. At last cooking smells called her to the common room and her dinner.

Liam suggested that they avoid notice in this restless town: he would not wear Shang insignia, and she and Coram should leave in their rooms anything to suggest that Alanna was a knight. That suited Alanna, who wanted to spend her time in Jirokan quietly. She dressed in boy's clothes, but to be safe, tucked a dagger at the small of her back. Whistling cheerfully, she slung Faithful over a shoulder and went downstairs.

Liam and Coram had waited for her. As soon as she joined them, the waiters brought their food. A charmed serving girl bore Faithful away "to see what we might get a handsome fellow like you." The cat shamelessly played up to his admirer.

Marenite Guardsmen and their women arrived to begin a night of drinking as the travelers finished their meal. Ignoring the soldiers, Coram and Liam played chess; Alanna divided her attention between the game and the Guards. Faithful rejoined them, his stomach full after his kitchen excursion.

The biggest of the Guards was a sergeant who looked as ill-tempered as he behaved. Clearly his men knew he was in a foul mood; they kept away from him. His lady, however, was bored by his sulks and didn't care who knew it. Alanna watched as the lady tried to tease her sergeant into a better frame of mind. When this tactic failed, her eye began to rove until she saw Liam. Until that point Alanna had no personal involvement in the woman's behavior. Forgetting that she was dressed like a boy—and that in the ill-lit room it would be hard to see the feminine shape under her clothes—she glared a warning. The lady didn't notice.

The sergeant wasn't aware that his companion's attention had strayed. "Back in a minute, darlin'," he belched. Getting up, he made for the privy.

The moment the huge Guard was out of sight, his lady came to Alanna's table. It was Liam's turn to move: his attention was locked onto the chessboard. Coram saw the expression on his knight-mistress's face. He looked up to see the reason for Alanna's scowl and grinned.

"So quiet ye lads are," the woman purred as she put a hand on Liam's shoulder. The Dragon glanced up, surprised. "Don't ye care for female...companions?"

Alanna rose and hissed, "Where I come from, it's considered polite to keep to the man you're with."

Startled, the woman glanced at her: she hadn't noticed anyone but the big fellow. Why did this youth interfere? "What—the boy's in love wiv' ye, then?" she asked Liam. Liam chuckled and looked the woman over.

Coram clapped a hand over Alanna's mouth, pushing her into her seat. "She can't see ye're a girl!" he whispered into her ear. "Liam can take care of himself!"

Coram took his hand away too soon. Alanna snapped, "What're you looking for, Liam, fleas?"

Her guardian sighed and corked his knight-mistress up again.

The lady ran scarlet nails through Liam's hair. "Lads're no fun, and this one don't look like he knows much. Now me, I *appreciate* a man."

Liam grinned at her as a muffled yell burst from Alanna. Coram put his lips close to the struggling knight's ear. "D'ye want him t'think ye're jealous? Ye're givin' a fair imitation of it."

His words nettled Alanna. She didn't want Liam Ironarm thinking any such thing! She quieted, and Coram loosened his grip. "I just don't like people who're so *obvious!*" she whispered back, knowing she *was* jealous.

A roar of fury split the air—the sergeant had returned. Anyone who thought he might be in the middle when battle lines were drawn moved quickly. The lady backed away from Liam.

Alanna saw the Dragon's eyes turn a pale green before he turned to face the enraged Guard. "This isn't what you think," he said quietly.

The sergeant wasn't interested. "On your feet!" He grabbed the Dragon's tunic.

Liam grasped the sergeant's wrist. "Forget this. I'm Liam Ironarm, the Shang Dragon—you'll get hurt."

The other man laughed. "Expect me t'think a Shang warrior'd sit with us ordinary folk?" His muscles bulged as he tried to lever his victim up.

Liam's hands tightened. For a second nothing

happened, then the bigger man howled in pain. Liam stood, and the Guard was forced to back away, unable to break his hold. Finally the Dragon released him. "The next time you're told someone is Shang, pay attention." He faced Alanna and Coram. "This place is too lively for me."

The sergeant threw himself at Liam's back. Alanna started to her feet, reaching for her knife; Coram tugged her down.

Liam dropped and twisted, boosting the bigger man over his shoulder. The Guard crashed into a table, to the fury of its occupants. He threw them aside with a curse and charged Liam. The Dragon pivoted, driving his left foot out into his attacker's belly, then his chin. The sergeant dropped like a stone.

Two of the Guards rushed to help their comrade. Liam kicked a sword out of one Guard's hand and flipped the other onto a table, then waited for the next attack—none came. He picked up the sergeant, asking, "Anything broken?"

"Hunh?" The Marenite was dazed.

Professionally, the Dragon checked his victim, then let him slide back to the floor. "You'll live." He glanced at the others, who seemed well enough, then beckoned to Alanna and Coram. "Let's find someplace quieter."

The crowd backed away as they made for the door. Alanna peered back: the troublesome lady knelt by her sergeant, cooing to him. Grinning, she followed her friends.

～

Midnight found Alanna and Liam seated on a wall overlooking the Shappa River. Coram had left in search of a card or dice game; Faithful went to meet a lady cat yowling in her master's garden. Alanna and Liam had visited the tent city to question the refugees about conditions in Sarain. Now they listened to the river and the distant howl of a wolf.

"I like how you fought back there," Alanna said sleepily. "No mess, no broken bones, no dead. Nice."

"I'm glad they took the hint," yawned Liam.

"Traveling with you is fun." She hesitated, then asked, "Did Coram tell you *why* we're bound for the Roof of the World?"

"He said you had a map for some treasure. It makes no sense, risking your lives for gold that might or mightn't be there. But you have no better plans—"

"It isn't gold," she interrupted quietly. "It's the Dominion Jewel. I want to find it and bring it home, for the glory of Tortall."

He smoothed his mustache, as he often did when he was thinking. "Not to mention that the deed would prove you're worthy of your shield." He jumped down and held his hands up to her. She slid into his grasp, and they kissed. "Gifted one, when it comes to a hero's deed, you don't think small."

"Liam?" She tried not to plead. "What're *you* doing next?"

"Riding with you and Coram, I expect."

⮠

*I*t was barely dawn. Liam was dressed when he woke Alanna. "You want to learn Shang, you keep Shang hours! Up!" He reached for the water pitcher.

She tumbled out of bed. "I'm up!"

"The stableyard, five minutes," he commanded. He slammed the door behind him. Alanna lurched to her feet.

You're ruining my rest, Faithful grumbled.

Alanna dashed cold water on her face. "Good!" Dressing, she wailed, "*Why* did I pick a man who's a grouch in the morning?"

⮠

*T*he Marenite Guardsmen said they were crazy to enter Sarain, but they let Alanna's party through. The difference between the nations was soon clear: healthy Marenite farms gave way to burned-out homesteads. Often they found the leavings of refugees who'd camped on the Great Road before crossing into Maren. The road was deserted.

Alanna worked at her lessons. Liam grew less gruff at exercise time when he saw she practiced longer than she had to and complained less than most beginners. He taught her only a few hand

blows, the arm blocks, and two kicks. But in these
he drilled her endlessly, watching for the tiniest
flaw. At night they shared a bedroll, with Coram's
unspoken approval.

The first evidence of fighting lay by the road,
four days' ride into Sarain, in a meadow beside the
road. Here the dead had been piled up and left,
until only skeletons remained.

Faithful came along as Alanna went to the
mound's edge. Whoever left the dead made no
attempt to separate the enemies: K'miri armor, lacquered bright red, blue, or green, shone against
rusted lowland metal. Bone hands still clutched
weapons. Kneeling, Alanna slid a lowland sword
out of the pile.

"Heavy fighting," she murmured, showing her
cat the nicked and scored blade. "Some archery at
first, but close quarters after. An ambush?"

"A world of difference between a good king and
a bad one." The voice was Liam's. He crouched
beside them, taking the sword to inspect it. "In five
years Adigun *jin* Wilima has destroyed the work of
generations."

"It looks as if he really tried," Alanna said. Was
this what might happen in Tortall if Jonathan died
without an heir or someone tried to take the
throne? Would the Dominion Jewel prevent this
kind of civil war?

"They deserved better." Liam touched a K'miri
arm guard decorated with a sunburst pattern. His

eyes were a stormy blue-grey. Turning abruptly, he rejoined Coram and the horses.

Alanna stayed, arranging twigs into a pyramid.

The Jewel doesn't create great kings, but it helps those who are to prosper, Faithful told her. *Never forget, though, it won't stop a king who wants to build an empire, starting with the conquest of his neighbors. It'll help him, too.*

"All good weapons can be turned against you." Alanna drew a piece of cord from a pocket, fashioning it into a knotted loop. Carefully she lowered it until the loop encircled the pyramid. She stood, dusting off her hands. "I suppose this will upset Liam. D'you think I made a mistake, being his lover when he's afraid of the Gift?"

Faithful retreated, knowing what she had in mind. *It doesn't matter what I think. You'll do what you want to—you always have.*

Reaching toward the cord-encircled sticks, she beckoned. Flames bit into the pile. Alanna touched the ember to see her spell: now the dead were covered by a purple haze sprouting flames. Her cord was a circle of power that kept the fire from spreading. Releasing the ember, she saw the fire of her Gift vanish. The flames were real; they mounted higher and higher among the bones and trappings.

Liam said nothing when she joined the men, but he was pale and sweating. *He really is afraid of magic,* she realized. The knowledge depressed her: it confirmed the end of their romance at its beginning. Someday she would have to leave him—no love would last when he feared part of her. They all rode on, watching the land, listening for any out-of-place sound. The mound of bones had made them nervous.

"I'd druther we was jumped. Get it over with," Coram grumbled softly. He and Alanna unpacked after stopping for the night; Liam had gone to hunt fresh food. Food was not a problem yet: knowing conditions ahead, they'd gotten extra provisions at the Mongrel Cur.

"I know what you mean," Alanna sighed. "Where are the armies?"

"Bedded down for the night, I hope." It was Liam, returning with a string of fish. "All the same, let's stand watches. I smell woodsmoke." He gave the fish to Alanna, whose turn it was to cook.

Coram built a fire, keeping it small and smokeless. They cooked and ate in silence, listening. The meal over, Faithful went out to prowl; the humans worked on personal tasks. Alanna was beginning to relax when the cat scrambled into their circle.

People, he hissed. *Women and infants. On the other side of the ridge!*

Putting their work aside, they buckled on sword belts. Coram indicated silently that he would guard the horses. Liam and Alanna made for the ridge, moving noiselessly through brush and trees. When they reached the top, Liam signaled Alanna to go to cover. She frowned: having grown away from a squire's obedience, resuming it even a little came hard. She also knew to bow to Liam's extra years on the road.

The people were below, following the stream. Alanna tried for a better look, wondering if she could get closer.

A voice growled, "Tell the big one to drop his blade, or I put a bolt through *you*."

three

The Warlord's Daughter

*A*lanna didn't have to repeat it—Liam heard. Rising from his crouch, he let his weapon fall. Alanna put Lightning down. To have Liam caught because a girl-child had the drop on *her* was humiliating. She was supposed to be able to take care of herself!

"Amazing," Alanna's captor said. "We go hunting for game, and we find you instead."

Alanna heard Coram swear in the distance. "Coram, are you all right?" she yelled

"Some lass is aimin' a crossbow at me," was the response. "Only my dignity's hurt, so far."

Alanna's guard called, "Thayet?"

"I'm all right, Buri." The voice was female, deep, and clear.

Black eyes locked on Alanna. "Start walking," Buri ordered.

"I won't leave my sword in the dirt," Alanna snapped.

The stocky girl stooped to grab Lightning, her crossbow sight never moving from Alanna's chest. "Now go," she commanded. "Hands in the air."

"Shame your mother didn't drown you at birth," Alanna muttered, obeying.

"What makes you think she didn't?"

Awaiting them were refugees; their belongings overburdened a donkey. The group itself was small: two teenaged girls, two boys aged ten or so, and a girl nearly the same age. One of the teenagers carried a baby.

Coram approached, leading their horses. Guarding him was a woman of Alanna's age, dressed in a split skirt, boots, a cotton shirt, and a fleece-lined vest. She bore her crossbow like one who knew its use. She was also the most beautiful female Alanna had ever seen. Her face—particularly her nose—was strong-boned; her hazel eyes were deep-set under even brows; her chin was determined. Her mouth was naturally red, accented by ivory skin. She wore her jet-black hair pulled into a knot.

Alanna sighed. "Cute" was the best description *she* could hope for.

Liam bowed to the young woman. "Your Royal Highness."

"Have we met, sir?" Hers was the voice that had answered Buri.

"No, Highness." Despite his peasant's accent, the Dragon was as gallant as a noble. "But I'd have to be blind not to recognize a daughter of the Wilima house."

Thayet *jian* Wilima smiled. "Sadly, I *do* take

after my father," the Princess admitted. She fingered the curve of her nose.

Alanna stared at Thayet. The Princess had once been considered as a wife for Jon, but the Queen had said no—there was bad blood in the Wilima line. But seeing her, Alanna thought it was too bad Jon couldn't marry this one. She didn't look as if she'd let him stand on his dignity for long. The idea made her grin.

Buri poked her with her bow. "Her Highness isn't someone to laugh at."

"Don't, Buri," Thayet said. "These people aren't enemies."

"We don't know they're friends."

Liam glanced at Alanna's guard. "Believe me, K'mir, if I wanted to turn the tables on you, I would." He feinted to the side and lunged forward. Before Alanna could see what he'd done, Buri sat in the dirt, her crossbow in Liam's hands. He offered it back to her as she rose. Buri took it, her eyes filled with respect. She put the arrow in her quiver and holstered the bow with a nod.

Her reaction made Alanna like her. From what she knew of the K'mir tribes to Sarain's north, Buri probably was reared a warrior. She took being disarmed well.

Liam performed introductions. When he gave Alanna's titles, Buri whispered, "A full knight is a *woman*—a *noble*woman?"

Coram bristled. "She has the bluest blood in Tortall," he growled. "There never was a *zhir* or *jin* anythin' fit t'polish a Trebond boot."

"Coram," Alanna sighed.

"The family's in *The Book of Gold*," added Coram. "No *zhir* or even *zhirit* were writ down till *The Book of Silver*—"

"I think it's wonderful," Thayet interrupted. "It's time we nobles showed we aren't delicate flowers, instead of leaving the glory to our Shang and K'miri sisters." Changing the subject diplomatically, she asked, "Where are you three bound?"

Coram told them about their journey (but not its object) as Alanna appraised Thayet's group. They were tired; the children's faces were grey with exhaustion. How long had they been traveling, and how much longer could they go?

Coram arrived at the same conclusion. "If ye'll forgive my sayin' it, yer Highness, ye need help. Where're ye and the young ones bound?"

"The Mother of Waters in Rachia," Buri replied. "All of us but Thayet and the baby and me were students in the convent Mother of Mountains. The baby, Thayet...found."

"Soldiers killed his family," volunteered the girl who carried the infant. "Everyone but him, poor little man."

Alanna did some calculations. "Rachia's four days' ride south," she said. "Except you're afoot—those of you who can walk."

"We had no choice," Thayet said. "*Zhir* Anduo's army was coming."

"Doesn't the Warlord have men to protect you?" Liam asked.

"They ran." Buri was plainly contemptuous.

Thayet protested, "Buri, that's not fair. They were afraid," she told Liam. "They had no way of knowing if their families were safe."

Buri shrugged. "In plain talk, it still means they ran." Thayet glared at her companion.

Smoothing his mustache, Liam said, "Coram's right, you need us. We'll get you to the Mother of Waters."

Buri wasn't willing to accept this. "We don't *need* them!" she told Thayet hotly. "We don't even know if they're on our side..."

"Don't be silly, Buri," Thayet replied. "I haven't heard Alanna's name, but I know about Liam Ironarm. People like this don't prey on people like us."

"There's a first time for everything," the K'mir muttered.

Thayet's response was in K'mir. Buri looked away, and Thayet turned to Alanna with a smile. "Please understand. Buri's family has served my mother's family for generations. That means I can't tell her to do anything. She'll always say what's on her mind—no matter how much it embarrasses me—and she behaves as she pleases."

Alanna looked at Coram, who hid a grin. "I understand, Princess Thayet," the knight said dryly. "I, too, suffer from old family servants."

"If this is settled, I want to set up camp," Liam

interrupted. "The little ones are asleep on their feet."

Alanna and Buri exchanged looks for a moment—Alanna's measuring, Buri's sullen. Finally Buri nodded. "If that's the way it has to be."

"It is," Thayet snapped.

∾

*T*hey camped where they were, the men settling the children after they'd been fed. Alanna took the first watch, enjoying the quiet. She had a feeling she wouldn't have too much quiet to enjoy for a week or so.

"Me and Thayet were fine before you came." Buri spoke unexpectedly, and Alanna jumped. Hadn't she learned once tonight, on the ridge, that this K'mir made no noise when she moved? "Thayet's K'miri-taught, and I'm K'miri-bred. We take care of ourselves."

Alanna felt a surge of empathy. She understood this girl-warrior's hurt pride. "For you and Thayet that might be enough, though I'm not sure. An entire army's looking for her. But what if something happens to you? The little ones will starve."

Buri sat on the ground beside her. "I'm *supposed* to look after Thayet," she explained. "I help with the children, but I'm not good at it the way she is. And I can't leave them to die. What've they done?"

"So the Princess is your chief responsibility. If

anything happens to her while you're worrying about the children, you will blame yourself."

Buri nodded. "You probably think that's foolish."

"Not at all." Alanna felt as if she spoke to herself when she was Prince Jonathan's squire. "Coram and Liam and I will help you make sure Thayet's unharmed, all right?"

They sat together for a while, saying nothing. At last the K'mir stood and offered Alanna her hand. "I'm glad you joined us," she said as the knight returned her grip. "I didn't like the idea of taking on any armies by myself."

Alanna hid a grin. "Thayet would've helped," she pointed out.

"Unh-unh," was the emphatic reply. "You think I'd let Kalasin's daughter endanger herself? I'd put her somewhere safe, where she couldn't get in trouble."

Yes, Faithful said when Buri returned to her bed. *She is very much like you at that age.*

"Surely *I* didn't think I could beat an army single-handed!"

You still do.

"The trouble with arguing with a cat is that cats don't hesitate to say *anything* about you, no matter how crazy it is," she complained. "You can't win an argument that way!"

Nor should you try. With that, Faithful trotted off for a walk in the forest.

∾

*T*he next morning Liam and Alanna did their dawn exercises. "I don't care how strange yesterday was," he told Alanna when she grumbled. "You don't get good unless you practice." The worst of it was that he was right. Were he and Faithful in a plot to make her feel young and ignorant?

Liam cooked breakfast as Alanna roused their companions. Once they were fed, the company was ready to set out. Buri and Coram erased signs of their camp: bandits who would ignore three people would attack a large party. Liam let the boys and the ten-year-old girl ride his placid Drifter. He led the horse, keeping a sharp eye on their surroundings. Thayet walked, the baby in a sling on her chest; Buri stayed with her Princess. Coram's Anvil bore the teenaged girls. Then came the packhorse Bother and the donkey (who kept well away from the bad-tempered Bother). Riding at the rear of the column, keeping an eye on their surroundings as Liam did, were Alanna, Faithful, and Moonlight.

At their noon stop, Alanna found the stream and splashed her face with cold water. Buri came to her, bearing an armful of baby. "Here." She gave him to Alanna, who froze—what if she dropped him? Sighing, Buri fixed the knight's hands in a better holding position before she turned away.

"Where are you going?" Alanna demanded.

"You act like you've never held a baby before!"

"I haven't."

Buri stared at Alanna as if she couldn't believe her ears. "Never? There are babies everywhere—"

"Perhaps so, but their parents didn't ask me to hold them!" The infant wriggled, and Alanna tried to give him back to Buri.

"You have to learn sometime." The K'mir turned away. "Stay there and don't clutch him. I'm going for a blanket. You'll be fine."

"I don't think child care is a necessary part of my education," Alanna said to herself. "It's not like I plan to stay anywhere long enough to marry and have children."

The baby sneezed and wrinkled his face, which made her grin. Gently she bounced him as she had seen Coram do. To her dismay, the infant started to bawl. She cooed and rocked him to no avail—he worked himself into a tantrum. Buri returned with her blanket.

"What's wrong?" Alanna cried. "I only joggled him a little—"

Buri opened the blanket on the ground and put clean diapers on it. "Probably wet," she said. "Change him." She left again.

Alanna looked at the child in horror. "I never—" She was saying that too much lately—surely a proven knight was equal to anything! Trying to remember how Thayet had done it earlier, she put the child down and unwrapped him. A stench rose from the diaper: the baby was more than wet.

When Alanna fumbled the knot open, she saw a damp brown mass was responsible. *This can't be worse than mucking out stables,* she told herself, fighting her unhappy stomach. *I've done that hundreds of times.*

Coram knelt beside her. "Take the diaper he fouled and wipe him with the edges," he explained, his eyes twinkling. When she looked at him pleadingly, Coram shook his head. "It's not hard. Lift him by his ankles—he's used to it. That's the idea— get rid of as much as ye can. Put the dirty one aside." He dampened a clean diaper in the stream and gave it to her. "Swab the poor mite down. Think how *ye'd* feel in that state. Easy, little lad," he crooned, giving the baby a finger to hold. The infant grinned, showing a bit of ivory. "Teeth, is it? Let me see." He ran his finger around the baby's gums. "And two more comin' in—no wonder ye're scratchy."

Alanna stared at Coram as he gave her a fresh, dry diaper. "Where in the Mother's Name did you learn all this?"

"Fold it like a triangle. I was the oldest, and four more after me. When I governed Trebond, I watched the little ones when their mothers were workin' in the fields. I like them fine." He shook the finger the baby clutched; the infant crowed and babbled happily. "A grip like iron: this one'll be a blacksmith, mark my words. No, no—if ye put it on him so loose, it'll fall off. And that's a fair knot."

Coram held the baby in the air and shook him gently, to be answered with a gleeful cackle.

Alanna felt odd. *Coram could've had a family years ago, if he hadn't been working for Trebond.*

Coram looked at her. "Don't start sayin' maybe ye should bring me home to Rispah. We've somethin' to do before we head back." He touched her shoulder. "I've been raisin' *ye.* I've no complaints of my life."

～

*B*uri showed Alanna how to feed the infant from a waterskin filled with goat's milk. When that was done, Alanna picked up the child as she'd seen Liam do, patting him on the back. *Now* she had the knack of handling a baby!

She was shocked by the infant's burp, unpleasantly surprised when dampness spread over her back. Seeing her face, Buri laughed until she cried. Liam gave Alanna a wet cloth, fighting to keep his face straight. "Put down a clean rag first," he explained. "They spit up when they're burped— and they fuss when they aren't." Alanna went to change, red with embarrassment.

When she returned, all the children slept on blankets in the shade. Even Buri dozed, one arm over the baby. Liam, Thayet, and Coram waited by the stream, out of earshot.

"They need rest," Liam told her when she joined them. "They won't make it to sundown, otherwise. We're used to the road—they aren't."

"Thayet tells me they've no supplies," said Coram. "Even the food we brought won't last."

"We tried to forage." The Princess cooled her feet in the stream. "The farms in these valleys were rich, and there was game—but not anymore. The land's picked clean. We ran out of food last night, and Buri and the older girls have been stinting themselves for days. They can't keep that up."

I bet they aren't the only ones who've gone short of food, Alanna thought, watching Thayet's too-thin face. *We have to do something, soon. But how, if we can't live off the country?*

"We have t'find humans, then." Coram was matter-of-fact. "If the land's picked over, let's find the pickers and clean *them* out."

✑

*A*lanna gave Moonlight's reins to Thayet for the afternoon. Sliding a quiver over her shoulder, she took her longbow and ranged up and down the road, watching for game. She bagged two squirrels, which told her more than Thayet's words how bad off Sarain was. At this time of year game should have tumbled into her lap.

Buri came to join her, with no better luck. After an hour's hunting, Alanna asked something that had been on her mind. "Why is Thayet roaming the mountains? Why isn't she with her father?"

"It's because of Kalasin," Buri said after a moment's consideration.

"Her mother?"

Buri nodded. "The most beautiful woman in the world. She was…amazing." Her black eyes were sad. "Kalasin asked the Warlord to deal fairly with the K'mir, because we're her people. Lowlanders take us for slaves; they steal our horses—" The dark girl stopped until her anger was under control. "*Jin* Wilima hates us—he's a lowlander completely. So he signed laws forbidding us to meet in groups of more than five people at a time. There's more than thirty in the Hau Ma clan, and they're our smallest! How can we honor the dead or a marriage or a birth if the clan is forbidden to meet?"

"Go on," urged the knight when Buri stopped.

"I'm sorry. What Kalasin did was a great thing, but it hurts to remember. She and Thayet tried to make the Warlord stop. They even *pleaded*—a K'mir never begs! But he signed the law.

"Kalasin knew what she had to do then. She sent Thayet to the convent, far away. My mother and my brother, who served Kalasin, kept the guards from breaking into her tower room. Kalasin stood at her window and sang her death chant, about her shame at *jin* Wilima's laws. A crowd was there to witness: nobles, commonborn, and slaves. My mother and brother were killed, but they held the door until it was too late for the Warlord's men to stop her from jumping. Mother and Pathom are buried at Kalasin's right and left hands. The Warlord will lie in his tomb alone."

"I'm sorry," Alanna said quietly.

Buri shook her head. "They had the best deaths any K'mir could have. My people did what was right, and so did Kalasin."

"But they're gone," Alanna pointed out, disturbed. "Being dead doesn't help anybody."

"That depends on the kind of death." Liam had drawn even with them. "If your death's wasted, that's one thing. By her example, Kalasin woke up a lot of folk who thought it was all right to abuse the K'mir. Buri's mother and her brother made it possible for Kalasin to tell *why* she killed herself."

"Dead is dead," Alanna snapped. "You can't do *anything* from a grave, Liam!"

The Dragon and K'mir exchanged looks that clearly said Alanna didn't know what she was talking about. Disturbed by their agreement, knowing she would rather change things while she was alive, Alanna moved ahead.

~

*W*hen Coram found signs that bandits had been in the area recently, Liam decreed it was time to stop for the night. Faithful found abandoned caves above a stream, where Thayet briskly set up camp. The children gathered firewood as Buri and Coram went fishing; Liam cooked. Once again Alanna got baby duty—diapering, feeding, and burping—this time with no mishaps.

Taking her bowl of thin stew outside, Alanna took a seat on a large rock. Homesickness had caught up with her that afternoon. She wanted to see familiar faces and scenes: she missed George, in spite of sharing a bedroll with Liam—or perhaps because of that. Since the night before, Liam had been careful and deadly serious, concentrating on keeping their company safe until they arrived in Rachia. She respected him but felt shut out all the same.

She missed George and his sense of humor. *If he were here,* she thought, *he'd be in the middle of things, burping babies, hauling the boys off to wash, stealing Sarain blind for our supper.* She blinked away unexpected tears. On the road she had no George to make her laugh, no Jon to say "Of course you can do it," no Myles to explain the history of Sarain. She hoped the Dominion Jewel would be worth the trip.

Faithful, who'd vanished when they found the caves, patted her foot. His coat was thick with dust and burrs. *Bandits,* he panted, *a large camp of them, east of here.*

～

*T*hayet, who protested, stayed with the children. The two men, Alanna, and Buri formed the attack party, moving quietly through the woods led by Faithful. They marched for half an hour before they came to a canyon. *Down there,* Faithful told Alanna. *Fifty of them and their women.* The four crept to the canyon's lip, where they could see the camp below.

Alanna beckoned the others to draw back while they talked.

"Faithful says there's about fifty people down there," she whispered. "We can't take on those odds."

"I'm not a good enough thief to get in there and take what we need," Liam told her. Buri and Coram nodded their agreement.

"I'll have to use magic." Alanna met Liam's eyes. She couldn't tell their color in the dark, but when she put her hand on his arm she found he was rigid with tension. "I'm sorry. I know you don't like it. Can you think of something better?"

"Magic's dishonorable," Buri muttered. "It's—*cheating*."

Alanna and Coram exchanged looks. "Do ye prefer ten-to-one odds?" Coram asked. "I don't. We've got some brave younglings and yer Princess who depend on us t'come back."

"I don't like this," protested the K'mir. "It's too confusing. I suppose you have a point. I can't exactly challenge all of them to single combat."

"What do ye have in mind?" Coram asked his knight-mistress.

Thinking, Alanna said, "I don't know. A net, maybe, to tie them down while you take what we need." Coram frowned, troubled. He knew she'd never done anything so big and real. He said nothing, for which she was grateful.

"Do your magic, then." Liam's voice was

hoarse. "If you feel like it when you're done, maybe you can lend a hand with the *real* work." He returned to the canyon's edge.

"That isn't fair," Buri protested softly, but the Dragon was out of earshot. "What he said isn't fair," she told Coram and Alanna.

"That's all right—I understand," Alanna told her. "You two had better get close to the camp. Don't worry about what I'm doing. It won't affect you." She watched them slip over the canyon's edge.

You used to feel like Liam, Faithful commented as he and Alanna went to the edge of the canyon. *Magic and fighting don't mix, and a fighter who uses magic is cheating.*

"I'm older now," whispered Alanna.

She heard Liam's feral battle cry, and the sounds of fighting. A sentry had seen the Dragon. Alanna had no more time to think. Reaching for the first image in her mind, Alanna saw the Dominion Jewel. Even a vision of it was a catalyst: Alanna's Gift rushed into and through it, swirling out over the bandit camp as a shimmering violet net. She maneuvered it into place, making sure each tent and bedroll was covered. It was hard to concentrate as elation filled her. Did Thom feel this powerful when he performed one of his great magics? No wonder he'd given up a normal life to become a sorcerer!

The net solidified. Coram, Buri, and Liam were unable to see it; they could only sense it. Alanna extended her magic until she could see what was happening below. Buri and Liam looted the bandits' supply tent to fill packs with food and goods. Coram met them, leading four horses. The others he'd turned loose, making it impossible for the bandits to follow them.

Now Alanna strained, trying to free herself from the spell while leaving it in place. She couldn't even banish the Jewel's image. It burned in her mind like a beacon, keeping her inner eyes riveted to it. Already she felt the peculiar sinking that meant she had gone too far.

Cut it loose! Faithful yowled in her ear. *Cut it loose, or you'll pour your life into it!* She couldn't hear him through the focus the Jewel-image demanded.

Pain broke Alanna's concentration as Faithful wrapped himself around her arm, his claws and teeth ripping into her skin. Now she could free herself of the Jewel's hold. Peeling the cat off, she lurched to her feet. The net itself would hold another half hour or so, time for them to get away. "Thanks," she told Faithful in a gasp.

When the others came for her with one of the spare horses, they saw she was unable to ride. Coram looked at Liam, but the Dragon's expression made it clear he would rather not be near Alanna just then. Coram pulled her up behind him onto the saddle.

∾

*A*lanna took two days to recover, sleeping to restore her strength. By the time she was on her feet, Liam had gotten over his anger with her enough to give a dawn lesson. That same day the small company took to the road once again, the teenagers each riding a horse, with a smaller child behind. Coram had the third ten-year-old, and Thayet rode with the baby in his sling on her chest. Buri rode the shaggy pony Coram had taken from the bandits.

Using the less-traveled paths, they moved quickly through the desolate highlands. They passed burned-out farms and cabins—all abandoned, their owners dead or run away. Almost every building had its own ugly reminder of the war in the shape of unburied bodies or skeletons. They saw and heard no evidence of human life, although the warriors all sensed watching eyes. Whoever spied on them stayed within the shelter of the trees, too frightened or too wary to approach.

These sights gave Alanna nightmares, dreams in which the bodies were Tortallan and the burned-out homes belonged to her friends. Liam soon found a way to deal with dreams: he gave an extra lesson in hand-to-hand combat after they stopped for the night. Between the new lessons, the regular ones at daybreak, and her turn on watch, Alanna soon was far too tired to dream.

∾

Rachia was a bustling trade city, her streets packed with things to see. Even the many soldiers present couldn't put a damper on people's spirits. The children wriggled in their saddles, trying to look at everything. Buri stuck to Thayet, scowling at anyone who came too near. Alanna found it difficult to breathe and was dismayed to think she was more used to desert and woodlands than to crowded cities. How would she feel when she returned to Corus?

They had crossed the marketplace when some instinct warned her—she looked up to see an archer on a nearby rooftop. Alanna yelled, "Thayet!"

Liam was afoot, leading his Drifter. Hearing Alanna, he dragged Thayet and the baby from their saddle as an arrow sliced past their heads. A second arrow followed; Liam grabbed it from the air.

Buri dismounted, dark with rage, and ran into the building where the archer stood. Dismounting, Alanna saw that the building supported a sturdy flower trellis reaching from ground to roof. She tested it and started to climb, trying not to think about rotten wood or loose anchorings. "Coram! Get them to the convent!" she yelled as twigs showered onto her face. She didn't look, but she heard Liam and Coram bellow orders.

She vaulted over the roof's edge, keeping low. The assassin—swathed in headcloth and scarf—shot at her, then leaped to the next building. Alanna dodged, unsheathed her sword, and pursued. Behind her she heard a rooftop door crash open, and another pair of running feet. Wary, she glanced back to find Buri catching up. The K'mir was a faster runner than Alanna. She drew even within seconds, with her dagger in her hand. "Don't kill him!" Alanna panted. "We need to know who pays him!" Buri nodded.

They raced from roof to roof, Buri and Alanna closing the gap. The assassin's breath came harder; his steps faltered. The next roof was a story lower than the ones they ran on—the assassin jumped and landed awkwardly. Rising, he stumbled on.

Buri jumped and fell, her left leg twisting under her, but she ran on, sweat pouring down her face. Alanna jumped and rolled, as Liam and her wrestling teachers had instructed her; she got to her feet without any hurt. Buri shook her head when Alanna hesitated. "Don't wait for me," she hissed. "Get him!"

Alanna raced on. Finally their quarry was forced to halt—he'd run out of roofs.

Alanna stopped, afraid to scare him. "Talk to me!" she called. "I just want to know why—"

He jumped. When Alanna came to the roof's edge, he lay in an alley below, sprawled and broken. Cursing, she returned for Buri. Ignoring the stares of the building's inhabitants, she and the hobbling K'mir went down to the street and into the alley. No one else had noticed the assassin's fall, Alanna was relieved to note. She didn't want a street urchin or his older counterpart stealing the dead man's belongings before she and Buri got the chance to examine them.

Buri knelt beside the body, turning out his empty pockets. "He could be anybody." She kept her voice low as she lifted the assassin's headcloth. The face, sickeningly misshapen after the fall, was male and coarse, the cheeks filled with a drunkard's broken veins. "Tavern scum," she said flatly. "You can buy a killer like this for a gold piece. He probably drank his money already." She covered the dead man once more. "Someone wants Thayet dead."

Alanna nodded. "She has enemies."

"Her *father* has enemies," Buri snapped, standing shakily.

"Does it matter whose enemies they are? They *want* Thayet."

You can discuss this at the convent, Faithful told them from the alley's mouth. *You're needed there, too. Now.*

✺

When she and Buri entered the convent visitors' court, Alanna smelled trouble. Their company should have been placed in a temple guest house immediately. That was the Daughters' policy everywhere in the Eastern Lands. Yet their party was here, outside the convent proper, watched by a Daughter Doorwarden. No other priestesses—a temple this size housed at least two hundred—were to be seen. Thayet was puzzled; the children was nervous.

"What's going on?" Alanna asked Liam quietly.

"I don't know." His eyes were blue-grey, revealing nothing. "Some Daughters came out, gabbled like geese, and vanished. The Doorwarden says we wait. I want Thayet out of sight."

Buri scowled. "Is this the honor given a Princess? I should teach these lowland hens some manners."

"Save your anger for Thayet's enemies," Liam advised. "You'll serve her best if you're careful."

"Hens," Buri muttered rebelliously.

Like Buri and the Dragon, Alanna wanted Thayet in a safe place, not this open courtyard. She went to the Doorwarden. "Please bear a message to the First Daughter of this House."

The Daughter nodded. Coldly the knight said, "I am Sir Alanna of Trebond and Olau, Knight of the Realm of Tortall, a shaman and rider of the Bloody Hawk Tribe of the Bazhir. Why are we kept outside the curtain wall? Why have we no explanation for this lack of courtesy? The children are tired and hungry, we are tired and dirty, and Princess Thayet is being shot at. The Daughters of the Mother of Waters owe a duty to travelers as servants of She Who Rules Us All. Why have you not performed that duty? I will be forced to report such a lapse to the Goddess-on-Earth in the City of the Gods." Her violet eyes dangerous, Alanna nodded. "Please deliver my message."

The Daughter bowed and hurried away.

In minutes they were shown to a guest house well inside the thick convent wall. Servants came to look after the young members of their group as the Doorwarden took the adults and Buri to a meeting with the leader of the Mother of Waters. Passing through a long courtyard, they entered a room where two Daughters sat at a long table. One was dressed in the black habit of the Hag, the Goddess as Queen-of-the-Underworld; the other wore the cloth-of-gold habit that marked her as First Daughter of a wealthy convent.

"I am First Daughter *jian* Cadao," she said when everyone was made comfortable. She avoided looking at Thayet. "Princess—Lady Thayet, we were… unprepared for your arrival. We want to extend every courtesy…" She stopped, looking flustered.

"There are problems." The woman in black was young, but she spoke with authority. "More than we could have foreseen." Buri stirred, thinking the Daughter was being rude to Thayet. The Hag-Daughter nodded to her. "Forgive my bluntness—I never learned to soften my words. Princess, your father—the Warlord—is dead. May the Black God ease his passing."

Thayet's ivory skin went dead white. "How? And…when?" she rasped.

"Illness," the Hag-Daughter replied. "Sudden and painful. We suspect poison, of course. But no one is anxious to prove it." After hesitating, she added quietly, "Forgive me if I am too abrupt. I was told you and your royal father were not on speaking terms."

"We weren't, not after my—mother," Thayet whispered. She tried to smile. "Still, he was all I had. Go on, please."

"Try to understand our position. His end places a different meaning on your presence in our Houses." Her eyes, unlike those of the First Daughter's, had been fixed on Thayet. Now she examined Liam; the Dragon shifted in his seat. "The rebel leader, *zhir* Anduo, is frank about his need to talk to you."

"Kill her, ye mean," Coram rumbled.

The Daughter's eyes went to him. "Not under our roof," she said coldly. "No priestess of ours will betray the Princess. Our House is a holy sanctuary; we will not be profaned." She glanced at the First Daughter, who looked away. "You say assassins already have made an attempt. We are not proof against them or against traitors. *Zhir* Anduo is not the only one to find the Warlord's child interesting." She met Thayet's eyes again.

"I understand," Thayet replied softly.

"The children are welcome," added the First Daughter. "Except...except for your personal guard..."

"Buriram," Thayet whispered.

Jian Cadao avoided Buri's glare and continued, "She is K'mir and closely linked to you. We cannot promise her safety. The children who were students at the Mother of Mountains we shall return to their families. We understand the infant is an orphan. He will be reared by us. But we dare not shelter you. I can give clothing, horses, whatever you need. You must go soon, before *zhir* Anduo knows you are here." Now she looked at the Princess. "I am truly sorry, Thayet. I have no choice. Already I have disobeyed orders to report your arrival. It won't be long before a spy sends word to the rebels."

ᔓ

*D*ismissed by the priestesses, they went back to the room Thayet was assigned. None of them were surprised to find packed saddlebags at the door. "They don't waste time, do they?" Buri sneered when she saw them.

Alanna combed mud and stickers out of Faithful's coat, a process the cat loved (and made difficult by wriggling in joy). "I liked the Hag-Daughter," she confessed, working on a clump. "She was honest."

"The First Daughter left a bad taste in my mouth," Coram remarked.

"Don't be hard on *jian* Cadao," Thayet said quietly. "She's a cousin on my father's side. It wasn't easy for her."

"Your own *family* throws you to the wolves?" Liam's eyes turned an intense green—he was furious.

"We prefer ambition to loyalty," Thayet replied.

She fingered the arch of her nose. "And she's in trouble herself. It'll be easier for all my family if I'm gone. With my father dead..." She looked away from them, swallowing. "Any power I had was through him. Now I'm a pawn. *Zhir* Anduo can strengthen his claim to the throne by marrying me. The ones who don't want him will use me to oppose him, because I'm *jian* Wilima—although a *jian* Wilima female." She started to pace, her hazel eyes stormy. "Where can Buri and I go? Please—I need advice."

"They can come along," Coram whispered to Alanna. "They're no hindrance—we saw that comin' here. The Roof can't be worse than what they face now."

Alanna looked Thayet over, fingering the emberstone. Thayet was dependable. She was a good archer, a necessity when they hunted to feed themselves. If she was nervous, Alanna had yet to see it. She never complained, never cried, never fainted. She never shirked her watch. Thayet and Buri would be an asset to an expedition like theirs.

Alanna looked at Buri and was surprised by a pleading expression in the girl's eyes. She replaced it with her usual scowl, but this time Alanna wasn't fooled. *Buri must be worried sick,* she thought. *And she knows Thayet will be safe with us. Besides, I'd miss them.*

"Thayet," she said aloud, "you know where we're going. We're on—a quest, I suppose. When I find what I'm after, I'll return home. If Liam and Buri don't object, why don't you ride with us?"

"Mind? Gods, no! Thayet's a better cook than you are," said Liam.

"The Roof of the World," Thayet whispered. Her face brightened.

"Leave Sarain?" Buri grinned. "Just show me the way!"

∽

𝒜 Daughter shook her awake. Glancing at the window, Alanna saw it was just before dawn—time for Liam's teaching. She directed a questioning look at the Dragon, but he only shrugged and tossed Alanna her clothes. They dressed and followed the priestess out into the corridor.

The black-robed Daughter awaited them with Buri, Thayet, and Coram. "No time to waste," she told them quietly. "*Zhir* Rayong, who is sworn to *zhir* Anduo, knows Thayet's here, and he's on his way. My people can delay him for three hours, but you must go if you want to escape."

Alanna looked at her friends, thinking fast. "We can't go as we are. When it gets out that we're gone, everyone will look for a group of nobles, or the Dragon and his friends. I can ride as a boy." She grinned, looking at the shirt and breeches she already wore. "Goddess knows I've had practice."

"We'll pass as mercenaries," Liam added. Coram nodded. They all gazed at Thayet, whose looks could not have been more distinctive if she had tried.

"I can disguise her Highness," the Hag-Daughter said. "My women will make your packs seem less well cared for. What of the horses?"

They conferred by glance, and Alanna shook her head. "We don't have time to dye their coats. If it's necessary, I'll put an illusion on them and my cat till danger's past." She looked apologetically toward Liam, who shrugged.

"Let's start," the Dragon said. "The sooner we're gone, the safer everyone will be."

Thayet and the Daughter disappeared while the others changed into their most disreputable clothes. Novices saddled the horses, rubbing dirt into their coats, manes, and tack, then covering the saddlebags in patched canvas. Alanna's lance and shield were put on Liam's Drifter, since commoner youths did not carry them.

When Alanna herself entered the courtyard, she barely recognized her own Moonlight in the dun-colored mare that awaited her. Using rawhide strips, the knight wrapped Lightning's gem-studded hilt until only the battered crystal on the pommel showed. Buri, dressed as Alanna was in a boy's shirt, breeches, and jacket, arrived next. She glared at Bother, who laid back his ears at the sight of her, and went to make friends with the pony she'd named Sure-Foot.

Thayet was transformed into a sallow-skinned female. Her hair was dull, touched with grey, and a purple birthmark spread over her nose and down her left cheek. She was swathed in a shapeless brown dress. The whole effect was so painfully ugly that no one would look at her for long.

"We provisioned you," one of the novices said, looking at Thayet with tears in her eyes. "The pack-horse, and your bags. Princess, the Goddess smile on you, wherever you go!"

Alanna gripped the Hag-Daughter's arm. "If you come west—"

She smiled. "Farewell, Lioness."

They galloped out of the convent gates, riding hard. Distance, rather than conserving themselves and the horses, was the important thing for this part of their journey. For once Faithful kept silent about the joggling, hooking his claws into his cup and holding on. Their route from the convent led past the city wall rather than into the city. The road was deserted by Rachia's early morning visitors, so no one would witness their flight. Either the gods smiled or the Hag-Daughter had weather-workers at her command: fog enveloped them, muffling the noise they made and sheltering them from sight.

The ride to the border took three days, with Liam setting a pace all of them could handle. Alanna relinquished command of their expedition to him: not only was he familiar with eastern Sarain and the Roof of the World, but he wanted to lead.

The countryside was deserted. The normal inhabitants—trappers, mountain men, K'miri tribesmen, a few Doi tribesmen from the Roof—

were not sociable at the best of times, and now they had fled the occasional patrols of southern armies. Alanna paid little attention to the deserted land. She worried about Thayet. She worried about herself. These days her old goals appeared silly—a child's dream, not an adult's. But what was she going to do with her life—after she found the Jewel—if she found it? What did acclaim matter if you had nowhere to go, nothing to do?

Three days after setting out from Rachia, they came to the M'kon River that formed the Saren border. On its eastern bank was Fortress Wei, a Saren outpost—there was no single government east of the river. Beyond Wei the ground formed hills and small valleys. Above those hills loomed a huge, purple band that hung too steadily to be clouds. Alanna squinted at it, curious.

Thayet brought her mare up beside Moonlight, observing the direction of Alanna's stare. "The Roof of the World," she said quietly.

four

The Roof of the World

Once they left the border, the road began to climb. The nights were cold, although it was May; Alanna was glad for Liam's warmth in their bedroll. Thayet was the first to don a fur-lined cloak, but the others soon followed suit.

Thayet and Buri joined the Dragon's morning exercises, learning Shang hand-to-hand combat. Alanna was surprised at how well she herself did. Evidently the years of training for knighthood helped her now. She could feel the difference in her body when they practiced, as her muscles took her smoothly from kick to blow and back. Filled with the optimism that comes from being physically fit, she mentally dared the Roof to do its worst.

The farther Thayet got from home, the more relaxed she was. She spoke about her childhood so frankly that Alanna thanked Coram for his affectionate, if gruff, raising of her and Thom. Thayet was the daughter of a ruler who wanted a son; only Kalasin made her feel loved. It was Kalasin who taught Thayet K'miri ways, Kalasin and Buri's family.

"I could never be as good a Queen as my mother," Thayet said. She grinned. "Not that it makes a difference now. I won't be a queen at all."

"Are you sorry?" Alanna wanted to know. She had been terribly frightened when Jon asked her to be his wife, knowing someday she would have to be his Queen.

"A little," Thayet admitted. "I'd like to change things. In Sarain, for instance, women have no rights—just those our husbands or fathers grant us. Estates and fortunes are held by men. Women can't inherit."

"That's barbaric!" protested Alanna. "At home women inherit. Not titles, but they have lands. I'm Myles's heir by law—it isn't common, but it happens."

"Tortall sounds wonderful," sighed Thayet.

"You'll find out when you get there," the knight promised. To herself she added, *We'll all find out a thing or two when we get there, especially Jon.* She grinned in spite of herself.

As the winter snows began to melt, traffic picked up. The roads were thick with miners, trappers, and merchant caravans. Alanna's company passed herdsmen driving flocks to the markets in the south. Farmers waved as they went by, their wagons filled with cheeses, brightly woven cloth, and chickens. Only the Doi tribesmen remained aloof. They were a people like the K'mir, though less fierce than their western cousins. They were expert at survival in the Roof; the most experienced guides were Doi, and the best furs came from their hidden villages.

The travelers rode deeper into the highest mountains in their world, where snow still lay in scattered drifts and patches along the road. Alanna battled rising impatience. For some reason, she felt that she ought to be on the way home. It would be foolish to turn back when they were so close, but she wanted to find the pass and do whatever it demanded, then leave.

She tried to reach Thom or Jonathan with her magic, but it was impossible. Too much distance lay between them. She hadn't been able to show Coram his Rispah since they'd left the convent. Perhaps Thom had the power to reach across the continent—she didn't.

Several days after they had crossed the border, she fell in beside Coram and signaled him to drop back with her. When they were out of their friends' hearing, she asked abruptly. "Have you been joining with the Voice?" She referred to a Bazhir rite: each day at sunset all who were Bazhir by adoption or birth entered into a magic communion with the Voice of the Tribes. The Voice heard news through this link, judged disputes, counseled his people. Since their adoption into the Bloody Hawk, both Alanna and Coram were able to enter into the joining, but Alanna had never done so. At first she refused out of a reluctance to let anyone, even someone as bound by duty and obligation as the Voice, into her mind. Later, after Prince Jonathan had become the Voice, and they had quarreled and broken off their romance, Alanna had decided she certainly didn't want Jon to know how she thought and felt. At the same time, she knew Coram took part in the rite and had done so ever since his adoption in the tribe.

Coram stared at her, startled. "Ye told me when we left for Port Caynn last fall that ye never wanted me to talk about it, or say what I knew..."

Alanna blushed. "Things are different now. Have you?"

"Not since we set out for Maren."

Alanna was startled by his answer. "You joined almost every night we were there. Why'd you stop?"

Coram shrugged. "It's different when ye aren't among the tribe. It's lonesome. I've been tryin', though, this last week. I knew ye're worried about things at home."

"And?" She couldn't keep some eagerness from her voice.

"I'm sorry—I must be too far away. I haven't felt a thing."

Alanna smiled with an effort. "That's all right. I'm probably worried about nothing." She caught up with Liam, pretending not to see Coram's troubled look.

⌒

They entered Lumuhu Valley the first week of May, and a day's ride brought them to the twin passes at its northern edge. An inn built solidly of wood and brick stood where the roads from the passes met. Snow lay in a tattered sheet in the meadow behind the buildings and on the sides of the northeastern pass. The northwest road was blocked with snow and ice; the pass itself was clogged. Alanna swallowed as she looked at this second pass. Why did she have a feeling this was Chitral?

The sky had been bleak all that day. It darkened even more as they stabled the horses, and sleet began to fall as they entered the inn.

"May blizzards is no joke," the innkeeper said, bringing them mulled cider as they waited for rooms to be prepared. "It's what we pay for bein' so high up. You'd best settle in. This storm'll close Lumuhu a week—maybe longer."

"What about Chitral?" Liam asked.

The man laughed. "Mother Chitral won't open till Beltane, and then only for the strongest. The snow never leaves. Him that told you Chitral's a good road was jestin'. I hope you never paid for the pleasure." He walked away, still laughing.

"Now we know why no one took this jewel before," Buri sighed. Thayet stared wistfully into the fire. Alanna huddled in her cloak, listening to the growing shriek of wind.

Liam stayed downstairs while Alanna went to their room to wash and dress in cleaner clothes. Unpacking her bags—since it appeared they were going to stay for a while—she found the violet gown she'd carried since leaving Corus. "How long's it been since I wore a dress?" she asked Faithful.

The cat looked up from his grooming. *You wore that one when you stayed with George, last fall.*

"That's right." She smiled at her reflection in the mirror. "This was his favorite."

It wasn't so wrinkled then, the cat remarked.

Alanna rang for the chambermaid.

∾

*T*hayet applauded when Alanna entered the common room in the violet silk gown (the maid had smoothed most of the wrinkles). Buri whistled; Coram grinned. Liam surveyed her from head to toe, an odd look on his face.

"Well?" Alanna finally demanded, blushing from the others' reactions. "Don't you like it?"

"It's well enough," he said at last. "Doesn't seem practical, though."

Would she ever understand him? "It isn't *supposed* to be practical. It's a dress. A dress that feels beautiful when you put it on."

"Feeling beautiful won't win a fight." His eyes were the pale grey that told her nothing about how he felt.

"I hardly think I'll fight anyone here, unless it's you," she snapped. "Why can't I wear impractical garments every now and then?"

"Suit yourself," he shrugged. "I suppose you'll want earbobs next, and bracelets and other frippery. What comes then? A noble-born husband and court intrigues?"

"I'm female." Embarrassed, she realized Coram, Thayet, and Buri were trying to slip away. "Why can't I wear a dress without you deciding I want to give up everything I am?"

"Our road is rough and cold and muddy. Maybe you realize now that a knight-errant's life isn't as glorious as you expected." There was enough truth in this to hurt. He waved toward her gown. "Maybe this is the Lady Alanna you mean to show your Prince when you go home."

She walked out, knowing that if she spoke she would cry. Running into her room, she slammed the door behind her. She *did* question her life as a roving knight, but not for the reasons *he* had claimed.

Alanna tore off the dress and threw it into the corner, following it with her shift and stockings. Her breeches and shirt were half on when she did begin to cry. Within seconds her handkerchief was soaked.

"I hate him!" She punched the bed for emphasis. "I hate him! It isn't right that one person can hurt someone else this much!"

"You scare him." Thayet closed the door behind her. "Just when he thinks he understands you, you do something new. He can't put you in a neat little box the way he does the rest of us."

"I never asked to be something new to him!" Alanna wiped her eyes on her sleeve and finished buttoning her breeches. "I never asked to be *any-thing* to him! It just—happened."

Thayet buttoned Alanna's shirt. "I have a feeling it 'just happened' to Liam, too, and that's what frightens him. Our Dragon is the kind of man who likes to be in control of everything, particularly himself."

Alanna stared at Thayet. Did this explain why Liam feared magic? "What's wrong with falling in love with me? And what does wearing a dress have to do with *any* of this, Thayet?"

The Princess smiled. "Alanna, when you wore that dress, he saw the daughter of a noble house—a woman whose family tree reaches back to *The Book of Gold*. Liam is common-born."

"If I don't care about that, why should he?"

"He's very proud." Thayet dipped her handkerchief in Alanna's water basin and wiped the knight's face. "Some women can cry and look beautiful," she said dryly. "You and I can't."

"I know," Alanna sniffed. "I get red and blotchy. When George told me he was, well, interested, I cared about his being a commoner. I even said 'like should marry like,' or something like that. George didn't care. But Liam— What difference can rank make to the Shang Dragon?"

There was a quiet rap on the door, and Liam came in.

"I was just leaving," Thayet said. She winked at Alanna and went out, closing the door.

His face scarlet, Liam watched the floor as he spoke. "You shouldn't've taken the dress off. You look very pretty in it. I guess sometimes we get used to seeing a person a certain way."

It was all the apology she would ever get from him, she knew. Alanna patted the bed beside her, and Liam sat. "I like dresses," she explained. "If you come with us to Tortall, you'll see me wearing more of them. Just because I'm a knight doesn't mean I don't like pretty clothes." She grinned at him. "I've even worn face paint, sometimes."

When he looked startled, she explained, "You know, lip rouge, and so on. I'm not ashamed of being female, Liam."

Tentatively, he brushed Alanna's hair with his hands. "I didn't think you were. I never forget you're a woman, Lioness." His first kiss was gentle, the second passionate. Alanna let him pull her into his arms, thinking, *We should talk some more about why he was angry. I don't think lovemaking will settle anything.* The Dragon was so determined, however, that once again she put her questions aside to be dealt with later.

∾

*A*n hour later, as they dressed for dinner, she asked, "Are there any Lionesses in Shang?"

Liam stretched, thinking. "Not for fifty years. The women prefer names they don't think are 'flashy.' That means not many Lionesses or Dragons.

My master in kick fighting was the Wildcat. She always said if the men wished to attract attention, that was their problem."

"But mythic beasts are 'flashy' by nature, I should think," protested Alanna. "Or don't you let women get to those ranks?"

"Try to stop them!" he grinned. "Right now there's me, the Griffin—also a man—and Kylaia al Jmaa, the Unicorn. She's the most beautiful thing on two feet, all silk and steel and lightning." He tweaked her nose. "Satisfied?"

Their group had dinner in the room Thayet and Buri shared, not bored enough to go down to the common room yet. They were filled with a weird sense of mingled excitement and apprehension, but no one cared to talk about it. What could they do now? Wait until Chitral cleared?

Alanna didn't think she could wait that long. Though she didn't know why, she had a strong feeling that she had to get home.

They amused themselves the next morning by catching up on chores that went neglected while they were on the road. Alanna and Coram spent the hours after breakfast mending tack in the stables. Liam worked on his fighting gear as Thayet mended clothes and Buri cleaned the weapons. By lunchtime all of them were ready for diversion. They went to the common room to see who else was kept there by the storm.

Two companies of merchants were present: one bore spices to the valley north of Lumuhu and

Chitral, the other furs and hand-woven goods south to Port Udayapur. They were joined by four locals— two shepherds, a blacksmith, and a guide—and a group of five Doi. The Doi were as interested in Alanna and her friends as the knight was in them. They exchanged looks with Alanna throughout the meal.

"Liam," Alanna whispered, trying not to seem obvious, "the Doi woman with the onyx in the middle of her brow—who is she?"

Liam nodded gravely to the Doi. They hid their eyes briefly, a sign the Dragon said meant respect. "A fortune-teller," he answered. "The Doi give them as much honor as you'd give a priest. Each fortune-teller works differently. Some read tea leaves in a cup. Some tell your future from the stars. I had my future done once. It's interesting."

She was surprised. "You don't like magic."

Liam shook his head. "This isn't the same. No sparkly fire, nothing flying at you, or things changing. A Doi looks at something *real.*"

One of the Doi men came over, covering his eyes briefly to show his respect for Liam. "Dragonman, we are of the Rockmouse people."

"I know the Rockmouse," replied Liam.

"Our Lady-Who-Sees, Mi-chi, she knows time lies heavy, out of the wind. If you wish, she will tell your hands, all of you."

"We will be honored." Liam stood, telling the others softly, "It's an insult to say no."

Thayet sat beside Mi-chi when the fortune-teller beckoned to her. "I read hands," Mi-chi said. Her voice was deep, her eyes dark and mysterious. "It is said the hand you use to draw a bow or to stir a pot will reveal that part of you others can see. The less-used hand, that is your inner self."

Thayet nodded. "I'm right-handed."

Mi-chi took the princess's left hand, holding it palm up. No one spoke as she ran her fingers over the lines in Thayet's palm. Curious, Alanna probed with her Gift. The fortune-teller's magic was like Bazhir magic; it was drawn from the land rather than from a source inside the person who wielded it.

"What do you see?" Thayet wanted to know.

Mi-chi smiled at her. "You have lost your chains only, great lady. Follow your heart. It leads you to a mighty place. And forget your home. You will never return there."

Thayet rose and walked over to the hearth, keeping her face away from them. Buri watched her royal mistress for a moment before taking her place beside the Doi woman. "Whatever it is you have to say, whisper it, all right?" she asked as she offered her right hand.

Mi-chi agreed, and afterward Buri refused to say what she'd been told. Coram was next, and he asked the same favor. When he stood, he was smiling—whatever his own future held, he seemed to like the prospect.

Mi-chi smiled at Liam. "You know your fate

already, Dragon-man. Nothing I may say will change it, or your knowledge of it." She looked at Alanna. "You, please."

Alanna took the seat beside Mi-chi, offering her left hand. Mi-chi took both, studying the knight's callused palms intently. When she spoke, Alanna could feel a power in her words that was nothing like the Doi magic she'd sensed earlier. This was stronger and untamed.

"He waits, old Chitral." Mi-chi's voice was harsh. "He knows you have come for his prize. He will not surrender it if you are unworthy." Alanna's friends gathered close, listening. "Do you think it will matter if you await *this* storm's end before you set out? He has others to throw at you."

"I'm not trying that pass in the middle of a blizzard!" Alanna protested.

"Then your desire, or whatever it is that drives you, is not enough." Mi-chi's eyes were mocking. "Make no mistake, hero from the flatlands. Chitral fights you with his snows and winds. All who would face him must battle on *his* terms, or not at all." Dropping Alanna's hands, the Doi looked at Liam. "Dragon-man, do you bring your kitten to us for testing? You may not want the grown cat."

"I don't bring Alanna anywhere, wisewoman. She picks her own road."

Mi-chi stood, shaking. One of her companions came to support her. "Do not forget that, Dragon-man." Her voice rasped with exhaustion. "She is a

champion, like you, but different. Always different."
The Doi helped her to her rooms.

Alanna rubbed her hands on her breeches—
they still tingled with both Mi-chi's Doi magic and
the *other* magic that had spoken through the fortune-teller. "It sounds...I don't know. I'm not a
hero, not yet."

Buri slung an arm around Alanna's shoulders.
"Glad to hear it. Come on out to the stables and
we'll practice some kick fighting."

∾

*T*he worst of it was that Alanna believed Mi-chi,
or she believed whatever had spoken through the
Doi woman. That surge of weird magic was impossible to deny. *Just what is sitting up in that pass,
waiting for me to come after the Jewel?* she asked herself time after time as that day ended and the next
crept on. The blizzard continued to blow outside
without showing any signs of letting up.

She thought about just going home, but at this
point, something inside Alanna balked. She knew
there had to have been other times in her life when
she'd failed to complete something she'd set out to
do. She couldn't remember them, however, and she
didn't want to. Furthermore, she did not want her
search for the Dominion Jewel to become the time
she *would* remember that she had started something and had given it up. Almost in spite of herself,
she began to remember what she'd known as a
child in Trebond about survival in the snow.

She was peering through a crack in a shuttered window shortly before twilight of their third day at the inn when she felt someone come up behind her. She knew it was Liam and didn't turn. "I think the storm's dropping," she said, trying to hope.

Liam turned her around, gripping her shoulders tight. "Don't even *think* of it," he warned. "And don't make your eyes wide and ask what I'm talking about. I'm not Coram, and your tricks don't work with me."

That made her angry. "Maybe Coram *lets* my 'tricks' work with him, and I *don't* know what you're talking about."

"Then why'd the innkeeper tell me you were asking about snow gear?" He gave her a little shake. "Do you think you're immortal? That's a killer blizzard! Entire herds are out there frozen in their tracks! Maybe that Gift of yours could shelter you from the little blows in Tortall, but this is the Roof of the World, and *you will die.* I'd never attempt it, and I *forbid* you to!"

Years of training stopped her from hitting him, although she'd never wanted to as much as right now. "You don't know what I can do, Ironarm." Her voice was icy as she jerked out of his hold. "I resent your acting as if I'd do something stupid if you weren't around."

"And wouldn't you do something stupid?" he snapped. "Sometimes you act like you have no more sense than the kitten I named you!"

That was unfair, and they both knew it was

unfair. Liam couldn't apologize; Alanna couldn't forgive. They were coldly silent through dinner, and the others retreated to their own rooms immediately after, rather than witness this quarrel. Liam stayed to talk with the Doi, and Alanna went upstairs with Faithful.

"We're not going to work this out," she told the cat as she undressed and got into bed. "We're too much alike, I guess." Then she began to cry, because it hurt, in spite of her knowing why things were going wrong. Faithful nestled beside her cheek, purring comfortingly. Alanna was asleep by the time Liam came to bed. She didn't feel him gently touch her tear-blotched cheek.

∾

*T*he dream was so clear it scared her: *Jonathan stood beside a coffin that held his mother, Queen Lianne.*

"She was not strong." Roger stood on the opposite side of the coffin, his face emotionless. "Her time had come."

Jon's eyes were tired. "She was healthy once, before you sent the Sweating Sickness. Before you tried to kill her with your spells."

"That was another lifetime for me," Roger said. Thom was a shadow at Roger's side. "I have no more magic," Jonathan's cousin went on. "I did not kill her."

Jonathan looked at his mother's face. "I know you didn't."

Behind Jon, in the shadows, stood George. His eyes were fixed on Roger.

Alanna's eyes flew open. It was very late—Liam was asleep, and the hearth-fire had burned down to embers.

That's it, she thought grimly as she slid out of bed. *I've wasted enough time. I'm going to claim that Jewel and go home.*

Are you sure? Faithful asked as he settled on Alanna's pillow.

"This is crazy," she whispered as she dressed. Liam slept peacefully, not hearing her preparations. "That Doi fortune-teller was making fun of me." Grabbing the bag that contained her next layer of clothing, she pointed to the door.

No, replied Faithful. *Someone has to keep him asleep.* He began to purr. A white, shimmering glow rose to cover him and Liam.

In the hallway Alanna shivered as she exchanged the clothes she'd put on so quickly for garments made of silk: shirt, hose, and gloves. The next layer was wool: leggings, stockings, another shirt. She'd begun to sweat, but she knew outside things would be very different. Discarding the bag and carrying soft-soled trapper's boots, she tiptoed out of the inn and into the passage that joined house and stables.

Underground hot springs made it possible for the inn to stay open. The stables were warm—in her clothes, *too* warm. Alanna cursed the heat until she spotted the stableboy, asleep in a pile of hay. When he stirred, she touched his forehead and told him to sleep, putting her Gift into it.

Moonlight pranced when she saw her mistress, but Alanna shook her head. "Not tonight, girl."

Next to the stable doors were the three large bins the innkeeper had described for her. The one marked in red contained heavy winter gear in the largest possible sizes; the yellow one held medium sizes, and the green was for small. Opening the last, she pulled out the next layer of clothing. Everything was Doi make: leather jacket and trousers lined with fleece, a vest filled with goose down, a knitted facemask, goggles.

She used a burnoose for a head-cloth and her own fleece-lined mittens. From her belt hung Lightning and a double-headed axe with a special blade for ice. Over it all she wrapped a fur-lined cloak. Scanning the racks of snowshoes hanging over the bins, she selected the smallest pair and fastened them over the boots. "I hope I still remember how to use these things!"

Standing, she took inventory. Had she left out a single piece of clothing or a single tool that might help?

If she had, she couldn't remember it now. Gently she brought up her Gift, filling every stitch she wore with it and binding the stable's warmth to every layer of clothing. She fixed it there with a word of command, just to be safe, and sealed it all with the ritual "So mote it be!" Heat settled over her like a blanket. Drawing a deep breath, she opened the stable door a crack and passed through. Before she closed it, she sent a bit of magic back to the sleeping boy, so he would wake in five minutes and bolt the door.

The stableyard held drifts of only a foot or so, protected as it was by the inn's high containing wall. She found the gate and opened it, bracing herself for the first unrestricted blast of the storm. When it came, it almost knocked her over. Slanting her body into the wind, Alanna passed through the gate and pulled it closed.

The wind made her gasp with its sharpness. Icy daggers bit into her chest as she started to shiver. *Cold,* a part of her wailed, *I hate the cold!*

Alanna forced a foot out in front of her, trying not to think of ice or wind. She stepped again, shoving her shoed foot down. *Step two.* She could barely see in front of her. How would she know which way to go? She raised a foot and brought it down, moving forward against the wind. *Third step takes all.* Somehow she was moving. Given what she already knew—that whatever ruled the pass was going to make this as hard for her as possible—she walked directly into the wind.

She hadn't used snowshoes much in the years since she'd left Trebond. It took her a few minutes to make her legs and feet remember just how they worked: long steps, lift the shoes clear of the snow, then put them down. Stop every six or seven steps to shake off the snow that piled on the top of the broad, flat shoe. It was hard work for her leg muscles, but she welcomed it. She welcomed anything that took her mind off the cold. Even her Gift couldn't ward off all of it, and her magic was burning up dangerously fast in the attempt.

Was she mistaken, or had the ground begun to rise?

She wasn't mistaken. With a thump she collided with a tall stone pillar, the one that marked the point where the road left the valley floor and climbed into the pass. Alanna sheltered herself in the lee of the rock for a moment, panting with the effort it had taken to get this far.

On a stormless day this walk would've taken me five minutes. How long have I been out here? An hour? She pushed away from her shelter and into the wind again.

A sudden gust shoved her to her knees. Clenching her teeth, Alanna got up and went on to ram into a tree. She stumbled and fell on her back in the snow. Afraid she'd get buried in snow if she stayed in one place too long, she struggled up again, hissing words she'd forgotten she knew at the clumsy snowshoes. Inspiration struck. She seized a tree branch and hacked it off with her axe to form a staff. *Miache didn't have to put up with anything like this to get the Jewel,* she thought grumpily as she shook the snow from her shoes and set off once again. *She stole it from a nice, warm vault.* Now she tested the ground ahead with the wood, always heading face first into the wind. She decided she'd rather face a dragon than this storm.

It helped to recite poems as she walked. First she went through those the Mithrans had taught her in the palace. When they ended, she started with those taught her by foot soldiers, thieves, and hostlers. She was halfway through "The Tireless Beggar"—the song that had almost gotten Coram into trouble in Berat—when she ran out of voice. Stopping to rest, she wondered how far she'd come.

Her internal clock said dawn was still a few hours away and that she'd been at this almost two hours. The innkeeper has said it was two hours' hard walking from his door to the top of the pass, but under these conditions, Alanna knew it might take her an entire day to cover the same distance.

I wonder if I can sense the Jewel? She reached for her Gift and stopped, feeling afraid. While she'd concentrated on pushing ahead, her Gift had poured itself into the effort of keeping her warm. It was dangerously low and flickering, burning itself up against the killer storm. She couldn't turn back—it would be gone before she reached the tree, let alone the valley.

Alanna climbed on. She thought wryly that she couldn't even blame Liam for forbidding her this climb and making her determined to do it. She was a grown woman, and the only person who had ultimate control of her behavior was she, herself.

Serves me right for losing my temper, she told herself. Carefully she began to cut back the areas her warmth-spell covered until it was in force only around her feet, hands, and face. Trying to ignore the increased bite of cold on the rest of her, she plowed back into the wind.

It took five minutes of uphill walking before she realized that the wind had dropped. Halting, she looked up. Drifting snowflakes were all that remained of the blizzard. She slipped up her goggles and turned to look for her tracks. They lay behind her, following an eerily straight line as far as she could see. A cold that wasn't winter-brought raced up her spine. Her trail should have swung back and forth in the snow. Instead it looked as if she could have drawn it with a straight-edge.

"I don't know if this is good," she murmured. "With the wind in my face, at least I knew where I was headed." Looking again at her tracks, Alanna shrugged and set off again. As her Gift burned lower and lower, staying in motion became a vital concern. Every few feet she'd look back to make sure she kept to her earlier course. Before her opened the pass, white and smooth along the road. Overhead the clouds broke up, revealing a sliver of new moon. The night was very quiet, the only sounds those of shifting snow and cracking rock.

Suddenly she heard in her mind a voice as terrible in its way as the Goddess's, filled with tumbling boulders and rushing streams. She dropped to her knees with her hands over her ears—it did no good.

So you have come this far. You took your time about it.

Alanna couldn't reply.

Look to your left.

She obeyed. A line of light stretched up the wall of the pass, over broken rock and pools of snow and ice. *The thing you came to take is at the end of this road—as am I.*

The voice—it had to be the voice of the being that Mi-chi had called "old Chitral"—was gone. Alanna listened apprehensively for a moment, then remembered the cold's danger and scrambled to her feet again. Drawing a breath, she turned away from the smooth path, which lay so invitingly before her. She strengthened the spell on her hands and feet, drawing it away from her face and wondering how long her Gift could hold out even now. She was sleepy. A nap would be—

She shook off the cold's growing spell and made for the slope, stopping only to remove the snowshoes and strap them to her back. Her temper came back with a rush—not at Liam, this time, but at Chitral. "Am I supposed to entertain you?" she yelled, climbing into the rocks. "Where I come from it's considered honorable to kill a victim outright— not play with her first!"

There was no reply, but she didn't want one. All

she really needed was the heat of her anger. She unhooked the axe from her belt once again, using it to pull herself up.

Her foot broke through a crust in the snow, and she went down, crying out as her leg got stuck between two rocks. Carefully she pulled herself out onto more trustworthy ground, using the ice blade on the axe. When she tried the leg, it throbbed but held.

"Are you *enjoying* this, Chitral?" No answer. On she climbed.

Within a few feet her staff slid on a hidden bit of ice. She struck the ground with her knees, biting into her lower lip. Alanna grabbed a handful of snow and pressed it against the mask, over her bleeding mouth. Adding another hurt to Chitral's account, she rose and went on. She knew she got hurt so much now because weariness and agitated nerves interfered with her judgment. The best solution was to stop and rest for half an hour, but she didn't dare try that. Instead she started to sing "The Tireless Beggar." She'd finished it and had sung halfway through "The King's New Lady" when she stumbled into the cave.

Her Gift flickered and died, leaving her with only a trace of its fire. She'd used it up.

Going home will be very interesting, she told herself as she looked around. There was a larger cave behind what seemed to be a small antechamber, and she went into it. Chitral's line of light ended here, in a large chamber with walls that glowed a dim, eerie yellow. At the opposite end was a tunnel.

"All right, Chitral!" she yelled when she'd pulled down her mask. "I'm here!"

Then prepare yourself for combat, came the nerve-shaking reply. *You asked for something you can fight. I will oblige you.*

The air in the cave was cool, but not cold. She began to strip, preparing herself mentally. She peeled everything down to her woolen layer, leaving the clothing in a pile on the cave floor. Her mind took careful inventory of her physical condition, and she was unhappy with what she found. She'd never taken on a fight in worse shape.

Nothing to it, she thought as she unsheathed Lightning and loosened her arms. *Next time I go after something, I hope it's in a dusty corner where no one sees or cares if I take it. I did ask for this.*

Something padded toward her in the tunnel. Moving into the center of the cave, Alanna set herself.

When it came into the light, she understood instantly that Chitral had assumed this form—she couldn't say how she knew it, but she did. He'd come as one of the great rock-apes that inhabited the Roof of the World. Incredibly shy of people, they were seldom seen, and they never carried short swords as this one did. The blade was black iron and very primitive, but Alanna had no doubt it would do the job intended for it. *Oh, gods,* she thought as the ape squared off against her, its deep-set eyes bright with intelligence. *I'm in for it now.*

He—it?—swung and chopped, forcing her back. She moved warily, her tired muscles sluggish at first. He jabbed; Alanna countered and thrust, making the ape skip away. Now wasn't the time for fanciness or art, now was the time to just stay alive. At least the knowledge of a fight sent adrenaline coursing through her body, putting a stop to the tremors of exhaustion. The ape pursued her, hewing with the short sword as if it were an axe.

The long hours with Liam began to show as Alanna automatically dipped, swerved, and twisted. Keeping out of the ape's reach—he could do as much harm with a hand as he could with his blade—she made him wary of Lightning. Her sword nipped and bit at him, leaving his fur dotted with blood.

Her injured knee buckled, and the ape's sword scored her from collar to navel, cutting through wool and silk to leave a shallow, bleeding gash. She faltered and lunged in, chopping at the ape's neck. He roared and smashed back with his unarmed fist, catching her on the elbow. Alanna fell forward and rolled out of the way. Her arm went numb; Lightning dropped from her fingers. Getting up, she staggered back as the ape picked up her sword. He peered at the grey lights shifting under the steel skin.

You did a work of art when you made this. As much as she might want to, she couldn't react to the pain of his voice in her head, not unless she wanted him to kill her as she covered her ears. She wondered how he even knew Lightning had once been two swords, and that she'd combined them to make one unbroken blade. The ape tossed the sword behind him, where it lay near the far wall of the cave. *I suppose you did it only because you wanted a whole sword you could command. Not because the magic was beautiful for its own sake.*

It wasn't true, entirely. He gave her no chance to answer as he attacked.

Alanna couldn't think, couldn't worry if her body might give out. She ducked and dodged. When he gave her an opening, she executed one of the jump kicks Liam had taught her, slamming into the ape's shoulder and making him roar. When he swung to chop her down, she was away and circling. She sought her chance and flew in again, hitting the same shoulder. It was his blade arm that she focused on, kicking every chance she had while keeping out of his range and grip. The fourth time she hit that arm, she kicked lower, into the same muscle he'd hit to make her drop Lightning. The iron sword fell to the cave floor, and Alanna went for it. Her hands closed on the hilt.

Pain seared her hands and arms, locking her muscles together. She screamed, her throat tearing with the cry. It hurt worse than anything she could remember. She held on—she couldn't let go—and rolled to her back, pointing it at the advancing ape. Crying with the pain, she yelled, "Don't! I don't want to kill you! Keep the Jewel!"

The ape stopped a foot beyond the sword's point, looking her over curiously. If Alanna didn't know better, she'd have sworn he smiled. Reaching forward, he plucked the sword from her freely bleeding hands.

You are a funny little thing. His voice hurt much less this time, which puzzled her. He seemed to have changed his mind about killing her.

He didn't choose to explain. Instead his thought-voice went on. *I suppose you have no idea why you are compelled to seek this Jewel.*

Alanna cradled her palms against her chest, too tired to rise. "It's for the glory of Tortall." Her throat hurt from screaming. "There isn't a nation existing that can't profit from the Dominion Jewel. And bringing it home would be to the glory of the knight who brought it. If it's yours, though, it's yours. Now that I think of it, I don't know how the famous heroes of the past *were* able to take things from the entities that guarded them—not if they were as noble as the stories claim. When you look at it right, it *is* stealing."

The ape shook his head, plainly amused. In a hand that was empty a moment ago, he offered a many-faceted purple gem. When she stared at him without moving, he placed it on her chest.

What use have I for a jewel? His outline turned blurry.

"Are you one of the gods?" she asked as he began to fade. Suddenly she had a hundred things she wanted to know from him.

No. I come from before. Your gods are children to my brethren and me.

Alanna could barely see the ape, and the air was getting perceptibly cooler. She scrambled to her feet. "Then who are you?"

I am this place, and these mountains. I suppose you might call me an elemental. Now his voice began to fade.

"How did you come by the Jewel?" She struggled to put on her clothing, trying to ignore the pain in her hands. The Jewel she stuffed into a pocket.

It finds its way to me from time to time. Not often, but now and then. I made it, and I keep it because I like to have company. I shall be entertained by your visit for centuries of human time. You mortals are quite interesting!

She could feel no sense of him at all when she finished dressing, which may have been just as well. She was not sure she liked the idea of being "entertainment" for anyone, elemental or no.

She found her way to the mouth of the cave and looked out, clinging to the rim of the opening. Dawn was coming, and she had no way to return to the inn.

"No wonder he gave me the Jewel," she muttered, sliding down to sit on the rock floor. "I'm going to die here anyway." She knew the idea should bother her, but it didn't. Her eyelids were getting heavy, and she barely noticed the cold. Pulling her cloak over her face, she went to sleep.

∾

She was warm—all of her, not parts. She could smell clean linen and herbal salves. Forcing her eyes open, Alanna wondered how long she'd been out.

"Never again." Her voice was harsh in her ears. "I won't spend another winter in the cold." Her eyes watered as she tried to look around.

"You could've fooled me." The deep rumble was Liam's voice. "If a man went by the way you act, he'd think you live to freeze!"

She sighed. "I'm sorry," she whispered. He was slowly coming into focus, and she wasn't surprised to see that his eyes were pure emerald in color.

"*Sorry*?" His voice cracked on the word.

"I'm sorry I had to go into a blizzard at all. I wasn't given a choice, remember?"

"You had your gods-cursed cat witch me!"

Alanna tried to push herself upright and winced: he hands were heavily bandaged and throbbed under the weight she'd put on them. "Ironarm, stop it! Aren't there times when *you* act alone?"

"This isn't the same!"

"Horse dung it isn't. People like us have to know when to break rules. This was one of those times, and I was right to do it. I *am* sorry I hurt you. Chitral didn't leave me much of a choice."

He walked out without looking at her.

Thayet came in a few minutes later with a pitcher of mulled cider. A maid followed with a tray of food, and Alanna's stomach growled a welcome. Seeing tearstains on Alanna's face, Thayet said, "The Dragon will be all right." She poured a cup of cider and helped Alanna to drink it. "He was worried sick about you. We all were."

"The Jewel?" Alanna didn't want to talk about Liam. "Where is it?"

"Under your pillow. Can you manage a spoon?"

Alanna looked at a bowl of porridge dotted with dried fruit and cream. "I'll manage if it kills me."

Unfortunately, she couldn't handle a spoon. Thayet fed her, ignoring Alanna's protests. "You've been asleep almost a week," the Princess said. "The storm was over when we woke up. You were out there when it stopped?" Alanna nodded.

"There was a tremor of some kind—a little earthquake—just after dawn," Thayet continued. "When it was over, the pass was clear. The innkeeper and some of the guests ran for a temple at that point, I think. You remember the Doi who were staying here? They went out and brought you down, slung over a pony. They said they found you in front of a cave near the top of the pass. You were a mess."

"Can I talk to them?" Alanna wanted to know. "Thank them?"

Thayet shook her head. "They're gone. They left when you started to get better. Buri says they don't like to be thanked."

"Did—the healers say how I am?"

Thayet put down the spoon. "You'll have a scar from your neck to your abdomen, right between your breasts. Your hands will mend. They said you'd do better once you woke up and used your own Gift on them." Reminded by this, Alanna felt for her magic and found it. Her rest had restored it to full strength. Thayet began to tidy up, saying, "The Doi healer said your hands will always know when it's going to storm."

"'Old swordsmen and their scars know the coming rain,'" Alanna quoted—it was a common saying. "I suppose I had to pay for this somehow."

"Was it worth the price?"

"I don't know." Alanna drew the Jewel from beneath her pillow and looked at it. The gem fit neatly into the center of her palm. "Thayet, do you want this? For Sarain? It seems as if you need it more than Tortall does right now." She offered it to the Princess, who stepped back with an odd look on her face. The Jewel began to shimmer with an internal light, until Thayet pushed Alanna's hand away.

"No female can hold the Saren throne." Her voice was soft. "*The Book of Glass* forbids it. Children hear tales of other lands, less wise than ours, who came to grief because they let a woman rule. The chiefs of the Hau Ma, the Churi, and the Raadeh are women, but they're K'mir, and everyone knows the K'mir are savages."

"Tortall isn't like the K'mir, but it isn't that bad, either," Alanna said. The bitterness in Thayet's voice hurt.

"All my life I've been worthless, the one who should have been a male and an heir. My father was kind, in his way—I take after him in looks." Thayet rubbed the arch of her nose. "But he never forgot I wasn't a boy. Every morning the Daughters of the Goddess and the Mithran priests have orders to pray for a *jin* Wilima in their daybreak services."

Alanna swallowed. If he'd loved his daughter, how could the Warlord have humiliated her like that? "Thayet, I'm sorry."

The Princess didn't hear. "I'll tell you something else, Lady Knight. In Tortall you lied about your sex and kept it secret for years, but when the truth came out, you were allowed to keep your shield. We heard about you at my father's court. The majority opinion was that you should be burned, although one group held out for death by torture." Thayet put the tray beside the door. "I thought Tortall sounded like Paradise. It's certainly an improvement on my father's palace or the convents, and it has to be better than what I'll get if I return to Sarain now."

"You didn't have to tell me any of this." Alanna slid the Jewel beneath her pillow again. "A simple 'no' would've worked."

The Princess's face had been hard and distant. Slowly she brightened. "A 'simple no'?" she repeated, amused. "Alanna, my very dear, you're an incredibly high-minded person, have you noticed? You take duty and responsibility *seriously*. If you believed I turned my back on Sarain for a whim or a fit of temper, you'd lose any respect you have for me." She put a hand on the knight's shoulder. "Before I met you, I thought the women of our class were useless. Those who go to Shang are commoners. Noble families chain their daughters in their rooms rather than permit them that life. The K'mir have no one of noble blood, only people who earn their honors. But you and I come from over-bred families, good as ornaments and nothing more. And *you* are far from useless."

Alanna blushed. "Thayet, you're flattering me. It was easier for me to rebel than stay and make something of myself. Why didn't I go to convent school and prove ladies are more than ornaments that way?"

Thayet's look was skeptical. "What I'm trying to say is that I look forward to creating my *own* life. In Tortall I can, because I'll be without rank or title." She sat on the bed. "I'm going to start a school for the children of commoners. Once I sell my jewels, I'll have plenty of money to do so."

Alanna, who had different plans for Thayet, said hastily, "I won't cast you adrift when we're there! You'll be our guest—Thom's and Myles's and mine. The school's a grand idea, but there are ways and ways to start one."

Thayet shrugged. "Look at me, rattling on when you just woke up." Firmly, she tucked blankets around Alanna. "Try to sleep some more." She left, carrying the tray.

Sleep was the last thing Alanna wanted. She'd had a week of it. With an effort she threw off her blankets and stood. Leaning against a bedpost for support, she took inventory: twisted leg—stiff but painless; assorted bruises—fine; gash on her chest and bitten lip—cleanly healed; eyes—teary but working; hands—she didn't want to think about her hands. Not bad, considering.

She dressed in garments that could be pulled on. Buttons and buckles were more than she could handle. She tucked her feet into slippers and clumsily ran a brush through her hair. Keeping a watch for well-meaning persons who might shoo her back to her room, she escaped to the stables.

The stableboy ran when he saw her, which was convenient. There are times in every rider's life when it is necessary to apologize to a horse, but Alanna preferred not to have witnesses. It was too embarrassing. Moonlight tried to stay aloof as her knight-mistress entered her stall. Alanna offered an apple stolen from the common room, stroking the mare and whispering compliments. Soon Moonlight was nudging and nuzzling, plainly checking Alanna's hooves, withers, and flanks. The salve on Alanna's bandages made the mare sneeze.

"I wish Liam forgave this easily," sighed Alanna. She looked up to see Faithful sitting on the gate. "Are you angry too?"

I know why you went. Moonlight and the others were worried, the cat said. *I've been staying her since the Dragon woke and found you gone. Horses are calmer people. They also don't throw things at cats.* He climbed onto her shoulder, draping himself around Alanna's neck.

"Poor Faithful. He didn't really throw things, did he?"

Only when he saw me.

Someone coughed. Coram had been grooming Anvil. Now he leaned against the bay's stall, watching.

"Are you going to yell at me, too?" Alanna asked warily.

"I should, I expect. I thought I raised ye to treat blizzards with more respect."

"I did. If you hadn't taught me how to dress, how to survive, I wouldn't be here now." Alanna wanted so much for him to say it was all right. She couldn't bear it if she lost Coram *and* Liam both.

"Surely ye're not tellin' me it was a simple matter of layerin' yer clothes and usin' snowshoes." There was a mocking gleam in his eye.

"No. I used my Gift. Coram, I didn't have a *choice*. If I'd walked out of here on a sunny day, Chitral—the being that holds the pass—would've dumped another storm right on my head. If there *was* a safe way to get the Jewel, I would've followed it gladly." To her shame, Alanna felt tears dripping down her cheeks. "Please don't be angry with me."

Coram walked over and put his arms around her. "There, now, Lioness," he whispered, holding Alanna tightly. "It's just hard to see ye all grown up and doin' mighty things." He wiped Alanna's eyes with his handkerchief. "Though I don't know why I'm surprised, since ye always told me ye would." He put the handkerchief to her nose. "Blow," he said firmly. She obeyed, just as she had when she was five. "That's my girl."

⤖

*B*uri, Thayet, and Coram came to share Alanna's dinner, setting their own meals up on tables so they could eat together. Since the inn's healer had examined and rebandaged her hands, Alanna could use her own knife and fork. That alone lifted her spirits—being fed made her feel helpless. Once the maids cleaned up, they roasted chestnuts in the hearth and told stories until everyone was yawning. Thayet was gathering up her beadwork when

Alanna said, "If it's all right, I'd like to go the day after tomorrow."

"Are you crazy?" Buri demanded. "You just got up! You said yourself you won't be able to grip anything but a fork or spoon for a week!"

Alanna shrugged. "I'd just like to set out. I'll be all right." Meeting Coram's eyes, she added, "Moonlight won't let me fall."

Shaking her head, Thayet sighed. "We'll see how you feel tomorrow."

Buri stayed when the other two went out. "I want you to know that it's an honor to ride with you, wherever," the girl said shyly. "I just hope someday you'll tell me what happened. It must've been *awful*, the shape you're in." She grinned.

"The innkeeper won't take payment, did Thayet tell you? The healer won't, either. The grooms fight over who works on our horses, especially yours. The maids cut up the napkin you used for lunch, so they can each have a bit."

"Buri, that's crazy!" Alanna protested.

"Ask them," Buri said impishly. "They say you parted the snows and walked up there to do battle with the God of the Roof for his Jewel."

"All this will happen to you someday, once you go out and start performing great deeds," Alanna threatened as the girl opened the door. Buri winked and left. "What nonsense!" Alanna said to Faithful.

The inn has filled up over the last three days, was

the cat's lazy reply. *The innkeeper raised his prices. He expects a very good year—several very good years, in fact. Word gets around fast.* He yawned and tucked his nose beneath his tail.

Muttering about human folly, Alanna tossed the bedclothes aside and went downstairs. Since her friends had been with her until late, only a few people remained in the common room, most of them drinkers who were oblivious to anything. The innkeeper and a maidservant were cleaning up. Liam sat before the fire in a low chair, feet crossed before him, frowning.

"I thought Shang warriors were too dignified to sulk." Alanna hooked a stool over so she could sit in front of him.

"Go away, Lady Alanna," he sighed, reaching for a tankard and draining it. The innkeeper came with another tankard and a pitcher, pouring mulled cider for them both before making himself scarce.

Baffled and hurt, Alanna pinched an earlobe to keep from crying. When she had herself under control again, she rasped, "What's wrong with you? Are you offended because I didn't take your manly advice? D'you think I did something you couldn't have? Is your *pride* hurt?" She looked at her bandaged hands; they were trembling.

A massive hand gripped her chin, turning her face so he could stare into her eyes. "Put yourself in my boots." His voice was soft, his face tight. "I sat here wondering if you'd live while all around me folk talked about those who died of the cold. Moonlight tried to break down the stable door. The hostlers had to drug her. Coram—I never want to see a man *that* drunk again. Thayet and Buri were fine. Why shouldn't they be fine? You witched them. Just like you witched me."

That's it, Alanna realized. She had known how he felt about magic, and she had let Faithful spell him anyway. Liam would never trust her again. "Are we finished, then?" she whispered.

He let her go. She continued to watch him, waiting. "I don't know, kitten."

At the use of her nickname she felt her chin tremble and her eyes fill. "I *am* sorry. I know it doesn't do any good, but I am. If you'd awakened, you'd've stopped me."

Liam nodded. His eyes faded from emerald to a blue-grey she'd never seen before. "Seems there's nothing we can do, right? I can't help the way I feel. Not about the Gift. And you can't help but use it, nor should you. A tool is meant to be used." After a moment he swallowed and added, "I'm sorry, too." His voice was cracking. "You probably saw I had my things moved to another room."

"Can we be friends, still?"

"I promise it." He couldn't keep the relief from his voice, which hurt Alanna more than anything he'd actually said. She made her excuses and went upstairs to cry over Liam Ironarm one more time.

∾

*T*wo days later they set out. Alanna couldn't shake the sense that she had to go home, and her companions had caught the feeling from her. Most of the inn's staff appeared sorry to say good-bye, although some—like the stableboy—hid their eyes in the Doi gesture of fear and respect when they passed. Alanna tossed a gold noble to the boy, wanting to make up for the fright her sleep-spell had given him. He dropped it with a yelp, refusing to touch it until a maidservant had picked it up.

On the road, Alanna stopped for a last glance at Chitral Pass. The snow was nearly gone after the spate of spring temperatures that had followed her adventure. Green showed on the rocky walls leading up into the surrounding mountains. A party of trappers was headed up into Chitral as another company descended from Lumuhu Pass. Alanna wondered if Chitral watched her and waved a farewell in case he did.

That night they stopped at an inn they'd used on the way north. Where before they had been treated no differently from other wayfarers, now they were honored guests. The news of Alanna's feat and her possession of the Jewel had spread rapidly, and the inn's staff made it plain they considered no service to be too small for them to give Alanna and her friends. The landlord refused payment at first but learned that the Shang Dragon could be very persistent. The company received the same treatment from the staff of the next inn, where they spent their second night on the southern road.

As their third day's ride drew to a close, Alanna thought wistfully of a camp under the stars. It would be chilly, like any other mountain night, but they would have privacy. If the next inn was like the last two, privacy would be in short supply. Burdened as she was with mending hands, Alanna didn't want to mention it. The others would have to do her work if they camped.

Buri halted when they saw the lights of a town ahead. "I'll meet the rest of you in the morning," she announced. "I'd rather freeze to death." She looked guiltily at Alanna. "Sorry, Lioness. I forgot you almost did freeze to—"

"*Enough,* Buri," Alanna growled.

"I have to stay with Buri so she can protect me," announced Thayet. "I'm tired of sleeping indoors anyway."

The men looked uncomfortable, and Faithful yowled his disgust with overly attentive maids. Alanna sighed in relief. "Let's find a camping spot."

ᑐ

*T*hey camped during the remainder of the ride to Port Udayapur, filling their bellies with game, wild greens, and oatcakes. Alanna performed any magic—such as mending her tattered hands—out of Liam's sight.

By the time they reached the seaport, Alanna had shed her bandages, and her friends were comfortable around her again. She sometimes felt a pang of sadness when she looked at the Dragon, but she also knew their friendship would last far longer than their romance.

～

*O*nce they were settled at one of Port Udayapur's inns, the travelers met in Alanna's room to discuss their next step. No one was surprised when Alanna said, "I still can't shake the feeling Coram and I are needed at home. Neither of us seems able to make contact with anyone. But I have this sense of trouble there. I'm thinking of hiring a ship."

"I thought you didn't like them." Liam sounded as if he didn't care one way or another.

Alanna grimaced. "I don't. Please, I'd like all of you to come with us. Actually, I'd *prefer* it. But you may have other plans."

Buri and Thayet exchanged looks. "We don't," Thayet said. "I still want to go to Tortall." Buri nodded her agreement.

Alanna smiled. "Good." She picked up Faithful, not wanting Liam to see how anxious she was. Things were so bad between them...

"The innkeeper says a Tortallan galley's in the harbor." The Dragon's voice was quiet. "I don't know if we can book passage—she's a diplomatic courier. But I can ask."

Alanna grinned. He'd said "we." "Would you?

Maybe if you use my name—Trebond and Olau—
they'll agree."

Liam nodded and went out. The others followed, Coram to take their snow gear to the market
and sell it now that they no longer needed such
things, Thayet and Buri to see the sights. Alanna
stayed in her room to nap.

She was roused from her sleep by a knock on
the door. When she opened it, one of the maid-
servants dropped in a curtsey. "Excuse me, miss or
lady," she began nervously. "The gentleman here
insisted that he see you." She indicated the very
large man standing behind her.

The man stood with his back to the hall's
torches, which meant Alanna was unable to see his
face clearly. *He* had no trouble seeing her, however.
A familiar voice said, "Praise Mithros, it *is* you!"
and Alanna was seized up in an enthusiastic hug.
Now she could see that his hair and mustache were
black, the same color as his wickedly dancing eyes,
and that his cheeks were tan and ruddy.

"Raoul?" she whispered, not sure if she believed
it. He grinned, and she returned the hug with one
every bit as fierce. "Goldenlake, you sly fox!" She
pounded his back in delight as he carried her into
her room and kicked the door shut. "Look at you!
Look at you!" He was as tall as ever. When he put
her down, she had to tilt her head to see him. "Sit,
so I don't hurt myself looking at you." He obeyed
briefly, only to jump up to hug her again. It was five

minutes or more before either of them had calmed down enough to make rational conversation. Faithful climbed into Raoul's lap to deliver his own welcome while Alanna poured fruit juice for them both.

Seeing him was almost as good as coming home. During her palace days Alanna's closest friends were all older than she was: Raoul, Gary, Jonathan, and sometimes Alex—Alexander of Tirragen. The older boys were squires to Alanna's page and knights to her squire. They'd taught her palace ways and let her join them in adventures and scrapes. She had introduced all but Alex to George, and they had advised her and looked after her.

"What are you doing here?" she finally remembered to ask. "Last I heard, you were riding desert patrols." Seeing his dark tan and the burnoose draped over his shoulders, she added, "I see the desert agreed with you. Did you like the Bazhir?"

He grinned. "They adopted me. Not your people, the Bloody Hawk. The Sandrunners." He'd named a tribe far to the south of Alanna's. "I like the Bazhir a lot. All they ask a fellow is to ride and fight and do his share of the work—no paying compliments to people you don't like or anything like that."

Alanna grinned. Both Squire Alan and Sir Raoul were notorious for their dislike of social functions. "So what brings you here now?" she wanted to know. "Is that courier vessel yours? Don't tell me you've turned diplomat." She sat on the bed as Raoul's grin faded.

Raoul looked at the cup in his hands. "I'm no ambassador yet. When Myles got your letter from Jirokan, the one where you said you might come here after the Roof, he told Jon, and Jon sent me to bring you home. He's got messengers all along the Great Road, in case you'd changed your mind and decided to return that way."

Faithful sat beside Alanna, who was now uneasy. "I didn't know Jon had the authority to do such things," she said nervously. "I thought only the King could dispatch the diplomatic ships."

"That's right. Jon—" He stopped, looking unhappy. "Look, Alan—No, that's not right. Alanna—"

"King Roald is *dead?*" she whispered.

Raoul nodded. "Let me tell it in the right order. I don't want to skip anything." Alanna nodded, feeling stunned. "See, her Majesty died around the March new moon. No one was surprised, not really. She wasn't very strong, after the Sweating Sickness—you remember. Then Roger tried to kill her, with that image of his. After you left, Thom destroyed the image so she wouldn't be hurt by it, but the damage was done. It was only a matter of time. Then, with the winter so bad, and everything else..." He sighed. "Myles and Thom said you were in Berat right about when she passed on."

"I wrote them from there. Black God, give her

rest," Alanna murmured. She'd never thought of the court without Queen Lianne, even when she tried to envision the hazy "someday" when Jon would be King.

Raoul gave Alanna his handkerchief and continued. "The King never got over it; you know how they were about each other." Alanna half smiled; the royal couple's devotion was plain to anyone with eyes. "It was three weeks later, something like that. Near the beginning of April. He went hunting and got separated from the rest of the party. He was dead when they found him, an accident. It looked like he tried to jump— Remember that gorge, the narrow one about half a league above Willow Falls?"

"Of course." She'd jumped Moonlight over that gorge many times. It was very deep, and the jump required skill and excellent reflexes. She whispered, "So Jon's King."

"Not officially. The coronation's set for the day of the July full moon. He's been acting as King ever since her Majesty died, though. The King just wasn't interested."

"Jon must be heartbroken."

"He is, but he's never had a chance to get away by himself to mourn. Not with things the way they are." When Alanna looked baffled, Raoul started to pale. "You don't know, do you?"

Alanna suddenly felt that something—something *more*—was seriously wrong. "Know what, Raoul?"

"You've had *no* word from Tortall this year? *Nothing?*"

"The hill roads were almost impassable when Coram and I rode for Berat." *What is wrong with him?* she wondered. Raoul's hands were clenched so tightly in his lap that the knuckles were white. "They were still bad in the south because of the winter rains. No messengers were coming through. And Berat's too far from the sea to get the news from the ships."

"Your Gift, though—?"

"I didn't want to contact anyone with it. I was...busy," she admitted, blushing as she thought of Liam. "What difference does my being in touch or not make? By April we were in Sarain. No messengers could've found us there."

"This was before April." Raoul's voice was tight. "Remember All Hallow? George told us you were with him in Port Caynn." Alanna's blush deepened. "Thom was doing experiments—that's what he told everyone."

"He borrowed my Gift." Her stomach sank. She sensed the worst was coming, and she wasn't sure she wanted to hear it.

"We didn't know," Raoul said disjointedly. "He kept it secret till late in February. It probably finished her Majesty...You remember Delia of Eldorne?"

"Raoul, *please* spit it out," Alanna pleaded. He seemed not to hear.

"She'd been after Thom since you left. Telling him that the *really* great sorcerers could raise the dead, playing off his pride. Sorry, Alanna, but you know how vain he is. Thom finally lost his temper. It was at a court ball; we all heard him. He told her he could do anything Denmarie the Earth-Shaker could do—"

Alanna felt dizzy. "Roger. He brought Roger back."

five

In the Capital of Tortall

*W*hen Queen Lianne died in March, Tortall mourned. Now, after the King's sudden death, the nation's feeling was one of shocked disbelief. To lose both in such a short time seemed like the work of an angry god.

"The Black God is taking his revenge on us," people muttered. "He's not pleased that the Lord of Trebond brought the Duke back from his grave. You can't go interfering with the gods without them extracting payment." The rumors spread, and gossips began to claim that Jonathan's reign would be cursed.

"As if I don't have enough problems," Jonathan told his acting prime minister, Sir Gareth (the Younger) of Naxen.

Gary looked up from the documents he studied, his chestnut eyes worried. His cousin looked worn out. "Talking to yourself again?" He said it like a joke.

"The rumors," Jonathan explained.

"They'll pass, particularly since there's no proof. If the gods are angry, why would they pick on their Majesties? Why haven't they struck Master Lord Thom down? If they want, I'll volunteer for the duty. Thom irritates me. A good striking-down might improve him."

"Does he look *sick* to you?" Jon asked abruptly. "Thom?"

Gary put down his papers. "I don't get close enough to notice how our bold sorcerer looks, if I can help it. He never sheathes that tongue of his anymore. Why?"

"George mentioned it to me, the other day. Thom does seem thinner."

"He's probably losing sleep while he looks up some old spell or the other. Jon, I need your signature on these."

Jonathan obeyed, writing his name over the royal seal on several documents. "I still can't get used to signing as ruler of Tortall. I didn't think I'd be King for…years." He swallowed a sudden lump in his throat. Sympathetic, Gary said nothing. After a moment Jon went on. "I feel helpless. I should have done *something* to keep them alive."

"What could anyone have done?" Gary asked sensibly. "Aunt Lianne never got really well after Roger's spell was broken. And the King—" He stopped, not wanting to touch an unhealed wound.

"He killed himself," Jon whispered. He always forced himself to see the truth, and Gary was one of the few who knew the King *had* deliberately killed himself. "How could he do that?"

"He loved her." Gary's voice was soft.

Jonathan shook his head. "Could I love anyone so much I'd forget that I have a duty to my people? George says you can *smell* their fear down in the Lower City. I can't blame them for thinking there's a curse—not with the famine last winter, and then…this. And what can *I* tell them that will give them confidence? They don't know me. They didn't *really* know my father." He returned the documents to his cousin. "Once things have settled down, I'm going to visit every corner of Tortall. I won't be a King who stays in his palace and waits for his people to come to him." His face was set and stubborn. "I hope Alanna really can bring us the Dominion Jewel."

"Do you think the messengers will find her?" Gary asked.

"One of them will. One of them has to."

⌒

*A*s Jonathan and Gary talked, George Cooper entered his mother's house. A message from Corus had brought him home from Port Caynn at a gallop. Claw, frustrated by months of trying to kill George, had done the unthinkable and attacked a noncombatant, Eleni Cooper. Men and women loyal to George had turned back Claw's forces, and now Mistress Cooper's home resembled an army camp, complete with wary sentries.

When her son walked into the kitchen, Eleni

was sorting and boxing the herbs she used as a healer. Pots holding some potions bubbled on the hearth, filling the air with the scent of herbs.

"It could have been worse," she told George. "None of your people were killed, and I'm all right."

George scowled. "*This* time, Mother. What of the next time, and the next? He attacked a woman who's not sealed to the Rogue. Claw will respect none of our laws if he breaks this one. He don't care who gets hurt. He don't care if my Lord Provost descends on us with soldiers to rid the city of us and our wars. He cares nothin' for them he bribes and forces to follow him. They can end on Gallows Hill, and Claw will make no move to save them. It isn't right. He wants to be Rogue, but he won't look after those sealed to him as is his duty." He accepted the cup of herbal tea she poured for him and sipped it without noticing what he drank. "Our greatest advantage lay always in never causin' enough trouble that my Lord Provost would be interested in cleanin' the Lower City of us."

"You'll find a way to deal with him," Eleni told him. She labeled a packet of comfrey leaves. "I've never known you to admit defeat, George."

"Sometimes *I* start believin' the rumors," George whispered, looking tired. "Let's face it, Mother—a man killed once should stay dead."

Eleni sat across from him at the table. "Thank the Goddess his Gift didn't leave the tomb with him."

"We've only *his* word for that, and Thom's." George spooned honey into his tea. "I think some- times *all* our troubles since October stem from those two. No, that's unfair. I let Alanna go myself."

"She could have waited for you in Port Caynn," Eleni reminded him.

George smiled ruefully. "I try not to ask the impossible of her, Mother. She's not a lass who waits at home for her man."

"She could have returned here with you."

George shook his head. "She didn't wish to face our nobles again. I think her memories of Jonathan still hurt."

"Perhaps you should go after her, then. You haven't been yourself since she returned to the desert." Taking one of his hands, she added, "It would please me to know you had stopped your courting of the hangman's noose."

George squeezed her hand. "I can't, Mother, not yet. I've a few things to finish up here, first." His face was bleak. "Besides, didn't I tell you? The news from Maren and Sarain is she's keepin' company with the Shang Dragon. How can a commoner and a rogue rival the likes of the King of Tortall and Liam Ironarm?"

Eleni frowned. "It's not like you to feel sorry for yourself, or to give up without a fight."

George patted his mother's cheek. "I haven't. I'm just givin' Alanna her head while I see to things here." He grinned, and Eleni grinned back. Finishing his tea, he added, "Speakin' of that, we need to take steps. Claw may be fool enough t'try this again."

"Be careful, George," she teased. "You risk getting tangled in the affairs of law-abiding people like me. Respectability might be catching." Seeing he continued to frown, she said tartly, "What would you do, surround me with the King's Own?"

He looked at her, and a wide grin spread over his face. "You know, Mother, you may have an idea there."

～

A few hours later George took his mother to call on Myles of Olau in his town house. Bazhir guards admitted them and escorted them to the knight's study. The servants hurried to bring Myles and his guests refreshments. George they knew for a frequent guest, but none of them had ever seen the woman who accompanied him. Gossip buzzed in the kitchens as the tribesmen who attended Myles looked on.

Alanna's father looked from George to Eleni after hearing George's request, tugging his shaggy beard. "I'd be delighted if Mistress Cooper wishes to stay in my house. I didn't know things were so bad for you, though."

"Claw's not givin' up easy," George said grimly. "And he knows he can hurt me through Mother. Here, with all these Bazhir about, she'll be safe. You have archers enough."

"It comes of my daughter being the Woman

Who Rides Like a Man," Myles told Eleni, his eyes twinkling. "I adopted her, and they adopted me." He took Eleni's hand. "Alanna's told me about you, and you are the mother of my friend George. I welcome the chance to do you a service, Mistress Cooper."

She looked him over. "I hate to leave my home," she admitted. "But while my son makes his life among rogues, I must be careful. Thank you, Sir Myles. I accept sanctuary in your house."

"Then it must be 'Myles.'" The knight kissed her hand.

"As I am 'Eleni.'"

Myles held Eleni's hand a moment too long, making George think. This possibility hadn't occurred to him before. *A fine thing, to be gettin' a new Pa at my age,* he thought with a grin.

ᖰᕝ

*T*hom dropped into an armchair with a sigh. The bright colors of his silk robe overwhelmed his pale face and dull copper hair, bleaching his eyes to a light amethyst. He rubbed a hand over his chapped mouth, wincing as a crack began to bleed.

Roger of Conté walked in. "So you're back. I was just finishing my notes on Palawynn the Windwaker."

"Thank you," Thom rasped, watching as Roger took a seat. In contrast, the Duke was the picture of health: gleaming brown-black hair and beard, brilliant sapphire eyes, glowing skin. He didn't look as if he'd spent ten months in a tomb, to emerge as a magicless sorcerer.

So here's an irony, Thom thought. *I raise him from death, and seven months later I look as if I just crawled out of the grave.* "I just had another cozy talk with his soon-to-be Majesty," he announced bitterly. "*This* time he brought my Lord Provost. I don't like that old man—I never did." Mimicking, he went on, "Was I *still* sure you have no Gift? Would I report it if you showed signs of getting it back? Have I noticed you conspiring with anyone? Do I suspect you of involvement in the King's death? or the Queen's? or my third cousin's, the one who was struck by lightning!" His face turned an ugly red. "They asked me if I trust you," he added sullenly.

Roger inspected his fingernails. "Do you?" he inquired in his melodic voice.

"Of course I don't. I don't trust anyone."

"Except your sister," Roger pointed out. "What did they say?"

"Nothing, this time," Thom replied, puzzled. "Usually I get a lecture about my duty to spy on you and report my suspicions, but this time— nothing."

"I see. Is there word of your twin?"

Thom glanced sharply at him, a look Roger met with a bland expression. "Jonathan's had word from some Udayan hedgewitch," he said reluctantly. "Sir Raoul found Alanna there. It's possible they'll sail to Port Caynn sometime next week."

"You must be pleased," Roger murmured. "Didn't I hear somewhere she is prone to sea-sickness?"

"Very." Thom grinned. "To think I'd forgotten that."

"Does gossip say if she found whatever it was that took her to the Roof of the World?"

For the thousandth time Thom wondered how Roger really felt about the woman who had killed him. "If his Majesty knows, he's keeping quiet about it. We'll find out for ourselves, soon enough. Are you looking forward to her coming home?"

Picking up a crystal, Roger shrugged. "I plan to stay out of her way. Shall I start on the Dragonbreaker scrolls next?"

"Do as you like," Thom snapped. "I'm not your jailer *or* your keeper."

Roger smiled, turning on his charm. "I owe you a great debt, dear boy. If not for you, I'd be caught still between here and the Realms of the Dead. If I can repay you, I will."

"They'll never trust you," Thom said, red with shame. "They watch everything you do for a sign you've regained your Gift."

Roger stood. "Believe me, Thom—if my magic returns, you will be the very first to know."

ᑐ

The Inn of the Dancing Dove was quiet. It was an hour before sunset, and the city's rogues still prowled the streets. George looked around the empty common room, aware—not for the first time—that he no longer enjoyed being master here.

In part it was his war with Claw. It had begun when George visited Port Caynn, to put down a revolt and then to have a love affair with Alanna. Four months ago Claw had moved to become King of Thieves in George's absence. He had used blackmail to force many to follow him, and then he'd tried to poison George. George had come to the city to save his throne, and Alanna had returned to her Bazhir. George had known then that he'd probably lost her.

When George was younger, things were different. A would-be king challenged the old one to a fight before witnesses. The winner took the throne-like chair at the Dancing Dove and a tenth of the profit on each major transaction and theft. He gave the choicest jobs and judged quarrels. He was king of the Tortallan underworld and received far more obedience than his people would ever give the King in the palace.

Claw would not fight. Claw swore loyalty to George while his men attacked George nightly. Many rogues changed their allegiance on a day-to-day basis, depending on who appeared to be the winner. Only George's oldest friends kept faith with him.

The only interest George now had in the Rogue was the effort to bring Claw down. And he hoped finding out who Claw really was would help. Myles had put a man to investigating Claw's secret past. The history the one-eyed rogue had given George on his arrival in Corus was as false as his name. In other thieves this hardly mattered, but Claw spoke and acted at times like a noble.

"Majesty!" A street boy George didn't know rushed in. "Majesty, come quick! Claw's took by Provost-men!" George followed the boy through the rear entrance, still deep in thought. When he emerged, a man struck him from behind, knocking him into the mud of the kitchen yard. George cleared two knives from their sheaths at his waist. *This is how you pay,* he thought grimly as he slashed and struck. *You forget to be watchful and the Black God taps your shoulder...*

He slashed again; someone screamed. The man on his back fell off. George lunged to his feet, his knives sweeping in a silver arc. Of the gang surrounding him, he took one in the throat and the next low. A fourth jumped from the kitchen roof onto his shoulders. George rammed backward into a wall to stun his assailant.

A swordsman attacked. A line of pain streaked from George's shoulder to his thigh. Gritting his teeth, George threw one of his knives, hitting the swordsman in the chest.

The kitchen yard boiled with enemies. Where were his own people? He found another of his many concealed knives and faced a man with a hand-axe. This one bellowed and charged, but four arrows cut his voice off. He never completed his attack. Black arrows rained as rearing Bazhir warhorses cut off all chances for escape. Within a second the only sound in the kitchen yard was that of the horses.

"You're lucky I was coming to visit," Myles said as he rode up. Dismounting, he caught George as the thief staggered. "You need a healer!"

George shook his head, as much to clear it as to say "no." "Solom," he muttered. Myles helped him into the Dancing Dove's kitchen. Just inside the door they found old Solom and two serving girls, dead.

∾

George was still recuperating in Myles's house two days later when a servant interrupted the knight at his lunch to say Dalil al Marganit awaited him in the library. Myles put down his knife and scrubbed at his face rapidly with a napkin. Al Marganit was the man he'd put to work seeking Claw's true identity. He'd used the little Sirajit agent before and could count on him to find out almost anything.

When Myles entered the library, the agent rose and bowed. He gestured to the bowl of fruit and the Tyran wine the servants had already brought him, saying, "I am treated like a noble in this house."

Myles sat behind his desk with a smile. "You

deserve that treatment, Dalil. Sit down, please. What have you learned for me?"

The little man took a notebook from inside his tunic and leafed through blotted pages. Nearsighted, he had to bring the pages so close to his eyes that they tickled his nose. He sneezed. "Regarding the matter of the thief Claw. Hm! Yes! Arrested by my Lord Provost's men two years ago. Charge of suspected robbery, released for lack of evidence. Our Provost is scrupulous in such matters, unlike many in his place, as your lordship knows. Arrested five months ago in the Dock Riots, escaped. He's now sought by Provost's men. They do not look as hard as they might; one assumes he has paid large bribes.

"I traced the subject Claw to Vedis in Galla, where he claims to originate. He is unknown in the cities Vedis, Nenot, and Jyotis in Galla, all having large communities of thieves. Going by my lord's guess that Claw's accent is that of the Lake Region in Tortall and that Claw was born of nobles either legitimately or illegitimately, I journeyed to the Lake Region with a good drawing of the subject Claw. Here is an accounting of my expenses." He gave Myles a sheet of notepaper, which the knight barely glanced at.

Al Marganit closed the notebook and looked at Myles. "Claw is Ralon of Malven..."

Myles turned white. Another of Alanna's enemies! No one had seen or heard from him in years.

While he'd thought Claw might be illegitimate and trained by his noble-born parent's teachers, he'd never considered the possibility that Claw was a true-born son of a noble family, hiding in the Court of the Rogue! He realized the agent was looking at him, worried. Forcing a smile, he said, "It's all right. Go on."

The little man shrugged and continued. Obviously Sir Myles wasn't going to tell him why he looked as if he'd just stepped on a grave. "He is the third son of Viljo, Count of Malven, and his lady Gaylyah. He was disinherited after the attempted rape of the second daughter of the bailiff, Anala, a village in Eldorne hold. Eldorne is the neighbor of Malven." *A connection between Claw and Delia?* Myles wondered. He scribbled a note to himself as Dalil continued. "The girl's maid threw acid in his face, thereby leaving the purple scars of which you spoke, and causing him to lose an eye. If I may refresh my lord's memory, Ralon of Malven left court at the age of fourteen, after months of feuding with the page Alan of Trebond. Or, if I may be so bold, in the matter of Alanna of Trebond and Olau."

Myles gave an absent smile. "Though blessed few of us knew it, then. Ralon of Malven! How could I have forgotten?"

"He is well disguised, my lord. He came, as bad men will, to make his name among rogues. He battles the present King of Thieves for his throne, but he will not call for an open fight as the custom decrees. Instead, he fights with treachery. Unlike the legitimate Rogue, Ralon as Claw will hire to do murder or to ruin a good name. He will betray those who follow him." The little man shook his head. "A noble gone bad, my lord. There's no stopping him, not at all. He will say that he is owed something, and he has come to collect."

Myles sent al Marganit home with well-earned praise and a fat purse. The agent had never failed him, and this time he'd succeeded past Myles's greatest dreams. The knight considered every aspect of what he'd learned for an hour or so, then went to tell Eleni Cooper and her son.

∽

Chance, and the first sunny day in more than a week, brought large numbers of people to the Corus marketplace that spring morning. Jonathan, after much persuasion, agreed to go riding—his first such outing since the King's funeral. He was a commanding figure in mourning black, flanked by Roger and Sir Gary, both also in black. With them rode other knights and ladies, including Delia of Eldorne, Alex of Tirragen, and Princess Josiane of the Copper Isles.

The company was a beautiful sight, even in their mourning colors of black, lavender, and grey. A crowd soon gathered in the market to watch them pass. The men of the King's Own—many of them uniformed Bazhir, these days—exchanged wary looks and kept an eye on the people who closed in on the riding party. They were disturbed by the crowd's silence. No one called blessings on the King-to-be; many made the Sign against Evil when Roger passed them. There were no cheers. The usual audible and sometimes satiric comments on the nobles' dress and private lives were missing.

George Cooper watched. He'd risked reopening his wounds and being spotted by Claw's or the Provost's men to see how people received their new King. He scanned faces in the crowd, trying to find any feelings other than suspicion or wariness.

"That Conté Duke looks like a *king,*" someone muttered. "Against him Prince Jonathan's a boy."

"I never heard bad of the Prince," someone else hissed. "I've heard plenty bad about his Grace! Ain't natural for a man t'live twice—"

"Th' Prince be cursed," came a third voice, cracked with age. "Th' Sweatin' Sickness when he was a lad, that took my Alish, and both his parents dead, and *him,* the sorcerer, come back—"

"He drove the evil from the Black City, away south," a fourth voice argued. "He made peace with the Bazhir. The old King, his grandda, couldn't even do that."

"He helped a woman make herself a knight. If that ain't unnatural—"

"Hush! Crowds is full of spies, and you've a loose tongue in your head!"

The people stirred with interest as the Lord Provost rode up to change places with Gary. George's long-time enemy was blue-eyed and lean, his face leathery from years in the sun and framed by heavy silver hair and a short silver beard. The Tortall rogues called him "The Old Demon" and were intensely proud of him; foreign rogues made the Sign when he was mentioned.

The people in the crowd, the honest ones, liked the fierce old man. Someone applauded, then someone else. A woman raised a cheer and was joined by others.

Jonathan smiled. Someone cried, "God bless you, Majesty!" This received a cheer from many, and George smiled at the fickle nature of the crowd.

A woman in front of the riding party held her child up to see, and shrieked when the toddler wriggled out of her hands and ran into the cluster of riders. Jon swung far to the right and down, seizing the child with one hand and scooping it up out of danger from the horses' hooves. Darkness reared and plunged at his rider's activity, but the King-to-be held him as the child wailed. The Provost gripped Darkness's bridle, forcing the stallion down.

Jonathan dismounted, carrying the squalling toddler. The mother ran forward under the glares of the King's Own, laughing and crying, to take her little one back. She hugged Jon in one arm and the child in the other, thanking the young man. Her words were inaudible against the cheer that went up as word circulated about what Jon had done. Uneasy for some reason, George left his niche and began to make his way through the crowd, heading for the group of nobles.

His intuition was good. A man near the party drew a knife from his belt and ran for Jonathan while George was too far away to help. The attacker was screaming something. Later the Provost told Myles it sounded like "Death to the unlucky King!"

Jonathan was tangled in woman and child. His companions were hampered by the crowd and their own horses. It was Darkness who came to his master's defense, rearing to strike the assassin with his hooves. The man went down as other killers swathed in cloaks appeared out of the crowd.

George tackled one and knifed another. The Provost had dismounted and was fighting with knives, grinning fiercely as he caught one man on crossed blades and kneed him. Horses reared, ladies screamed, and the Great Market Riot had begun.

Of it all, George remembered only the moment when he and the Provost—for the first time in their long war—came face-to-face in the melee. Given a choice, he would have relinquished the honor. Now he froze, letting the assassin he'd targeted get away. The Provost looked at him, turned, and disappeared back into the crowd. Had he *winked*?

Accompanied by his most trusted people—the brothers Orem and Shem, the knife masters Ercole and Marek—George reached Jonathan's party to find the King-to-be nursing a wounded arm. The King's Own closed in, forming a tight circle around Gary, Jonathan, and Josiane. Roger was nowhere to be seen, the thief noted. The Provost was mounting his horse, secure in the middle of a second ring of guards. George's shoulder wound had opened and was bleeding again.

He ignored it. "I know a way out!" he called to Jon. "If you'll trust me!"

The leader of the King's Own glanced at the Prince, who nodded. George guided Jon's party into a side street and out of the riot, keeping an eye out for assassins. He and his people left the nobles on the Temple Way when others of the riding party arrived and a second company of the King's Own came riding down from the palace.

"It was Claw," George told Eloni and Myles at House Olau soon after. He winced as his mother applied yet another poultice to his reopened shoulder. "The assassins were his, every one, and they wanted Jon."

"What does *Claw* gain if anything happens to Jonathan?" Myles wanted to know. "He's not connected to anyone at the palace who would benefit—not as far as I've heard. Although *Delia*—"

"I find it interestin' that his Grace of Conté got out so easy," George drawled, propping his feet on a hassock. "But you're right, it still makes no sense. 'Twas too easy for the innocent to get hurt along with the guilty this mornin'. If he planned it, he ran as great a risk of bein' trampled as the rest of us."

Eleni shook her head sadly. "I'm worried about those who got hurt in this madness. I'd best go see what I may do." She stood, shaking out her skirts. "But isn't that always the way when folk plot to steal power? The innocent get hurt."

The final toll of the Great Market Riot was fifteen dead, thirty-six hurt (including the King-to-be), and untold damages to shops and stalls. The atmosphere of suspicion and fear thickened. In spite of it, or perhaps because of it, Jonathan began to ride once a week through the capital and the surrounding countryside.

⌒

Jonathan watched the stars appear from a castle balcony, relaxing as he prepared himself for a night among his court. Again Josiane would try to win him back, and again he'd keep her at a distance. Not for the first time he regretted his involvement with the Princess from the Copper Isles. He'd tired of her quickly, and she'd been reluctant to understand that. Now that he knew her better, he also realized that, in spite of his mother's plans for Josiane, the Princess would have made a very bad Queen.

Still, he had to smile. He'd just come from his time as the Voice of the Tribes. In touch with Coram for the first time since January, he'd learned that the wayfarers had reached Maren's western border and would anchor in Tyra in the morning. Soon Alanna would be home, and he could put his Lioness—and the Dominion Jewel—to work.

～

"*T*hat's all of it, Majesty." The humpbacked man known as Aled the Armorer fidgeted. "I wish Claw'd never come t'me. I don't like this, nor the consequences if words leaks out of what's afoot."

George sprawled in his chair, rubbing his chin as he surveyed his informant. His hazel eyes glittered through his lashes, making the armorer twist his cap into a knot. "Mayhap Claw fed you a tale, Aled. It won't be the first time a man tested loyalty by givin' out a lie."

"He paid gold for his tale, then," Aled whined "Asides, he don't know I've been sellin' t'Isham Killmaster and Kasi the Spy these five years. Only Killmaster favors armor in the K'miri style but lacquered black like they never do. And the Spy—"

"Enough. If *you* say that's who's involved, I must trust you. I pay you enough."

"T'ain't just the gold, Majesty," Aled protested. "My mam raised no fools. They's one fate for them as kills a king." His gesture illustrated the fate clearly. "I'm afeared of Claw, bein's he's crazier'n a priest, but Provost's justice is *fast*. Our folk be crooked, but loyal all the same. If they knew Claw was up t'this, them that helps 'im wouldn't *live* t'face the Provost. I'm between Goddess and Black God with no place to run."

George tossed a silver noble to the Armorer, who caught it and bit it (to make sure it wasn't fake). "Not a word to Claw, Aled."

The other man winced. He knew what Claw would do to him if the news he'd talked to George leaked out. "No, indeed, Majesty!" He left the Dancing Dove, muttering.

George stared into the distance. When Alanna had introduced him to Jonathan, he knew the day might come when his duty to the Rogue would conflict with his friendship with the Prince. That time had come. What was he to do? A rescue in a riot, with everyone too excited to think clearly, was one thing. Informing on a plot was another. The marketplace assassins were dead and Claw in hiding, so no good would have come of his saying who'd started the whole thing. But Aled's tale had concerned corrupt servants, and a new plot that reached from the palace to Claw.

George grew up in the Lower City, learning the underworld's laws: obey the Rogue; pay his tax; and—most importantly—*never betray a fellow Rogue to the King's Justice.* The penalty was slow death. A year ago George would have been the last to consider such a betrayal. But that was before Claw changed things.

Jonathan was his friend. They'd spent many good evenings together; they'd loved the same woman; they both knew what kingship meant. In some ways Jon was closer to him than Alanna—she couldn't conceive the burdens of a king, and Jon had never known anything else.

Either I've turned stupid, or life's turned hard, he thought with a sigh.

∿

The first thing Thom of Trebond noticed, returning late to his palace rooms, was that the door to his study was not closed. "I'll turn the maids into fish if they left the door ajar!" he roared, slamming the door open.

The shadowy figure sitting by his hearth was thrown into relief by the glow from Thom. "I can see we'll not be needin' candles," George drawled. "Close the door. There's a good lad."

Thom stared at his guest, then obeyed. As he slumped into a chair, he demanded, "What're *you* doing here at this hour? Up to no good, I bet."

"Why must you ask? Don't you see all that happens in your tea cup in the mornin'?" George's voice was bitter. He'd just come from telling Jon about the newest threat to his life—*from betraying the Rogue,* part of his mind insisted.

Thom tried to read George's face, but the glow he cast wasn't that strong. *Not yet,* he thought bitterly. "You haven't done something...Rogue-ish, have you?"

George glared at him. "Don't play me for an innocent, Thommy my lad. If I wanted to tell you, I would. It chances that I don't."

Thom shrugged. "As you wish." He threw fire at the candles beside George; it was too much, consuming half of the fat wax sticks. He looked at the thief to see what he made of it, but only a slight crinkling around George's eyes gave away that he'd noticed anything unusual.

"Say something." Thom's voice was tight. "Everyone else has! I heard Baird tell Jonathan perhaps the Mithrans let me go too soon." When George didn't reply, he yelled, "*Say* it, damn you!"

"You keep things chilly in here," was the mild reply. "I know this old pile's hard to warm, and it's near midsummer and all—"

Thom laughed and could not stop. He buried his face in his hands, his thin body shaking. George rose, a worried look in his eyes, and put a hand on Thom's shoulder.

"Don't!" the sorcerer cried, but it was too late. George pulled back his hand after only a brief touch: Thom was far hotter than any mortal could be and still live.

"Black God's belly, Thom! How long've you been like this?"

The younger man shook his head. "I have no idea." He saw George shiver. "Go ahead—start a fire. It doesn't make a difference. I'd do it myself, but—" He looked at the candles.

George knelt to use flint and steel to start a blaze. Watching it burn, he said cautiously, "I was struck by old Si-cham, when we visited you at the City."

"No. No, I tell you! Have him come, and gloat—"

"He didn't look like the gloatin' kind to me, lad. He would've liked you, had you given him a chance. He was a bright young sprout himself, once."

Bloodshot amethyst eyes stared at him. "D'you think this is some trouble I stumbled into, that my teaching-master can get me out of? A safety measure I didn't take? Some bit of carelessness that can be mended by someone older and more experienced?"

"No. That kind of mistake's known right off, and it's often fatal. But Si-cham may've seen what's wrong with you before—"

"I don't want to hear it." Thom's voice was flat as he wiped his eyes on his sleeve. "They were jealous of me in the City, all of those masters. There's nothing they'd like better than to see me caught in a mistake."

George considered his next remark carefully, knowing he was on dangerous ground. Finally he decided to speak anyway. "What of Duke Baird, him that's chief of the palace healers? Mayhap he—"

Thom giggled in earnest, his laugh hoarse with disuse. "Baird! What do I tell him? That—that—" He caught his breath. "I have a *cold* in my Gift?"

George smiled. "Does your friend know?"

They both knew who he meant. "If he does, he keeps it to himself. I can't—won't—ask him." Softly

Thom added, "I'm afraid to." He looked at George, his face white and pinched. "I believe he knows exactly what it is." He jumped out of his chair. "Are you happy? Will you tell Myles *he* was right all along? Why not tell Jon, while you're at it? You have no proof he's whole again, *no* proof!" Tears ran down his cheeks.

"Lad, calm down," George said, keeping his alarm hidden. "You're wearin' me out."

Thom laughed. "I don't have any proof, either," he went on tiredly. "But what else *can* I think, except that somehow he can do this? It's that or…I have to believe the gods turned away from me. Because I thought and said it would be easy to make myself a god."

"If there's anyone you can ask—"

"No one. I made sure of that, didn't I? This will pass. I'll find a cure—something. I haven't looked in the right places."

George knew a dismissal when he heard it. He gathered up his cloak.

"Thank you." It was a whisper.

"I did nothin' to be thanked for this night," George said harshly. "Not for you, not for anyone."

"You listened, even though I've tried my best to discourage you. And you didn't say you've warned me. If he *is* doing something."

George nodded and left. Thom watched the fire for a moment, then rasped three words. A wave of sea water broke over the hearth, toppled the candles, and doused the fire before vanishing. He sat for the rest of the night, smelling scorched wood, ocean, and wet carpeting.

The thief, who was gone from Thom's thoughts when the door closed, went to his most recent hideout. At dawn George's messenger rode north to the City of the Gods with George's urgent letter to Si-cham, First Master of the Order of Mithros.

∾

Several nights after George had passed on his information, Jonathan and the Lord Provost laid their plans to catch the conspirators. They met in a room near the servants' quarters. By Jonathan's command, Roger was also present. "You are in charge, my lord," Jon told the Provost when his cousin arrived. "Give us your instructions."

The Provost opened a hidden panel that led to the maze of secret passages and servants' corridors in this section of the palace. "We'll be able to see and hear everything. My boys were able to fix the room, thanks to all this advance warnin'. But neither of you make a sound, or you'll blow the game." The old man was common-born and it showed in his speech. "If they say what it's claimed they will, I'll signal the arrest."

"I cannot see why *my* presence is necessary," Roger commented. He looked bored.

Jonathan glanced at him and snapped, "Call it my whim, Roger."

"Since when does the King-to-be take part in spying, even on a whim?" Roger's melodic voice was filled with sarcasm.

"We're spyin' on would-be regicides," the Provost said dryly. "King-killers."

"A plot against my cousin? What folly!" Roger's voice sharpened. "You suspect *me*, Jonathan?"

"You haven't been implicated," was the cool reply.

"I thought I was to be forgiven my…earlier errors," said Roger bitterly.

"Do your friends feel the same way?" Jon demanded. "Perhaps you should ask them. If you don't know the answer already!"

"Enough!" the Provost ordered. "Let's get movin'."

They threaded through the corridors until they met one of the Provost's men. Quietly the three of them were guided to spy holes in the corridor wall. Shielded from notice inside the room, the holes nevertheless allowed them to see and hear what took place inside. Three servants stood, sat, or paced the room, according to their natures. With a start Jonathan recognized his groom of chambers and the maid who brought him food or drink late at night. The third man, a nailbiter, wore the uniform of the Palace Guard, the rivals of the King's Own.

Jon sneaked a look at Roger to see his cousin's reaction. Roger's mouth was set in a grim line as he watched the scene before him. He didn't appear upset or worried, reactions Jon had half expected.

"When're they coming?" the Guard snapped. "If my sergeant inspects—"

"You said he *never* inspects." The girl's voice was clear and cold.

"But if he does, tonight—"

"Keep your breeches on," the groom ordered scornfully. "If you followed your orders, everything will proceed according to plan."

There were two raps on the door—everyone inside stiffened. There were two more raps, a pause, then two more. The maid undid the bolt and let four men in. One was Jonathan's favorite palace scribe, who had apparently guided those with him to the meeting place. Putting aside his bitterness over the scribe's betrayal, Jon turned his attention to the outsiders.

He recognized Claw—Ralon of Malven—from his description. The other two he assumed to be the assassins, the Spy and the Killmaster—they had the look of paid killers.

The maid bolted the door as Claw looked around. "You were careful on your way here?" he demanded of the servants. Jon smiled grimly. Unlike Myles, he knew Ralon's voice instantly. "No one followed?" Claw went on, checking the corners of the room. He apparently was unable to keep still. "Woe to any of you if you betray me."

"None of us dare betray anyone," the groom answered. "We're all in too deep." He tossed a packet of documents on the table in the center of the room. "Here's my part of it. Diagrams of the King's rooms and every way to get in or out."

The Guard put a paper on the table. "Here's the nights I'm on duty at the kitchen gate. But I don't want to hear details—"

Claw put his hand on his dagger hilt, his single eye suddenly wild. "You hear whatever I want you to hear! And when I want your opinions, I'll tell you to give them!" The Guard shrank back, frightened. At the edge of his vision Jon saw the Provost give a hand signal to one of his men. The man nodded and trotted away silently.

"Memorize their faces," Claw was telling the assassins when Jon focused on the room again. "So you know who to kill if we're betrayed." The assassins looked slowly at each of the servants until the others were clearly frightened. Suddenly Claw leaned over the table and drew his finger over the surface. He stared at his fingertip for a moment before turning on the maid.

"You said no one ever uses this room. But there's no dust on the table."

The maid steeled herself. "I came in and dusted around. I didn't want to breathe ten years' worth of dirt—"

Claw backhanded her viciously. "Stupid female!" Walking straight back until he was inches away from the Lord Provost's spy hole, he drew a finger down the intricate molding of the screen that masked the wall and the openings in it. He brought it away clean.

"And you dusted back here, too?" he screamed at the maid. He ran for the door and yanked it open as he drew his sword.

The Provost's men outside were caught unaware and unready. Claw cut down one of them as the assassins rushed to follow. The Provost had already left at a run. Jonathan and Roger drew back from the wall.

"Tell me you knew nothing of this—*cousin,*" Jon snapped. "Tell me this isn't yet another of your plots to gain the throne. I don't care if you didn't bespell my mother one more time. It was because of your past work that she lost the strength to live. What is there to stop me from believing this is just another of your schemes? That you want my throne as badly as you ever did?"

Roger gripped Jon's arm. "I had no knowledge of a plot. I'll swear it by any of your gods," the Duke hissed. "If those who planned this did so for reasons they claim involve me, I shall hunt them down and...disabuse them of their mistake. In the name of the Goddess and the Black God, I swear I do not want your throne. Does that satisfy you?"

He'd just invoked two deities famous for their fierce punishments for oath-breakers. Reluctantly, Jon nodded. "You say 'your gods.' Don't *you* believe in them?"

Roger's smile was bitter. "I believe in them. Only a fool does not. Since they have made it very clear they do not like me, I refuse to worship them." He stared into the distance, his eyes glittering. "But they can be defeated, Jonathan. The right man can shake their thrones."

A few minutes later a slightly mussed Provost found Jonathan alone in the passage. "We have all of them but Claw," he said wearily. "And two of my lads are dead. The others might wish *they* was dead, once I get through with them for lettin' Claw escape."

"He's slippery," Jonathan said absently. "I have every faith that you'll get another chance at him, though."

∽

*E*leni Cooper came awake, feeling uneasy. In her own home that feeling meant someone needed her as a healer. Deciding it couldn't be different here, she pulled on a robe and ran downstairs. A bleary-eyed maidservant held up a lamp as Bazhir guards helped three people in at the door. One Bazhir gave orders to others outside: Eleni saw the glitter of drawn swords as the door was closed and barred.

"Mistress Cooper!" Relief was in the maid's sleepy face. "These people say they're friends of Master George."

Eleni recognized them. "Marek Swiftknife, can't you keep yourself in one piece?" She ran forward, taking charge of a pale and bloody Rispah while still lecturing Marek. "It's only six months since I patched you up last!"

Marek tried to smile. "Sorry, Mother Cooper."

"We need the empty storeroom," Eleni told the maid. "And wake Myles—"

"Unnecessary." The knight hurried downstairs, his hair and beard in disarray. "Mistress Cooper needs her bag, Tereze. Wake the housekeeper. We need clean linen and boiling water!" He opened the storeroom.

"You're learning," Eleni said with a smile. She helped Rispah onto a clean table in the unused room. "Who's the worst hurt?"

"Ercole, then Marek," Rispah whispered. "I'm all right, Aunt."

Marek held a wadded burnoose to a wound in his side; another in his thigh bled freely. "They got Ercole five times," he told Myles as Eleni laid the oldest of the three on his table.

The healer looked at one of the Bazhir. "Someone must go for Mistress Kuri Tailor, House Kuri on Weaver's Lane. She's a friend, a healer, and I need help." The man bowed and was gone as she stripped Ercole down.

Myles's servants brought Eleni everything she needed. As she cleaned Ercole's wounds, Marek talked to Myles. "It was Claw—he found us, him and his people. He said he had a job, a secret job, and he was betrayed."

"Betrayed?" Myles frowned.

"Just as we was betrayed." Marek looked away, wiping his eyes on his sleeve. "They're dead Myles—Scholar, Red Nell, Orem, Shem, Lightfingers, the Peddler, and Zia the Hedgewitch; we was the only ones t'escape."

Kuri arrived, her red-bronze hair flowing down the back of her cloak. Throwing that garment onto a chair, she came to Marek with her healer's bag. She tied back her hair and rinsed her hands, appraising Marek's wounds with level brown eyes. Eleni finished cleaning Ercole's wounds and began to stitch them, her hand steady. Fortunately for healer and patient, Ercole was unconscious.

"How did they find you?" Myles's voice broke. Scholar had been a friend.

"Anci," Marek whispered, gritting his teeth as Kuri probed the wound in his side. "She brought them in."

"Your *lady*?" Myles asked, horrified.

Marek nodded. "Claw told her one of us sold 'im to the Provost. She gave us over because we broke Rogue's Law."

Kuri stitched Marek's wounds quickly and went to Rispah. The redhead who'd promised her heart to Coram bore a long gash on her left arm from shoulder to wrist. Kuri went to work as Rispah fought to keep still.

"I hope someone did turn that crazy bastard over," she snapped, her voice tight with pain. "Since he tried for George last Midwinter, more than a hundred of us've died. And it hasn't mattered if the dead was for him or against him or innocent altogether. I haven't forgotten the Market Day fight. Who could? With Claw loose, we don't need my Lord Provost to weed us out!"

"What if Claw's not wrong entirely?" George had come at last, hooded and cloaked like the Bazhir to escape detection. "What if I made sure he and his people were taken up before they killed Jonathan? What then?"

The room was silent as everyone but Eleni and Ercole stared at him. Then Myles whispered, "*Regicide.*" Kuri made the Sign.

"Remember the tale of Oswan that murdered King Adar the Weak?" Rispah asked. "The law said he wasn't to be let die till he was tortured three days, dawn to dark. The gods turned their faces from him and he lived six days."

"Royal dynasties get their right from the gods. Only the gods can take it back—not men," Kuri added softly.

"I don't know if you did right, George." Marek lay back, his face white. "I only wish you'd'a shivved Claw yourself afore lettin' him escape my lord."

～

*T*he room was a parlor decorated in pale green and cream, perfect for the emerald-eyed brunette on the sofa, less perfect for the striking blonde beside her. A swarthy nobleman lounged in an armchair. It was a room meant for chatter and flirtation. The fourth man, with his battered clothes and ravaged face, was wrong here. He stood before the cold hearth, hands jammed into pockets.

"We erred in letting you join us, Ralon," Delia of Eldorne said coldly. "Last fall you said you would be Rogue in a matter of weeks. You are *still* not master among the thieves. You tell us, leave the killing of a certain Prince to you. Now the Provost has your people who were to handle the matter, and Jonathan is alerted to his danger."

"I was betrayed!" Ralon of Malven was rigid with fury. "No one knew Cooper would—"

"*I'm not finished!*" Delia rapped out. "Explain this!" She thrust a parchment at him.

The drawing was clearly one of Ralon. Beneath it was written:

**WANTED BY MY LORD PROVOST
FOR TREASON AGAINST THE CROWN
ONE CLAW, BORN RALON OF MALVEN
REWARD: ONE THOUSAND GOLD NOBLES**

It described him in detail. "How did they learn my name?" he whispered in horror.

"That is immaterial," Princess Josiane said coldly.

"You're useless to us," Alex of Tirragen pointed out. "More than useless—you are a danger."

"No!" Claw yelled. "You need me—"

The door slammed open. Alex stood, sword

unsheathed; Claw's hands were filled with two sharp knives. Roger of Conté swept in, followed by a frightened guard. "My lady, I couldn't stop him, not *him*—" the guard stammered.

"Return to your post," ordered Delia, and he obeyed. Delia, who'd once been Roger's mistress, rose to curtsey to the Duke. "Roger, this is a pleasant surprise—"

"I wanted no independent action on your parts." They stared at him, seeing he was in a rage, and were suddenly afraid. "Do you think you *assisted* me? Now the King-to-be watches me; my Lord Provost suspects me. And I find I owe this happiness to *you four*."

Delia sank prettily to her knees, skirts billowing. Reaching up, she touched his hand. "Forgive our enthusiasm, dear lord," she murmured. "We meant to bring you to your rightful throne—"

"Enough." He dragged her to her feet. "You cherished dreams once of becoming my consort. Unless you wish to be the consort of Carthaki snake-breeders, you will *await* my orders." He threw her into Alex's hold and turned to Josiane.

"Josiane of the Copper Isles, I have known you only since my return from the dead, but I understand you well. Jonathan courted you to spite Alanna of Trebond. Still, you might have kept him, with some restraint on your part. Now you want to punish him, and so you meddle with things that do not concern you. *I am not your pawn.* Stay out of my affairs. If you wish to be a part of this, you will await my commands—either here, or on the river bottom. Do not cross me again!"

He looked at the thief. "Ralon of Malven. The present Rogue is worth twenty of you. Your choice of tools is bad, Delia. He'll betray you when he's done with the thieves."

Turning to Alex, the fury in Roger's sapphire eyes faded to puzzlement. "I am surprised at *you*, my former squire."

"I told them to do nothing," Alex shrugged. "I said you'd have different plans. They thought matters could be…hastened. Frankly, I didn't think it was important enough to bother you for."

Roger smiled grimly. "You might have been right. The trouble with ambitious plots is that those who are not involved get wind of them—as they did this time. That person, or those persons, took what they heard to Jonathan, and he took their information to my Lord Provost. But you—I know you are not a plotter, and I know you are not ambitious. What do *you* want from this?"

Alex met his eyes for a long moment; then, smiling slightly, he bowed. He knew Roger would guess what he desired of any plan to take Jonathan from the throne.

Roger tugged his beard. "We shall see. Perhaps…You haven't changed. As for you others," he said, looking at them, "no more plots. No more assassins. Steal nothing for me, bribe no servants for me. My plans are my own, and you will await *my* instructions. I warn you this once."

He raised a hand. Slowly blood-colored fire— the fire of magic—collected in his palm. With a savage gesture he hurled it at a small table, which exploded into chips of burning wood and molten pieces of brass and porcelain.

In the silence that followed, Roger whispered, "Don't think to disobey me." Turning, he walked out.

Delia was ashen. "But his Gift was bright orange…"

Alex picked up a cooling bit of glass in his handkerchief. He looked it over and began to smile.

six

Homecoming

The travelers set out from Port Caynn immediately after landing, eager to reach their destination. Riding slowly, to reaccustom themselves after several weeks out of the saddle, they would be in Corus before nightfall. They halted shortly after midday at an inn Alanna and Raoul remembered, where the squires had often stopped on trips to Caynn. The food was good, the place so quiet that a rest seemed in order. Buri and Thayet napped; the men played chess. Alanna took Faithful to sit under a courtyard tree, scratching his ears and enjoying the sun. She was half drowsing when she heard an approaching rider.

Someone in a hurry, the sleepy Faithful remarked. Alanna nodded, refusing to open her eyes. The buzz of summer crickets was soothing after days of waves and gulls. *Never* would she board a water vessel again!

Curious, she peeped through her lashes; the rider entered the yard. With a yell she leaped up, dumping Faithful to the ground. "George!"

The thief grinned and grabbed her. His brawny

arms closed tight; she was lifted, spun, then well kissed. Alanna looked up into dancing hazel eyes. "How did you know we were here?" she asked, wiping teary eyes on his sleeve.

"Stop that, lass," he whispered. "Messenger birds, remember? You're thin. Haven't you been eatin', my hero?"

"I was seasick." She grinned. "It was the only way to get home in time. Are *you* all right? You look worn."

George kissed her again, taking his time to convince her of his health. He released her, a wicked twinkle in his eyes. "Now your Dragon can kill me—I'll die happy."

"You know about Liam?"

He chuckled. "Sweet, everyone knows the Lioness and the Dragon were prowlin' Sarain. I heard two songs about you this week."

"Have you counted her fingers yet, Cooper?" Liam walked toward them, his eyes pale crystal.

George smiled. "I never thought you wouldn't take care of her, Dragon." He held out a hand, keeping a grip on Alanna. "I assume you're used to bein' sung about."

Liam's eyes darkened to blue-grey; he shook the offered hand with a smile. "They'll have more to sing about, I guarantee."

George stared past Liam, eyes wide. "Bless me, Crooked God," he whispered.

Thayet and Buri emerged from the inn, still

yawning. Alanna knew what had caught George's attention: the afternoon sun sank into Thayet's midnight hair while it turned her skin a deep cream. *Thayet would look good anywhere,* Alanna thought, with only a touch of envy. "Princess Thayet *jian* Wilima, may I present George Cooper? George, this is Princess Thayet of Sarain, and her guard Buriram Tourakom."

"Don't bother," muttered Buri. George released Alanna to bow and kiss Thayet's hand. "He won't remember anyway."

George straightened and winked at the K'mir. "I'm awed, Buriram Tourakom, but I'm rarely *that* awed."

Charmed in spite of herself, Buri smiled. "Alanna told us about you," she said gruffly. "We've been warned. It's Buri, anyway."

"I told you I'd bring them back," Raoul said.

George looked at Alanna and gave her a squeeze. "I'll never doubt you again, lad."

"Ye *would* be the first," Coram announced. He and Raoul had brought the horses around.

George laughed. "Were I you, I'd treat my wife-to-be's cousin and king better than that." The two men gripped each other's arms in greeting.

George exchanged his tired horse for a fresh one, joining them for the ride to Corus. His presence made the journey pass quickly. He refused to relay the news, but had no trouble wheedling tales of their adventures from Buri and Thayet. Alanna was not fooled. The past months had taken a toll on George: he was thinner, small lines fanned out from his eyes and framed his broad mouth. She wondered precisely what had been going on. Where was his court—Scholar, Solom, Marek, Rispah, and the others? If she asked now, she knew he would laugh and ask the questions *she* didn't want to answer.

"Has he *always* been this obstinate?" she asked Faithful.

The cat sniffed. *You're a fine one to talk.*

She grinned. "If *I* don't know obstinacy when I see it, who does?"

At the crest of the hills between seaport and capital, Buri drew up her pony. "Mountain gods," she whispered, her black eyes huge with awe. The others stopped beside her.

Corus lay on the southern bank of the Oloron River, towers glinting in the sun. The homes of wealthy men lined the river to the north; tanners, smiths, wainwrights, carpenters, and the poor clustered on the bank to the south. The city was a richly colored tapestry: the Great Gate on Kingsbridge, the maze of the Lower City, the marketplace, the tall houses in the Merchants' and the Gentry's quarters, the gardens of the Temple district, the palace. This last was the city's crown and southern border. Beyond it, the royal forest stretched for leagues. It was not as lovely as Berat nor as colorful as Udayapur, but it was Alanna's place.

"Glad to be home?" George asked.

"Yes."

He reached to wipe a tear from her cheek. "It's been that long a journey, has it?" he whispered.

Alanna met his eyes. In their hazel depths she saw a degree of love that frightened her as it warmed her.

∾

*I*nside the City Gate waited a small company of Bazhir, Hakim Fahrar at its head. They bowed to Alanna from their saddles. She bowed in reply. Hakim fell in with Coram; the others formed a loose circle around the travelers.

"Is this necessary?" Alanna asked. "We *wanted* to be inconspicuous." She and Thayet exchanged rueful glances.

"It is," George said. "You wouldn't've been able to do it, anyway—not with yon big, brawny lad amongst you." He nodded toward Liam, who talked with a Bazhir rider. "Things've changed somewhat, and all Corus knows you're Jonathan's knight. You'd do worse than ride with a guard."

The gate at House Olau was open. The hostlers greeted Alanna cheerfully, showing no surprise at the size of her party. It was Thayet who hesitated, a worried frown on her face. "Buri and I should find an inn somewhere," she pointed out. "If you can direct us—"

"I know one," Liam said. "We can stay together—"

"Don't be ridiculous," Alanna interrupted. "Why should we split up?"

"He's expectin' you," George told them.

"Oh?" commented Thayet. "Where'd he learn about Buri and Liam and me?"

"The Voice?" Alanna asked Coram.

The burly man chuckled. "Ye have to admit, Lioness, the Voice is a useful man." Turning to the others, he explained, "I've been in contact with the Voice of the Tribes since we entered Marenite waters. We're expected, all of us."

"You'll hurt Myles's feelin's if you go else-where," George said. "He's that hospitable. He puts up my mother and cousin also. The man shouldn't be a bachelor, not with a fine, big house like this."

Thayet smiled ruefully. "If you're certain…"

George bowed. "I can't lie to a pretty lady."

Alanna dismounted, giving her reins to a hostler. Faithful leaped down to vanish into the shadows as Eleni Cooper and Rispah came out to the courtyard. Alanna rushed to hug them, trying not to cry anymore. How could she have forgotten what being home was like? She introduced Thayet, Buri, and Liam. She didn't know what George's mother and cousin were doing in Myles's home, but she was glad to see them.

Glancing to her left, in the shadows she saw Coram taking Rispah in his arms. Smiling, she looked away.

George nudged Alanna, pointing to the wide-open front door. "Go say hello to him. He's been up since dawn."

Alanna ran to Myles and hugged him. Neither of them required words, which was just as well, since both were unable to speak. Myles wept unashamedly, soaking his beard as he beamed at her with delight. He too looked older and worn, with bits of grey in his hair. *He doesn't think Roger isn't dangerous,* Alanna realized. She had to find out what was going on.

"Come in, come in," Myles told the others. "Welcome, all of you!"

After dinner they gathered in the library. The others talked, but for the most part Alanna listened, happy to be there. Grim subjects and the Jewel were left for the next day. Thayet, Buri and Liam were never given a chance to feel left out; once they were introduced to Myles, the knight made them welcome. Thayet's offer to find somewhere else to stay was brushed off by their host, as Alanna had known it would be. Coram stayed close to Rispah, and Alanna realized with a twinge of sadness that his days as her mentor-companion were done. It surprised and delighted her to see Myles take Eleni's hand; George saw her looking and winked. Later she accused him of matchmaking, and he made no attempt to deny it.

Finally Alanna dozed off in her chair, waking slightly as Liam carried her to bed. Kissing her forehead, he whispered, "Sleep well, Lioness."

"I don't *like* being 'Lioness' to you." He didn't seem to hear. Gently Liam closed the door, and she slept again.

She woke instantly some time later. What had roused her? She listened, but the house was silent. Looking around, she saw a blot of brownish light by the window. Lightning hung nearby; she lunged and unsheathed it as the blot gained size and substance.

"Put that thing down," a familiar voice snapped. "I haven't hurt you."

"Thom?"

Even before he finished materializing, he glowed enough for her to see his features. Crossing his arms on his chest, he lifted an eyebrow. "Don't you have any nightshirts?" Liam had removed only her boots and stockings.

Alanna jumped up and grabbed her twin, holding him tightly. Thom's embrace was as hard as her own. He buried his too-hot face in her shoulder.

"Thom, what's wrong? D'you have a fever?" Her voice faltered. "You're…*glowing*…"

He gripped her shoulders. "Calm down! The heat's part of it, so just—calm down." He touched the crow's feet at the corners of her eyes, traced the hard line of a cheekbone, smoothed over the thin crease that edged her mouth. He too had lines that weren't his before, and he was even thinner than she. He looked tired—mortally tired. On impulse she touched the emberstone at her throat.

With the talisman's aid she saw that Thom shone with a rust-red fire, the color of old blood. "How do I look?" he whispered, knowing the ember's properties.

She tried to smile. "You don't want to know." Swallowing, she added, "It's as if you have another Gift, or your own is—"

"Corrupted," Thom finished. "Enough. We'll trade stories later. You look half dead." He smoothed her hair with a shaking hand. "I just wanted to look at you, and see if…if you forgive me."

"There's nothing to forgive," she insisted. "You did me a favor. Now I can talk with him. I can see for myself if I made a mistake when I—you know. If he could've redeemed himself, somehow."

"Nice try," he scoffed in his old way. "I think you could've lived with it if he'd stayed in his tomb."

"But it's true," she protested.

"Go back to bed, all right?" He began to fade. "Get some rest." He vanished.

She stared at the spot where he'd been. Did anyone else know Thom was dying? Couldn't they have warned her? But what was there to warn about—besides the fact that he glowed in the dark?

Her eyes blurred; she sniffed. Was Myles still up? Slipping barefoot out of her room, Alanna made for the library, Myles's favorite room. The library door was open. She froze on the landing, not wanting to intrude on any private reunions.

"I couldn't get away sooner." The deep voice was Jonathan's. "We don't have *parties* because we're in mourning, but these 'quiet get-togethers' take hours, all the same."

"You should've waited." Alanna recognized George's lilt. "She fell asleep in her chair, poor thing. She's weary. They all are."

"And there's little rest for my lady knight here," Jonathan sighed.

"Does he know she's back?"

"He knows. I just don't—what?"

George came out and bowed to Alanna, indicating she should go into the library. Pushing her inside, he closed the door, leaving her alone with Jon.

He stood before the hearth, cradling Faithful. She'd forgotten he was a head taller than she. His black clothes emphasized his sapphire eyes; his mustache and hair were darker than his velvet tunic. She looked at his elegantly carved mouth and straight nose, thinking, *Jon's still the most handsome man I've ever seen—and that includes Roger!* He'd changed since their angry parting; his face had stubborn lines, and there was a seriousness about him she liked.

Deeply moved, she knelt and bowed her head. "My liege. I am yours to command."

He put his hands on her hair. "You're sure, Alanna?"

She met his eyes. "Until death and after, Jonathan."

He swallowed. "I accept your fealty, Sir Alanna. I accept, and I vow to return fealty with fealty, honor with honor, until death and beyond it." Lifting her to her feet, he kissed each cheek. The kingliness faded. "You don't know what it means to have you home." His eyes filled suddenly. "He killed himself, Alanna. He made it look like a hunting accident, but it wasn't. Oh, gods! Why did I have to lose both of them?" He covered his face with his hands and cried. Alanna held him, shushing him and weeping herself.

When he was calm again and she had dried her tears, Alanna said, "We may not have another chance to be alone for a while. What do you want me to do with the Jewel?"

Jonathan drew a deep breath. "You really have it?"

"I'll get it, if you like." She tried to pull away, and Jonathan tightened his arms.

"Not yet, all right? This is so comfortable. It's been almost a year since I held you, remember?" He sighed and released her. "Keep it safe, for now. I need to think of a way to present you—and it— suitably." He smiled briefly. "You don't know how much it means to be able to tell people we have the Dominion Jewel. Perhaps it will even stop the rumors of a curse."

A short time later, George rejoined them. "All's well, then?" Alanna and Jonathan smiled at each other. "At last," George sighed. "I never felt right when you two were on the outs with each other. We were havin' tea," he told Alanna. "Will you join us?" At her nod, he got a third cup and filled it from a kettle on the hearth, refreshing Jonathan's cup and his own. "It's Copper Isle Red Griffin," he explained to Alanna, who squinted at the scarlet liquid. "The taste grows on you."

Jonathan raised his in a toast. "To old friends, the best friends."

"So mote it be," Alanna replied.

"Hear, hear," George added.

"Oh, I'm sorry!" a low female voice exclaimed.

Jon turned to the door and froze, eyes widening in awe. "Great Merciful Mother!" he breathed.

A tousled Thayet stood there, clutching a dressing gown at her throat. "Faithful woke me up, and then I couldn't sleep." The cat jumped into Alanna's lap, startling her. She hadn't even seen him leave. Thayet, flustered, avoided Jon's eyes as she tried to tuck her bare feet under the hem of her robe. Alanna concealed a grin with her hand.

George drew the Princess into the room. "We're havin' a bit of tea," he told her, closing the door. "There's a seat by the fire—over next to Jon."

The King-to-be stood and raised Thayet's hand to his lips. Their eyes met; Thayet's puzzled, his searching. Quickly the Princess drew her hand away, saying dryly, "We haven't been introduced."

Alanna couldn't speak until she could master her amusement. Already Thayet had Jon off balance, and already they seemed attracted to each other. *I knew it!* she told herself triumphantly. *I knew I was right to bring her!*

"Thayet *jian* Wilima," George said, eyeing Alanna, "may I present Jonathan of Conté? Are you officially 'King' now, Jon, or does that wait till the coronation?"

Jonathan was not listening. "Does the introduction meet your standards, your Highness?" His voice matched Thayet's for dryness.

The Warlord's daughter curtsied to just the degree proper for a princess to greet a king—not an inch more. Instead of modestly looking down, she kept her eyes on Jon's. "I am 'Highness' no longer, your Majesty. My father is dead, and I am an exile. I hope to become your Majesty's loyal, low-born subject." She inclined her head graciously, her curtsey not wobbling an iota.

Alanna sighed wistfully. She could never match Thayet's skill at courtly female behavior. Thayet glanced at her, knowing the reason for the sigh, and her gravity gave way. She began to giggle, then to laugh. A fourth cup of tea was poured, for her, and she took the seat beside Jon.

Ꮿ

*T*he next morning Alanna and Liam met for their dawn work-out. Buri and Thayet, half awake, joined them shortly after they began. The four worked silently and hard for an hour before splitting up for the day. Alanna bathed, deciding to pass up a morning meal. Her nerves were wound too tightly for sleep or food. Despite a short night and excitement the day before, she was wide awake and ready for something she'd wanted to do for weeks.

Duke Roger was on the wall overlooking the City Gate as she rode into one of the many palace courtyards. Alanna stared up at him for a long moment, then glanced at the four Bazhir who had accompanied her this far. How far would their unasked-for protection extend?

Their leader bowed, interpreting her look correctly. "We await you here, Woman Who Rides Like a Man." Glancing up at Roger, he added, "As long as we may see you plainly."

She nodded. Leaving her mare to the hostlers and draping Faithful over a shoulder, she climbed the stairs up the wall.

Roger leaned against the battlement, waiting. Alanna was surprised to see his hair was too long and there were foodstains on his robe—he used to be vain of his appearance. Drawing a deep breath, she put her cat down. "Behave yourself," she told him firmly. She approached to within arm's reach and stopped; the cat, his tail dancing with badly contained hatred, crouched at her feet.

"So," Roger said, his light voice poisonous, "you survived. What a pity."

Alanna grinned with relief. She didn't have to pretend everything was fine and she liked this man. Open war was declared. "Hello, Roger. You look pale. Not enough time in the sun?"

His eyes, lighter than Jon's, narrowed. "You're cocky, aren't you? Killed anyone recently?"

"No. It's so depressing to come back and find one's work reversed." Her nerves hummed as if she were in combat.

A cruel smile curled his lips. "You know who to thank."

Alanna shrugged. "I know. Tell me something, will you? You meant to kill her—the Queen? And the King, and Jon?"

Roger tugged his beard. "If you ask about the days before you killed me, yes, I did. You doubted it? Or did you persuade yourself a court trial would have absolved you from complicity in my death?" She flinched and looked aside. "You aren't absolved. If not for you, I would have been King. Those were my plans. Now, of course, it's different. I had nothing to do with their deaths. I have promised to behave. Not that I can *mis*behave, since my Gift stayed behind when I came back to the living." He grinned wolfishly. "It keeps my tomb warm for me, against my return." Alanna shuddered. "Don't you want to assure yourself my fangs are drawn? Use your keepsake." He pointed at the ember. "I know all about it from Thom."

Alanna did not like that Thom had seen fit to tell Roger that bit of news. Still, she touched the ember and saw only him, not even a tinge of orange fire. Disquieted, she released the ember. "You're still a dangerous man, Roger. Your Gift just made things easier for you."

He reached out and gripped her wrist, searching her eyes. "You've changed, Squire Alan. You're very much the experienced knight, aren't you? And you don't fear me anymore—not as you did once." He let her go.

Alanna tucked her hands into her pockets to warm them. Thinking about what he'd said, she replied slowly, "You know something? There are sandstorms that strip man and horse and bury them—I've seen them. I saw bones piled higher than my head for the folly of a bad king and those who wanted his throne. I lived through a blizzard that froze every other living creature solid. Against those things, you're only a man. I can deal with you."

Delight played across his face and eyes. "I'm sure you can, my dear. But I won't give you the chance—not a second time." He walked away, climbing to a higher level.

Alanna watched him go. At last, she sighed and picked up her enraged cat, warming her nose against his fur. "Calm down," she whispered. "I'm not fooled, it that's what you're worried about." She felt cold. "He's up to something. I'll stake my reputation on it."

ᐁ

Raoul awaited her at the foot of the stairs. Instead of the rough shirt and breeches he'd worn aboard ship, he wore the royal blue and silver of the King's Own, with the silver star of the Commander on his chest. Alanna stopped to admire him.

"I know you told me you were commanding the Own," she said as she joined him, "but hearing it and seeing it are two different things." They started walking deeper into the palace grounds. "Did they run to seed while you were off fetching me?"

Raoul shook his head, grinning. "Mahoud ibn Shaham, my Second—he kept them on their toes. Still, I'm glad to be back. I worry when I'm not able to look after things. I saw who you were talking to, by the way."

"And?"

"What do you make of him?"

"He's crazy," Alanna said flatly. "I don't know if it's because he's above ground when he should be in his tomb, or if the spell that brought him back rearranged his mind, but it doesn't matter which. He's crazy, and he's dangerous."

Raoul nodded. "I agree; Gary agrees; sometimes I think *Jon* agrees. But what could we do? King Roald—gods rest his passing—you remember how much he disliked a ruckus. He wanted to forgive and forget, *especially* forget. He restored Roger's estates, his titles—everything. So now we're stuck with a crazy royal Duke and all those people who think we're cursed for keeping him. Can we talk about something else? I'm getting depressed."

Alanna smiled. "All right. Tell me how you like commanding the King's Own."

"It's all right," admitted Raoul. They walked through a passage to emerge in the training area for knights, squires, and pages. "It's not like the border patrols. Commanding the Own means you have to sneak and spy, what with people conspiring to kill Jonathan—"

"What?" she whispered.

Raoul turned red. "Forget I said that. It's taken care of—ask Jon. Listen, I don't want to talk about *me*. What've *you* been doing? What's the Dragon like? And why in the name of Mithros did you go to the Roof of the World?"

"It's a long story." Alanna looked around at the open-air courts, the racks of wooden swords and staffs, the practice dummies, the targets. At this early hour only a few knights were out—Gary, Alex, Geoffrey of Meron. They gathered around, clapping her on the back and demanding to hear all of her adventures. Laughing, she refused, telling them she'd have plenty of time to spin tales.

As they talked, she examined each face. Alex's was as closed as ever, although he seemed pleased about something. Gary stopped to think before he spoke, so he wasn't as sarcastic as he used to be. Myles had said Gary had taken up Duke Gareth's duties; Alanna thought the responsibility was good for her friend. Even Geoffrey seemed sharper, more *honed*. He told Alanna Scanran raiders kept him hopping all winter on the northern borders.

"Come on, Alan—*Alanna*," he corrected himself as the others laughed. "Let's see if you're still in shape." He tossed her a wooden practice sword.

"Of course she's in shape," Gary said tartly.

"I doubt she did much fencing with the Shang Dragon," Alex commented. When Alanna looked at him to see if he meant something nasty, he explained, "I know Ironarm prefers hand-to-hand techniques over weapons."

Alanna hefted the practice sword, testing its weight. "That doesn't mean he avoids weapons."

Gary, Raoul, and Alex sat on the railings to watch. "Is it true Sarain's a shambles?" Gary called as Alanna and Geoffrey squared off.

"Yes." Alanna sidestepped Geoffrey's lunge and engaged his blade, twisting down and up. He freed his sword and darted back, looking at her with respect. Alanna concentrated, knowing she was being tested to see if she'd changed. From what people had said the night before, she knew Jonathan needed her as a knight, to point out to skeptics that his vassals were loyal and strong. That she was female was a source of trouble, but she could balance that by proving—here and now—her abilities were the same.

Geoffrey came in with a series of chopping blows, trying to limit her to defense. She slid away and kept him turning. He faltered and she darted in, her sword coming to rest at the base of his throat. Geoff lowered his blade.

"I'd forgotten how gods-cursed *fast* you are." He grinned.

Gary climbed down. "My turn."

Alanna got into position. Part of her was aware that servants and nobles were coming into the yard to watch. With a grim smile she went to work, forcing Gary to attack. She beat him with a disarm like the one she'd tried on Geoff, hooking his sword out of his hands. Raoul didn't last as long as Gary; he wasn't really trying, and she told him so.

"I'm used to you beating me," he told her with a grin. "It's hard to change an old habit. From the evidence, I needn't bother. You're still best, except maybe for Alex." He nodded at the dark young man, who was seated on the railing. "Come on, Alex. Give the Lioness a try."

The hair on the back of her neck stood up. It was weird to hear her warname on an old friend's lips. It told her—more than anything else she'd seen or heard—how much she'd grown away from her fellow knights.

Alex shook his head. "I want to catch the lady knight when she's fresh." His eyes met Alanna's with an expression she couldn't read. "Some other time, I promise."

Others volunteered, eager to try a pass or two. Alanna had another five practice bouts before she bowed out—she was getting hot. The men and boys protested her departure, but she noticed they began to fill the courts as soon as she stepped out of hers. *I should be flattered they held off practicing to watch me*, she thought, accepting a towel.

Gary walked her to the stables, an arm around her shoulders. "Were the last two even Tortallan?" Alanna panted, wiping her face.

"No." The big man was pleased. "One was Gallan, and the black was Carthaki. They're here for the coronation."

"A little early, aren't they?"

"Everyone wants to know what Jonathan's like. They particularly want to know if he'll be King for long. That's why it's good to have you at home. Most of us younger knights aren't known outside Tortall. The *Lioness* is known and respected. A king who commands your loyalty is worth paying attention to." They'd reached the stable doors.

Beet red, Alanna muttered, "Hogwash."

"To you it's hogwash," Gary agreed. "To foreigners it's important. They'll keep their fingers out of our business until they know more about Jon." With a cheerful salute he left her to return to the palace and his new duties.

Entering the stables, Alanna found them deserted. Most of the hostlers were in the courtyards or the paddocks, which suited her. Putting fingers to her lips, she gave an ear-splitting whistle. A stock man slipped down from the haymow above, not bothering to pick dried grass from his strawlike hair.

"So there you are," Stefan commented, bowing

and tugging a forelock. "It's that good t'see you. Mayhap now his Majesty'll perk up. It's been that gloomsome, Mistress Alanna."

The knight leaned against a post. "Why don't you tell me what's going on to make things so 'gloomsome.'"

Stefan looked around, wary. "Come up," he invited, climbing a ladder to the mow. "And keep your voice low."

ꙮ

On her return to House Olau, Alanna found the premises occupied by seamstresses. "It was Eleni's idea," Buri explained. "She says you and Thayet need clothes. Good luck!" Faithful saw the welter of fabrics and earnest-looking women and fled with Buri; the men had already vanished.

"I know you'd rather do other things today," Eleni explained as she hauled Alanna into the fitting room. "But his Majesty wants you to bring Thayet to court tonight. He left you this." She handed over a sealed parchment.

Breaking the seal, Alanna read Jon's note while George's mother divested her of sword belt, tunic, and boots.

Lady Knight, Tonight would be a good time to present you officially at court, and to formally introduce Princess Thayet. The longer more conservative souls have to get used to you, the

*more productive your presence will be. This
will also be an excellent opportunity—with so
many there to witness—for you to present me
with the object we spoke of.*

She nodded in approval of Jonathan's strategy
as she threw the note onto the fire. A formal introduction was a grand occasion; foreign diplomats
and Tortallan nobles alike would be present. By
virtue of her rank, Thayet was due such a reception,
even though the court was in mourning. While
Alanna preferred an informal welcome, she knew
her life would be easier if Jonathan gave her public
approval. Also, giving him the Jewel would help—
both her and him. No one would wish to unthrone
a king who held the Jewel. And once presented,
word would get around. The sooner the better, after
all the news she'd heard that day!

With a sigh, she removed her shirt and
breeches as an assistant came to take her measure-
ments with a knotted cord. Grimly, she looked
at the ceiling while the cord snaked around her
body.

The fitting, however, was almost over before it
began, when the chief seamstress showed Alanna
dress designs. "I won't wear a gown, not tonight,"
the knight said firmly. "They'll think I'm crawling
back with my tail between my legs."

"Ye can't show your legs to the whole court and
his Majesty that's to be," the seamstress replied. "It's

indecent and disrespectful, and all the nobles will talk about ye."

"They do that already," Alanna retorted.

The woman shook her head stubbornly. "The only ladies as wears hose are them that's no better than they ought to be." Rispah turned a laugh into a cough when the seamstress glared at her.

"I'm not a lady—I'm a *knight,*" Alanna growled. "And I'm making my bow to the court as one. Dresses are fine sometimes, but not tonight."

"Sir Alanna is right, and *you're* right," Thayet put in diplomatically. She held up a sketch she'd been working on. "Is this a suitable compromise?"

"With a bit of gold or silver stripe along the seam?" Eleni suggested gently as the seamstress frowned.

Alanna peered at it. It was a shirt and tunic, with soft, full breeches instead of hose. The tunic was longer than usual, coming to the knee, yet splits in the sides to the waist ensured the wearer's freedom of movement.

"All right?" Thayet asked.

"I like it," replied Alanna.

"Hmm," the seamstress commented, still skeptical.

Rispah put a friendly arm around the woman's shoulders. "The dark grey silk, with—oh, of course, I can see where it might be too much trouble, with Princess Thayet's and Mistress Cooper's ballgowns besides. Perhaps Mistress Weaver, as has a shop over in—"

"It's no trouble," snapped the seamstress, pulling out of Rispah's hold. "No trouble at all, for a shop of the first cut, like mine. Weaver! She sells inferior cloth and stitchin' that comes undone in the first bow—" Rispah winked at Alanna; the skirmish was settled with honor to both sides.

The gleam in Eleni's eye made Alanna uncomfortable. George's mother was looking her over, inch by inch, leaving no part of Alanna unscrutinized. The knight hurriedly began to dress.

"Earrings!" the older woman exclaimed.

Alanna forgot her trepidation and looked at Eleni, hardly believing her ears. "*Could* I?" she whispered. All her life she'd envied the court beauties their eardrops, to the point that she'd refused to get the single earring a man could wear—it just wasn't the same.

In a twinkling Eleni and Thayet had her in a chair while Rispah heated a needle. "This shouldn't be any trouble at all," the redhead grinned, "bein's how you're a blooded knight. Hold still!"

Alanna gritted her teeth as the needle punched into a lobe; the bottom dropped out of her stomach, and her ears roared. "I'll tell you what the Daughters told me when I had mine done," Thayet said as Rispah replaced the needle with a bit of silk. "'Beauty is pain.'"

"Is that supposed to be a consolation?" Alanna gasped. She closed her eyes against the next punch of the needle. This time the bottom of her stomach continued to drop, and the roar was deafening. She opened her eyes onto more blackness.

Someone was waving aromatic salts under her nose. Alanna sneezed and sneezed again. "What happened?" she asked, struggling to keep her stomach in place. Rispah stopped trying to fight laughter; Eleni wiped teary eyes with a handkerchief. Even the seamstress showed signs of amusement. Alanna fixed Thayet with a darkling look. "*Thayet?*"

"You fainted," the Princess gasped, and surrendered to whoops of mirth.

◡

Rispah and Eleni told the travelers what had been going on in the palace and city, while the seamstresses worked nearby. The picture drawn for Alanna was grim, grimmer than she had thought from the recital in the stable. Jonathan's future subjects wondered if he was cursed. Duke Gareth had taken the deaths of his sister and brother-in-law hard; he was in retirement, and Gary was virtually Prime Minister. No one questioned Gary's ability, but everyone had known and respected his father, and few people outside the palace had ever met the younger Naxen. Many of the older nobles, who normally could be relied upon to support the King, had withheld support from Jon without giving reasons. Their excuse was that they waited for the coronation, which was the proper time and place; but Myles and Duke Gareth told Jonathan that the same lords had pledged to support Roald before his coronation. Claw appeared to have vanished, but Alanna knew from Stefan that his followers still made trouble for George. A wet spring and cool summer this far meant sickly crops, a bad omen in a king's first year on the throne.

"Everyone's waitin' to see which way the cat will jump," Rispah said as Alanna submitted to fittings. "With no reason at all. They're hopin' for another claimant to the throne, but who's it to be? The Conté Duke's givin' them no encouragement, for certain."

"With some, all it took was the Bazhir coming here in great numbers," Eleni explained. "Plenty of northerners hate them, and any King liked by the desert men will find he has trouble."

"Some folks say Duke Roger's older and more experienced than Jonathan," Rispah added. "They say what happened two Midwinters ago—" she nodded to Alanna, "was Jon's plot to get Roger out of the way."

"Easy, child," Eleni cautioned, putting a hand on Alanna's arm. "It's just talk. No one's doing anything, not even speaking out publicly. But Jonathan could do with a miracle."

To her surprise, Alanna smiled. "Then we'll give him one."

∼

She found Myles in his study late that afternoon, napping. Once he was awake, Alanna sat down to discuss the events of the past year with him. He could fill in the blank spots because he knew better than anyone else why nobles behaved as they did, and his merchant friends were always honest with him. "They don't think Jonathan can hold the throne," he told Alanna bluntly. "Until they see proof that he can, they're going to hold back. It isn't that many of them expect Roger to try for the throne. Well, those who live at court don't expect it. But Tortall's a big kingdom, and it's hard to keep it knit together in the best of times. If Jonathan can't rule, the fiefs on the borders will start to break away and form their own kingdoms. Tusaine, Galla, and Scanra will nibble at the edges. That's what people fear. Roald let them be, and twenty-odd years of that kind of beneficent neglect is bearing fruit now. Does that answer your question?" Alanna nodded. "The Jewel will help. After that, it's up to Jonathan and the use he makes of you bright young people."

Alanna laughed. "Don't forget, he's got you on his side, too."

Myles chuckled. "By the way, I have something for you. Eleni told me you'd had an ordeal this afternoon. I bought these to make you feel better." He dug in a pocket and handed Alanna a small box. "Don't open it in here. Expressions of gratitude embarrass me." He leaned back in his chair, putting up his feet. "Now, if you don't mind, I'd like to finish my nap."

Outside his study, Alanna opened the box. Inside was a pair of black pearl earbobs.

❧

*E*very Tortallan girl dreamed of descending the Great Stair in the Queen's ballroom with all eyes fixed on her, the knight of her dreams singling her out and bearing her away to a life of bliss. Minstrels made their living off tales of common-born girls presented at court by mysterious—wealthy— guardians for just that fate. Now it was Alanna's turn to descend; she felt a degree of panic she was unaccustomed to as an old palace hand. She had seen hundreds descend the Great Stair to cross the long room and kneel before sovereigns. In the ball-room she'd met girls who came to court to make good marriages, foreign diplomats and their ladies, merchants, visiting warriors—the list was endless. If they had been as terrified as she was that night, they didn't show it.

They stood in the chambers outside the ball-room's great doors: Thayet, Buri, Eleni, and Liam for official presentation; Myles to bolster their con-fidence; and Alanna to be— *Reintroduced? That can't be right,* she told herself. The Jewel, snug in its box, seemed to have caught her case of nerves; she could feel it humming through her black kid gloves. "Jump up," she told Faithful, wriggling her shoulder. "I need the reassurance."

No, the cat replied, shaking his head. *I'll muss*

your pretty clothes. Startled, she pulled away. He'd actually sounded serious!

Eleni Cooper fussed with the gold lace at her throat. "I wish I hadn't agreed to do this, Myles." She was elegant in mahogany-colored silk, her grey-streaked hair in a heavy knot at the back of her head. "I am suitably entertained in the Lower City."

Hazel eyes met hazel eyes, with a depth of love that made Alanna wistful as Myles raised Eleni's hand to his lips. "This will be just as entertaining, my dear. Perhaps more so."

Strong fingers brushed Alanna's new earbobs. "Pretty," Liam approved. "A nice touch."

Alanna's heart skipped a beat. The Dragon did not have to wear dark colors or pale greys or lavenders of mourning for Lianne and Roald. He was magnificent in blue-violet satin over silvery shirt and hose. His hair flamed in contrast.

"It isn't fair of you to look so good!" she hissed.

"I could say the same about you. You think I don't have regrets about us breaking it off?" His eyes were the bright aqua he seemed to reserve just for her. "When you're Queen of Tortall, you'll thank me."

She was opening her mouth to say, "I'm not *going* to be Queen," when Gary joined them. "Liam Ironarm? I'm Gareth—Gary—the Younger of Naxen. My father's Prime Minister. Can you tell me about Shang?" He put his arm through Liam's and walked him away, calling, "I'll talk to you later, Alanna."

Timon, once Duke Gareth's personal man-servant, now chief of the palace footmen, arrived looking harassed. Gary bade a swift farewell and went to stand by the throne. Timon nodded to Myles, who took Eleni's arm. "You're worth any of them, Mistress Cooper," Alanna heard him whisper. The chief herald bowed and opened half of the great door, admitting the couple.

"Am I all in one piece?" Buri wanted to know. She wore a deerskin jacket richly beaded in red and silver, tight deerskin breeches, and soft boots. She bristled with silver and black daggers; both the short and long sword were thrust in her sash. Her thick hair was tightly braided and coiled; the pins securing it were silver. She slapped black gauntlets nervously against her arm as Alanna looked her over.

The knight smiled. "You look splendid. Your mother and brother will be proud."

"*We* are proud," Liam added. The herald beckoned to him. He drew a breath. "Shang Masters, I hate this kind of thing." Leaving the two women staring in astonishment, he went through the open door.

Buri poked Alanna's arm. Thayet had emerged from the robing room. Alanna's voice caught in her throat as the Princess tried to smile. "Do I look all right?"

Her hair was a mass of ringlets cascading from crown to shoulders. Her hazel eyes were big against her creamy skin, her lips crimson. Her flame-red gown left shoulders and an expanse of bosom glowing against the muslin, then blossomed into a wide skirt. Rubies set in lacy gold shimmered in her hair and against her neck.

The chief herald stared at Thayet too, stunned. "Don't ask *me*," Alanna grinned. "*He's* seen all the beauties come and go. He told me they didn't impress him anymore."

Thayet looked curiously at the chief herald; he bowed to her, as deeply as he would to a king. "Princess, may you always grace our halls," he said with feeling.

∾

*B*oth doors at the head of the stair swung open. The silence in the crowded ballroom was abrupt: both doors were used only for visiting royalty. The herald walked to the head of the stair; he struck his iron-shod staff three times on the floor.

"Her most Royal Highness, Princess Thayet *jian* Wilima of Sarain, Duchess of Camau and Thanhyien." Alanna walked forward with Thayet on her arm. "Sir Alanna of Trebond and Olau, Knight of the Realm of Tortall. Buriram Tourakom of the K'miri Hau Ma."

Jonathan rose, watching them. The awe-stricken look on his face was all Alanna needed to see. She gave herself a pat on the back for an idea well conceived. Thayet descended the stair as if she were floating, her face impassive. Only her tight, somewhat damp grip on Alanna's arm revealed the state of her nerves. Jonathan walked down the scarlet runner between door and throne, to meet them in the ballroom's center.

Alanna gently withdrew her arm from Thayet's clutch, letting the Princess walk the few steps to Jon alone. The King-to-be embraced Thayet gently and kissed her on both cheeks. "Cousin, welcome," he said, using the form of address common to royalty. "We regret the sad event that drove you from your home."

"Thank you, your Majesty." Thayet's gaze was stern; plainly—to Alanna—she was trying to remind Jon of her wish to become a private subject.

Jonathan ignored the hint. "Until such time as peace returns to Sarain, know that Tortall is your home." Offering Thayet his arm, he led her to the chair placed for her just below his own. She sat gracefully, her skirts settling around her feet in a perfect fan. Buri took up her station at her side. No one knew who began it, but a patter of applause turned into a roar of enthusiasm. In Sarain she was the female who should have been a male heir; the Tortallan courtiers accepted Thayet for herself.

George also enjoyed Thayet's entrance, but he was not blind to her companions. He nodded his approval to Buri. And he was acutely aware of

Alanna from the moment she appeared. In her dark grey and black, she was elegant and somber; her hair and eyes blazed. No one could miss the sword belted at her waist. Beneath one arm she carried a box not much bigger than her fist.

Remembering his disguise as a stern-faced Bazhir, George defeated the urge to beam like a proud lover. *She's done it,* he thought. *My darlin's made them pay attention and dance to her tune. And I thought only common-born knew how to do that.*

Waiting for the applause to quiet, Alanna looked around. Even in his disguise she knew George. She bit back a grin—she should've known he'd come!—and winked at him, enjoying the approval in his eyes.

Behave, Faithful scolded. *You have business to take care of!*

The noise was finally dying. Jonathan nodded. "Sir Alanna, come forward."

She continued down the carpet, hand on sword hilt, Faithful beside her. Thayet smiled encouragingly as Alanna knelt before Jonathan.

"Your Majesty." She drew Lightning and laid it on the step at his feet, in token of her allegiance. "This I swear: to serve you and your heirs with all I possess, in the Mother's name." Taking the box in both hands, she flipped it open. The Jewel lay on a black velvet bed. She held it up to him. "I bring you the fruit of my traveling, Majesty—the Dominion Jewel."

Jonathan reached for it as total silence fell. The moment his fingers touched the Jewel, it flared into life, blazing like a small sun in his hand. Jonathan held it aloft, and first one courtier, then another, knelt, until everyone but Jonathan and Thayet was kneeling.

"We thank you, Sir Alanna." His voice was audible in every corner of the room. "And we praise the gods for sending us this Jewel—and our Lioness—in this time of need."

seven

Period of Mourning

The next morning Jonathan called a meeting of his most trusted advisors: Myles, Gary, the Provost, Duke Gareth, Duke Baird, Raoul, and Alanna. Feeling uneasy, Alanna went. In the last year she'd grown more used to taking action than to sitting in meetings. Also, she was unsure of her place in such a gathering. She was a knight; all the others had great responsibilities or wisdom, like Myles. She didn't even hold a large fief.

Arriving early, she found the King-to-be in his small council chamber. He rose and kissed her cheek. "Thank you for coming," he said. "I hate to plunge you into things just when you've come home, but we have a great deal to do." As she took a seat a little way down the table from him, he asked, "Have you given some thought to the place you'll hold in my reign?"

Alanna was startled by the question. "What place—? I never thought that I'd hold *any* place, not really. Although it would be nice to have *something* to do," she admitted. "I like roaming around, but I like it far better when I have a purpose. Maybe

Liam is happy wandering from country to country like the wind. I feel as if I'm a sort of weapon, but a weapon must have someone to wield it, or it just lies around rusting." She grinned, suddenly embarrassed. "Listen to me. Next thing you know I'll start sounding like our old philosophy master."

Jonathan groaned. "That old bore!"

Gary peered inside. "Is this a private gathering, or can anyone come?" He took a chair, plumping a stack of documents on the table in front of him. Seeing Alanna's horrified look, he said kindly, "Don't worry, the papers aren't for *this*. They're documents I refer to constantly, so I carry them around. It saves waiting for a servant to fetch them."

"Gary, how awful!" she exclaimed.

"Nonsense," Duke Gareth's son retorted. "I had no idea before how interesting a kingdom's business can be. To put diverse things like rainfall, the number of people leaving their farms, and the price of iron goods together and find out how they affect each other—"

"He'll go on all day if you let him," Raoul interrupted as he took his seat. The Lord Provost sat beside the big Commander and nodded a greeting; Alanna nodded back. Raoul went on, "Me, I have no talent for administration. Give me a good horse and a patrol any day!"

"You underestimate yourself, Raoul," said Jon. "The Bazhir love him," he explained to Alanna. "He's made a good impression on the northerners and the foreign soldiers in the King's Own as well."

Alanna beamed at her large friend, who blushed. "I always knew you'd be a credit to us," she teased him.

When she saw Duke Gareth at the door, Alanna got up and went to greet her teacher, hiding her shock as she knelt before him. The Duke, always lean, was rail thin. Streaks of grey had turned his hair a muddy yellow-brown.

Gary's father looked Alanna over as she rose. Finally he smiled. "You have lived up to your promise," he said quietly. "We are all very proud of our Lioness. Welcome home."

Coming from Duke Gareth, who had always been sparing of praise, it was the highest honor she could receive. "Thank you, sir," she whispered as she blinked tears away. "You're very kind. I tried to be a credit to my training—to you." She bowed herself back to her chair as the Duke sat beside Gary. The others busied themselves with papers, pretending not to notice.

Baird and Myles arrived together while Alanna mastered herself. The Duke greeted her cheerfully. At the reception the night before he'd complimented her on her work as a healer among the Bazhir. Myles winked at her as he settled into place.

Alanna fidgeted as servants put out water, paper, ink, and fruit. *How long will I be stuck here before I can go riding?* she wondered. *I don't have any place at councils like this!*

Jonathan cleared his throat, and the conversations stopped. "Thank you all for coming. I know the sixty days until the coronation seems like a great deal of time, but we have much to do." He glanced at Duke Gareth. "I've given some thought to the appointment of a King's Champion." Alanna's throat went dry. "Uncle Gareth was my father's. It seems to have been an easy post for him—"

"Thank the gods," the Duke said dryly. "None of the others were."

Jonathan joined the company's chuckling before he went on. "Except for taking part in the coronation of my father, he was never called on to represent—or defend—the throne. I think many have forgotten the post exists. Uncle no longer wants it." Duke Gareth nodded. "We feel someone young should be Champion. A proven warrior, of course. One who is known to our people and our neighbors."

She saw all too clearly the direction this was taking. "Raoul," Alanna croaked, looking at the Knight Commander. Grinning, Raoul shook his head. "Or Gary," she tried as Gary tugged at his mustache to cover a smile. "Both fine, strong fellows, liked by—"

"No," Jonathan said firmly. The others in the room fought their amusement. "I want them where they are—Raoul with the King's Own and Gary as Prime Minister."

"Geoffrey of Meron." She wiped sweat from her upper lip. "Noble, far more respectable than me—"

"I've made up my mind." The Provost was the last to grin as Jon spoke. All the others had seen such confrontations between the Prince and his obstinate squire.

"You'll make enemies," Alanna said flatly. "There's *never* been a female Champion, not even when women *could* be warriors! Not in Tortall!"

"That's true," Myles said. "And it's understandable that you would be concerned about your standing in the eyes of the people. There are some, still, who feel a lady knight is unnatural. And at first there was a lot of feeling against it. Even the King—" He stopped and looked at Jon. "But a lot of that thinking has changed."

"Like it or no, you're a legend, after the Bazhir and winnin' your shield," the Provost said in his blunt way. "Girls play at bein' Lioness. I saw one chasin' her brother down the street, wavin' a stick and callin' for the Conté Duke to submit to her sword."

The men laughed. Alanna blushed and continued to shake her head.

"Should we call a minstrel and have him sing all the Lioness songs in his memory?" Duke Baird asked, his eyes kind. "The newest is the one in which the Lioness and the Dragon defeat whole armies of Saren mercenaries. *I* like it, although now that I see you again, I remember you aren't ten feet tall."

"The Bazhir are for you," Raoul added. "You're the Woman Who Rides Like a Man. You also helped to bring down the Black City. The other one to do that will be King. Your own tribe would be the first to say it's your right to stand beside Jon."

Jonathan met her eyes, his gaze friendly but determined. "And let's not forget that you journeyed into the stuff of fables and brought back the Dominion Jewel." He took it from his belt-purse and set it on the table, where it shimmered. "This alone would cause you to be given a high place, even without everything else you've done. So say 'thank you,' Alanna."

"Jonathan," she whispered, knowing it was useless.

"Say 'thank you,' Alanna," Myles told her gently.

She looked at the others, but they weren't looking at her. They watched the Jewel, speculating or wondering, as their natures dictated. She realized then that even they had changed the way they thought about her. Only Jon met her eyes, and he would give no quarter. She *had* earned this honor. Did she really want to refuse?

"You said you wanted to be useful," Jon pointed out.

Alanna had to grin—*trapped by my own tongue,* she thought. "Thank you, Jonathan," she whispered.

He smiled. "You won't regret it—or at least, *I* won't." He gathered in everyone's attention. "Let us discuss the situation in Tortall. I refer to the interesting rumor that my reign is cursed and that I will be unseated from the throne."

"As it stands, there *is* no 'situation,'" growled the Provost. He ran his fingers through his hair in vexation as he explained. "It's all rumor and whispers. There are no plots afoot, none that I can find. Except that Ralon of Malven is loose, and he's still got followers. When I get my hands on him, he'll give me their names." He closed his black-gloved hands with a predator's grin.

"And Duke Roger?" asked Duke Baird.

"Innocent as a bird," said Gary with disgust. "His every movement can be accounted for. He either studies manuscripts and scrolls with Master Lord Thom or he's in plain view of the court."

"Does anyone watch Alex of Tirragen?" Alanna wanted to know. "He was Roger's squire."

The Provost, Raoul, and Gary exchanged glances. "Alex we don't know about," Gary admitted. "He locks himself for hours in his palace rooms—"

"He's in one of the old wings, where the floor plans've been lost," the Provost explained. "It's possible there's passages in and out of there we know little of. But we've no proof, of course. Unless his Majesty gives us a King's Writ, we cannot search Sir Alexander's rooms without evidence of wrongdoin'."

"I won't give such a writ," Jon said. "If I give one now, with only rumor and imagination to support it, I'll issue the next one more easily. If I wantonly break into any of Alex's homes, even the one he keeps in my own palace, what is to stop me from breaking into yours? Of all my subjects, I am the least able to break the law."

"Let's see what the news of the Jewel does over the next few weeks," Myles suggested. "Send out messengers, until even children know we have it. Perhaps knowing it's in his Majesty's possession will give people confidence in his reign."

"And we'll stay vigilant," Gary promised. "I'd hate to learn, sixty days from now, that there is fire under all this smoke."

～

They went on to other topics. It was noon by the time the meeting drew to a close. Jonathan signaled Alanna to remain behind while he showed the others out. She obeyed, still considering all she'd heard since meeting Raoul in Port Udayapur.

Jonathan closed the door after Gary and came back to Alanna at the table. "Please don't feel that being Champion traps you in some way," he said, somewhat concerned. "We're far past the era when a Champion had to defend the King's law with his sword. I imagine you'll have all the time in the world to continue roaming."

Alanna smiled at him. "That's good. It's not that I don't like being at home. I just know there are places I haven't seen. I'll always be here when you need me, though."

"That's a comfort." An awkward silence descended until she asked, abruptly, "Are you still courting that Princess I heard about—Josiane? The once I met last night?"

Jonathan blushed and shook his head. "She likes being a Princess too much. And she's cruel. She hides it well, but she is." He fiddled with the papers in front of him. "Are you jealous?" he asked sharply. "I noticed you didn't waste time finding somebody to replace *me*. Two somebodies, if you count George *and* Liam Ironarm."

It was Alanna's turn to blush. "I'm not jealous," she said at last. "I just thought you had better taste."

Jonathan stared at the table. "My offer of marriage stands, if you want."

She looked at him. Part of her wanted to say "yes," but it was a very small part. "I don't know if you've noticed, Jon, but we're very different people these days. I didn't realize *how* different until this council meeting."

"It's funny," he replied, thinking. "I look at you and realize you've been to places I'll never visit." He smiled regretfully. "You turned into a hero when I wasn't watching."

"Don't say that. I'm still me." Alanna walked over to sit on the table in front of him. She took his hand, and feeling more at ease, she tickled his palm. "Jon, if we were married we'd make a mess of things. You know it as well as I do."

Now he *did* look at her. "I don't want to go back on my word," he explained. His eyes gave his other feelings away. "I asked for your hand—"

His obvious relief hurt, but it didn't keep her from knowing she did the right thing. "And I said no. Thank you, but no. I love you, Jon. We've been through a lot. But what we want from life—" She pointed to his papers. "You *like* this king business. I like action. I like to say what I think." She saw a rough sketch half hidden by other documents and pulled it free.

"Don't, you—" Jon started to say, but he was too late.

Alanna waved the drawing of Thayet in front of him, grinning wickedly. "You still want to marry *me*, Sire? Or were you just checking to see if the road is clear?"

Jonathan was beet red with embarrassment. "Don't tease. You know I'd marry you if you said 'yes.'"

"Then thank the gods one of us has sense." She examined the drawing closely. "Your artwork's improved. The one you did of Delia made her look like a cow." Pursing her lips, she added thoughtfully, "Though now that I think of it, maybe that was your subject matter—"

Jon laughed so hard tears gathered in the corners of his eyes. When he regained his self-control, he said, "I need you home, if only because you make me laugh."

"I'm not sure that's a compliment," she said dryly as she gave him the sketch.

Jonathan caught her hand, his eyes serious. "I love you, too, Alanna. You're a part of me—my sword arm."

She kissed his forehead. "Fine. I like that. But you need a Queen, too. Thayet would be a good one."

"Are you *sure*?" he wanted to know. "Are you positive we couldn't make a good marriage?" She returned his look, equally serious, and he sighed. "You're right. Still, it would have been interesting."

～

*H*er head spinning from the events of the last three days, Alanna went to earth. She was all but invisible at palace social functions. Jonathan, knowing that she needed time to think, left her alone. Instead he asked for Thayet when he called at House Olau, taking her for rides or to the palace. He invited Buri on these excursions, guessing— accurately—that the little K'mir would prefer several deaths to making polite conversation with noblemen. Thayet could make no threat that would cause Buri to act as a chaperone at such times. Instead the Princess's companion joined Alanna as she refamiliarized herself with Corus and the palace grounds.

Alanna introduced her to the remnants of George's court and to her friends among the palace hostlers and servants. They joined Liam in extended hours of exercise and sparring. George took them on picnics beside the river and on explorations of the city's catacombs. Buri learned how to pick pockets, and Alanna relaxed in the thief's company. The pair found themselves drilling the city's urchins, boy and girl, in staff- and sword-play, and running races with local youths. Alanna brought Buri into the morning practice sessions in the palace, where the K'mir met Raoul, Gary, and the other knights and squires. Many of these young noblemen, particularly those who didn't know Alanna well, were unsure of what to make of *two* females—one an unproven stranger—joining their practice. Their attitudes soon changed to respect for Buri and awe for Alanna.

Because the body concerned was hers, Alanna didn't know how much she'd improved under Liam's teaching. If she beat her old friends, which she often did, she decided they had been riding chairs too much recently. Alex never challenged her, George could still best her with knives, and Liam always won.

"It keeps me humble," she told Coram with chagrin after one session with Liam. Coram laughed and ruffled her hair.

She watched Duke Roger. He was often present when she visited Thom. These glimpses were enough to confirm her feeling that she trusted him less than ever. She relayed her suspicions to everyone who mattered; there could never be too many eyes on the Duke. Still, he continued to act conspicuously innocent. Instead of easing her fears, such behavior only increased them.

The days slipped away. She was fitted for dresses, which she wore during quiet evenings with her family and on leisure excursions with George or her friends at court. Summer began with the June festival of Beltane. Since this was the time of year men approached their chosen ladies (the excuse being the custom of leaping over fires hand-in-hand to ensure a bountiful harvest), she looked for George to renew his courtship. Certainly he'd had time to see that she no more belonged to Liam than to the moon! George, however, remained simply friendly; after his enthusiastic greeting on her return, he showed no other signs of warmer feelings.

"I'm doomed to be an old maid," she told Faithful mournfully, surveying her image in a looking-glass the morning of the festival.

There was a time when you wanted to be a spinster, he reminded her as he washed his glossy fur. *A warrior maiden, with no one to tie her down—*

"Oh, shut up," she said crossly. "Must I have everything I said as a girl thrown back in my face?"

You seemed positive, the cat taunted her wickedly.

A serving girl peered in. "Excuse me, your ladyship, but the King says, if you're awake, will you come down? He's in his lordship's library."

Alanna tugged on one of the new gowns, listening with enjoyment to the rustle of lilac silk as she tugged a brush through her waving hair. She put on slippers as she went downstairs, nearly killing herself by hopping first on one foot, then the other. While she knew Jon rose quite early, it was rare for him to leave the palace at this hour: he must have an important errand.

"Hello," he greeted her as she rushed into the library. "That's a pretty dress. Are you wearing it for anyone in particular?"

"Yes," she snapped. "Myself."

"Ouch. You should be nicer to your King, my Champion."

"No I shouldn't," retorted Alanna. "Duke Gareth says the Champion must always be honest, even when others lack the courage."

Jon smiled ruefully. "Lacking the courage to speak out has never been one of your problems, I admit."

She looked him over with some concern. "Are you taking proper care of yourself—eating right, getting your sleep? It won't do for you to fall ill for your own coronation."

"I'll be fine. I've been up late the last week or so, working with the Jewel."

"How is that going?"

Jonathan smiled. "Very well. Thom has been a great help, finding spells and writing new ones for the Jewel. Its power can be limitless, if you know how to use it." He sighed. "That's a temptation I'll always have to fight. The minute I start relying on the Jewel to rule is the minute I court disaster. There's no substitute for a human touch."

"Do you always think like this?" she wanted to know. "Or do you rest sometimes and think about ordinary things with the rest of us?" She couldn't tell him that she was in awe of him when he spoke of such things. *If ever a man was born to be King, it's Jon*, she thought.

"Of course I do," he replied tartly. "There are plenty of ordinary things for me to think about—the future, and love, and—" He stopped, turning red.

"How *are* things with you and Thayet?" Alanna inquired, interested.

Jonathan scrubbed his face with his hands. "Baffling." He sighed. "I don't know if she goes riding with me to be polite, or because she likes my company—"

"Good," his Champion said. "You're too sure of yourself with women. It won't hurt for you to have to struggle a little."

Jon picked up Faithful and smoothed the cat's fur. "Thank you, dearest Alanna. I *knew* I could depend on you to salve my wounded pride."

"You always take care of your own pride," she reminded him. "You've never needed me for *that*. By the way, what *do* you need me for this morning? Or are you here for the conversation?"

He shook his head. "I'm here for a talk with George—who is late. I thought your presence might smooth things."

"You aren't angry with George, are you?" she asked, concerned.

"Quite the opposite."

The subject of their conversation strolled in, mussed and sweat-streaked. "Sorry I'm late," he told Jonathan, collapsing into a big armchair. "I had a bit of a scuffle with some hotheads. Nothing serious, but it delayed me." Alanna poured George a cup of the fruit juice left on Myles's desk by the servants. He accepted with a murmured word of thanks, and drained it. She poured him another, checking him for wounds from beneath lowered lashes.

He still knew what she was doing. "I'm all in one piece, lass," he grinned. "Never tell me you were worried."

Alanna scowled, prodded by his mocking tone. "I wasn't," she retorted.

George winked at her. "That's my girl!"

Jonathan opened a manuscript case that lay on the desk before him and drew out two scrolls, both adorned with heavy seals and tied up with royal blue ribbons. "Enough squabbling, you two." He passed the first to George. Alanna noted the flowing writing was a court scribe's and not Jonathan's precise hand.

George read for only a moment before he stood

and tossed the parchment on the desk. His mouth was tight with anger, his face white. "A royal pardon! What d'you take me for, Majesty?" His big hands were clenched. "You've had fun with the lowborn, and now you'll throw me a bauble as reward? I want no charity, Jonathan!"

Alanna forced herself to sit, gritting her teeth. She could not interfere.

Jonathan refused to be provoked. "I'm not charitable," he said coolly. "My father was. Now the results of...certain of his charities threaten this kingdom. I wish he had been more just and less kind."

He leaned back. "You were the best teacher I had. Must I list what you made me learn? The reaches of men's trickery. Making even those who mistrust me follow where I lead. The extent of human greed. The things that can't be bought. The need for ruthlessness. The ability to recognize—and trust—loyalty." Jon smiled grimly. "I've often wondered—would I have survived the Ordeal of the Voice, if you hadn't taken me under your wing?"

He tapped the pardon. "'The teacher earns his wage,'" he quoted. "But it's more than that. This is to prevent the day when I have to sign a writ for your execution."

George went to the bookshelves, staring at them. "You needn't go so far. I've lost my taste for the Rogue. I'll leave Tortall, settle elsewhere."

When Alanna would have started forward, Jon

gripped her arm, keeping her beside him. "Must you desert me when I need you?" he asked the thief. "Never again will I have any freedom. And our hero is easily recognized, which limits *her* movements." He smiled at Alanna and let her go. She stayed where she was, tense.

Jon continued, "I need someone unusual to serve as my confidential agent. I'd trust such an agent implicitly. He must be clever and unorthodox, someone who could venture among all classes without trouble."

George looked at Jon, his face unreadable. "What's t'other writ, then?"

"A grant of nobility and the title of baron. The deeds to the lands and incomes traditionally belonging to the lord of Pirate's Swoop, a day's ride south of Port Caynn."

"I know where the Swoop is," George snapped. "Why? Why must you go and make me respectable?"

"A confidential agent needs a home and income," was the simple reply. "His comings and goings, particularly at court, *cannot* be remarked upon, which means he must be a noble."

"I want to travel, Jon. Before I'm old and know nothin' but the Rogue."

Jonathan smiled dryly. "Is life here so dull that you two think of nothing but roaming? Never mind. I *need* you to travel. I have to know what's outside my borders, too." He let George think for a few moments before adding softly, "I can't do this alone. Say you will." Both Alanna and George heard the real pleading in his voice when he added, "Please."

George picked up the pardon, re-reading it. He tapped a large seal in silvery wax. "How in Mithros's name did you get my Lord Provost to sign?"

"You'd be surprised. He's an amazing fellow." Jonathan's tone was filled with wry respect, making Alanna wonder just what the Provost had done to put that feeling in his voice.

George sighed, rolling the parchment up. "With so many good reasons for me to accept, I'd be touched in my wits to refuse." With a lopsided grin he told Alanna, "He's grown up with a vengeance. I wonder if I shall be glad or sorry."

∾

*A*lanna rode to the palace that evening as the sun set against the Coastal Hills, paying her daily visit to Thom. When she left him, as always, she was troubled and uneasy. He looked no better than he had when she first returned to Corus. If anything, he looked worse, and she was frightened. She'd also noticed that Faithful stayed away from Thom, and that Thom deliberately avoided the cat. To her there was no better sign of something dangerously wrong; but when she questioned Faithful, he refused to answer.

Instead of riding home or seeking out her

friends, she and Faithful wandered idly through the maze of the palace, thinking about the coronation. It was hard to believe only three weeks remained.

Their walk finally brought knight and cat to the Hall of Crowns. This room had one use: Tortallan sovereigns were consecrated to the realm there. At all other times it was closed, its windows covered by heavy velvet curtains.

They entered, smelling beeswax, spices, and incense. The servants had worked hard, cleaning the dust-covered draperies, polishing wood- and metalwork until it shone, scrubbing the many-paned windows. Tiny votive candles winked on the altar, where a Mithran priest and a Daughter of the Goddess would bind Jonathan to the crown and the land.

Her steps echoed to the ceiling as she walked around. Here were the wooden benches where the nobility sat. She climbed the stone risers that would seat the principal merchants, guild-masters, and their families until she reached the top. Here were the City Doors, the height of five men and the breadth of seven. These would be open during the coronation. All who could fit in behind the wealthy and powerful commoners would do so, relaying what happened inside to the less fortunate.

Once crowned, Jonathan would mount Darkness at the City Doors to ride down to his new capital. Alanna would stay a pace behind as he rode through the packed streets.

Thank the Goddess Moonlight isn't some skittish yearling and hard to control in a crowd, she reflected. *Still, I can think of things I'd rather be doing that day.*

She sat on a riser, almost on top of Faithful. "Oh, stop it," she muttered when he yowled. "You aren't hurt." Propping elbows on knees, she put her chin on her hands, staring at the distant altar. "I'm getting old," she whispered. "I should be excited about the coronation. I wish I knew for certain he'd be safe."

You wanted to be a hero, Faithful said. *Heroes have responsibilities.*

"I'm not sure I want to be a hero anymore," Alanna sighed.

Then you are in trouble. That's the one thing you'll never be able to change.

"I know. I think about marrying, though, if I could do it and still see the world. It wouldn't be such a bad thing. Not if it was someone I liked *and* loved. Someone I could laugh with."

You want to be warrior and woman. You want to travel and serve Jonathan. Can't you make up your mind about what you want? complained the cat.

"Who says I can't have a little bit of each?" she wanted to know. When she realized what she'd said, she began to grin. "That's right—why can't I? And I've done pretty well, I think!"

I suppose so, he replied grudgingly. *For a person. Mind, be careful in your choices—particularly if you want to marry. You need somebody who isn't as noble-minded as you are. Otherwise you take yourself much too seriously. I won't always be around to correct you.*

"I am *not* noble-minded!"

Yes you are. You hide it well, but not everyone knows you like I do. And you think you can solve all the world's ills. You need someone who will cheer you up when you can't.

Abruptly Alanna sneezed four times without stopping. She got to her feet, blinking teary eyes. Something took form before the altar, something with substance enough to obscure the votive candles. It was the Goddess, her white skin and emerald eyes gleaming in the dark. Impossibly tall, she smiled at Alanna. *Of course she's here,* Alanna thought, awed. *It's Beltane. Every couple tonight will ask her blessing on the summer crops. Then why has she come here? I'm alone, without a lover, and I'm more worried about the coronation than the crops.*

The gentle whisper nonetheless drove Alanna to her knees. It took all her willpower to keep her hands from her ears: that voice still embodied huntress and hounds and the storm. In the Hall of Crowns even the Goddess's whisper rolled like thunder. "We meet again, my daughter. You have traveled a long road since last we spoke. Surely you must be pleased, now. Your labors of all these years, here and in the Roof of the World, bear fruit. Your Jonathan is to be King. He will bear the Dominion Jewel."

Alanna looked up eagerly. "Then he *will* be King? Please—can you give me a sign, some hint of what is to come? I sense trouble, but...and my brother. What's wrong with Thom?"

The Goddess shook her head. "I may not answer these questions. The gods cannot reveal all things; otherwise, where is men's right to choose their fates? Where is *your* right to choose?"

"I think I chose well," Alanna said, getting to her feet. "How can I thank you for your favor?"

"Your life is my thanks. I have guided you as best I can, but the time for guidance is past. You are fully grown into all your powers, Alanna. The days to come are what you make of them. The coronation is a crossroad in Time. Bend it to your will—if you have the courage!"

Alanna's blood thrilled to the challenge, but her common sense made her beg, "Just a *hint!*"

The Goddess shook her head, smiling with amusement. The air brightened. Alanna could see other figures before the altar. The shining warrior could only be Mithros, the divine protector. On the Goddess's other side, hooded and cloaked, waited her brother the Black God. Alanna knew him and bowed her greetings; the great head nodded in reply.

Behind them were ranged others, only some of whom she knew: the Crooked God, his smile as wicked as George's own; the Smith's God; the Sea Goddess. The array of immortals stretched on and on, but somehow she saw each face clearly. Awed and frightened, she covered her eyes like a Doi tribesman.

Slowly the glory faded. When she uncovered her eyes, she and Faithful were alone. She stayed where she was for a while, remembering what she had seen. At last she shook her head. "Ask a silly question."

It always comes to this, Faithful remarked. *A god can guide a mortal, nurture, teach. And yet there comes a moment when the god must stand away from the fosterling and let the inevitable happen.*

"Why?" she asked, curious.

That's how the universe is fashioned, Faithful replied. *There are moments when only a human can affect the outcome of events.*

She picked him up, letting him perch under her left ear. "You mean they don't *know* what's going to happen?"

People like you are the fulcrums on which the future turns. He gave her ear a nuzzle. *Don't mess it up. I have a reputation to maintain.*

∿

*L*eaving the Hall of Crowns, she was surprised to come face-to-face with Delia of Eldorne and Princess Josiane. Both wore plain dark gowns and veils over their hair. Plainly they were as surprised as she was.

Delia recovered quickly. "Well, if it isn't 'Sir'

Alanna," she sneered, her green eyes glinting. "The Woman Who Rides Like a Man!"

Taking her cue from Delia's words, Alanna bowed as a man would. "Princess Josiane. Lady Delia."

"I used to have to dance with her when *she* posed as a *he*," Delia told the tall blonde. "I *sensed* something was not right."

"Funny," Alanna said thoughtfully, "as *I* recall, you chased *me*. You made a point of flirting with me, because the men said I was a woman-hater, and you wanted to make me fall in love with you."

"Liar!" Delia hissed.

Alanna shrugged. "As you like. I was taught not to question a *lady's* word."

"I'm told you were Jonathan's lover once," Josiane said abruptly, veiling her blue eyes with her lashes. "Is that why he made you Champion?"

Surprised by the attack from this unknown source, Alanna took a step back. She clenched her hands, her nails biting into newly formed scars, as she controlled her temper. "I'm told you replaced me in his affections—for a little while," she replied sweetly. "Why didn't he make you Prime Minister?"

Josiane's beautiful face changed into an ugly mask. "No one gets the better of me," she hissed.

"Did you plan to be King's Champion?" Alanna wanted to know. "You don't have the training."

Delia gripped Josiane's arm; Alanna could see her blood-red nails digging into the Princess's flesh.

"I don't waste time in conversations with sluts, Josiane," she snapped. "Neither should you." She literally dragged the Princess away, quite a feat in so delicate-looking a woman.

∾

"She could do harm," Alanna told Liam and Myles later that night as they sat over brandy. Outside they could hear the sounds of the Beltane festival. "I'm no expert, but that Josiane is crazy!"

"There's bad blood in the Copper Isle kings," Liam drawled, his eyes sleepy. "They birth a mad one every generation. Josiane's uncle is locked in a tower somewhere. It comes from being an island kingdom—too much inbreeding."

"I think it might be a good idea if the Provost's spies kept an eye on her," Alanna said frankly. "I don't trust her."

"He has her watched," Myles said reassuringly. "Any foreign noble is suspect at a time like this."

Alanna fidgeted in her chair. "I wish the coronation was over. The waiting is getting on my nerves."

"Once he's sealed to the crown and the land, he'll be hard to dislodge." Liam yawned. "And if the Jewel's all it's supposed to be, so much the better."

"In the meantime, we still can find no traces of a plot or plotters." Myles sighed. "With people starting to arrive for the ceremonies, it will be hard to spot fighters coming to take part in an overthrow."

"George and I ride through the city every day," Liam said unexpectedly. "The Lord Provost and Duke Gareth, too. Between the four of us, any group of warriors will be easy to spot. The Provost's men stand alert as well." He noticed Alanna staring at him and grinned. "Did you think you could leave me out of your worries? I'm still your friend. I won't sit idling when there's a hint of a fight in the offing."

Alanna smiled gratefully at the Dragon. "It *is* a weight off my mind, knowing you're keeping an eye on things, too."

George glanced into the library. "Ah, here you all are. Myles, I've another visitor to cast upon your tender mercies." He bowed gracefully, ushering the guest into the room.

"Master Si-cham!" Alanna cried, jumping up. The tiny old man in the orange worn by Mithran adepts smiled and held out gnarled hands for her to kiss.

"*And* Liam Ironarm," he said, nodding cheerfully to the bowing Dragon. "What a pair of warriors to grace your house, Myles!"

Alanna looked from Si-cham to Liam to her father, baffled. "You know Liam?" she asked. The redheaded man winked at her. "You know *Myles*?"

"I traveled more when I was younger," Myles explained. "Si-cham, have a seat. George, thank you for bringing him. Where was he?"

"Cornered near the Water Gate by a set of

young louts. The drunken fools wanted him t'dance for the Goddess," George said, pouring tea for the Mithran priest. "There's no respect for old men anymore."

"I've danced for the Goddess in my day." Si-cham admitted with a grin. "Not after such a journey, though." He drank his tea. "I'm sorry to be so long in answering your summons, George Cooper. I had a thousand loose ends to tie up in the City of the Gods once they realized I was *truly* going. Also, I do not cover so much ground as I did when I was young. I had to be carried in a litter—a sad comedown for me, when I rode so well."

"But why are you here?" Alanna wanted to know.

Si-cham put down his glass, his face tired. "George tells me your brother is ill—desperately so, perhaps. He asked me to come to Master Thom's aid."

"Now all we have to do is convince Thom he needs it," admitted George.

∾

*A*t first Thom refused to consider talking to his former master. His rage on learning why Si-cham was in the city scared Alanna, not so much because she feared his temper, but because she heard despair and fear in Thom's voice as he screamed at her. This made her determined that Si-cham should meet with her twin. Thom resembled a skeleton now; his skin was dry and cracked with the heat that ate at him from within.

A week before the coronation Thom gave in. Even Roger was banned from their meeting, a ban he accepted gracefully. When Thom and Si-cham instructed the palace servants to bring their meals to Thom's rooms, Alanna gave up waiting for word. They would send for her when they needed her.

She had a number of mundane tasks that needed to be taken care of in the days remaining. Visiting the palace scribes, she had a new will drawn up: the last had been done prior to her Ordeal. They were disturbed to see such a document when death should be the last thing on her mind, but she could not shake uneasy feelings about the coronation. She wanted nothing left to chance, just in case. She took her mail to be polished and her sword to be sharpened. While neither her gold mail nor Lightning required the extra attention, she felt better for having it done. When the hairdresser came to style Eleni's hair for a court party, Alanna asked him to cut her hair as well. Everyone but George and Buri cried out when they saw her. The coppery locks that had fallen past her shoulders were trimmed back to her ear lobes in the short cut she'd worn as a page. She shrugged at the protests. "I couldn't keep it out of my eyes," she explained.

Finally one of the palace servants came to House Olau, four days after Thom and Si-cham had cloistered themselves, to ask Alanna to visit her brother. She did so, wondering what delightful surprise the sorcerers had ready for her.

Thom was pacing when she arrived. Alanna dropped into a chair with a grateful sigh. "It's baking outside." *About as much as you're baking inside,* she added to herself, noting that his skin was peeling and his lips bled.

Thom looked at her quizzically. "Tell me, Sister Mine, when is your Dragon going to make an honest woman of you?"

She made a face at him, thinking he had to feel a little better if he was nosing into her affairs. "He isn't. We were done before I came home. He doesn't like magic."

"Silly man. What about Jonathan, then? Everyone knows you two used to be lovers, even if he *is* a prig about other things. Maybe I should talk to him. Having sullied your reputation, he can't be allowed to abandon you. You have a good name—"

"I'm not amused, Thom."

"*I* think you should take the thief, if you must take someone. If you marry George, I'll give you my blessing."

"If I marry anyone, I'll let you know. Can you change the subject?" She shifted in the big chair, hooking her legs over one arm. "I love you dearly, Thom, but you're prying, and I don't appreciate it."

He grinned. "What sort of twin would I be if I didn't pry?" That made her smile. Sitting on the edge of his desk, he tugged his beard as he looked her over. "It's changed you—the Jewel. Time was you'd've lost your temper with me for calling him a 'prig' or teasing you about the Dragon. You only save your anger now for big things, is that it?"

"Thom, do you *mind*?" she snapped. "I didn't come here to be analyzed by my own twin, thank you very much!"

He looked away. "Sorry," he murmured shyly. "I forgot how much *I* dislike it. And you *have* changed. For the better, I think."

"Thank you," she whispered, touched by the rare compliment.

There was a rap on the door; it opened to admit Si-cham. "There you are, Lady Alanna. Now we may begin."

Alanna looked at Thom, feeling the first pricklings of mistrust. "Begin *what*?" she wanted to know.

"We've been going over the books in Jonathan's sorcery library," Thom explained. "And we found some possibilities. For now, I want to drain off a little of the power that burdens me. Without it, I can think clearly. Because you're my twin, you're the best person to carry it."

"Wait a minute—" Alanna began, rising out of her chair. "What if it poisons me like you've been poisoned? Even a beginning hedgewitch knows you can carry your own Gift and no more!"

"That would be true, if we spoke of weeks or

months or years. This transfer is for a week. Our spells will enclose it, keep it from leaking into your Gift," Si-cham reassured her. "We are sure of it." He met Alanna's eyes, smiling.

Alanna stared at the sorcerers for a long moment. "A week?"

"No more," Thom said. "The most important of the infusions I need takes that long to make."

Alanna bit her lip. He was so thin! "It'll help? It won't interfere with my participation in the coronation?"

"It will help," Si-cham affirmed. "It will not interfere. You won't even notice it after the first night, unless you try to use your Gift, of course. I would not advise it."

She sat down with an exhausted sigh. "What must I do?"

∽

*A*lanna kept to House Olau for the next few days while her head buzzed and her stomach lurched. Grimly she continued her exercises with Liam in spite of it, fearing to slack off for even a day. At last her body adjusted to the new burden. But she refused to do so tiny a spell as the one for lighting candles, fearful of what might happen. Visiting Thom once more, she was glad she'd given in— he looked better already. Together with Si-cham, he had embarked on the beginnings of an intricate spell. It would be finished several days after the coronation, and—if Thom was lucky—it would purify his magic.

～

Three days before the coronation, Jonathan summoned Alanna to the palace to discuss how the Jewel would fit into the ceremonies. "It seems like a silly thing to worry about," he admitted with a smile, "but the Master of Protocol wouldn't let me alone until I agreed to do it his way. You see, I can't take it up when I'm crowned, or when I get the scepter and the Great Seal. Those are all Tortallan things, and the Jewel isn't Tortallan."

Alanna had to laugh. "Poor Jon! Maybe I should've given it to you for your birthday, or something."

The King-to-be grimaced. "Very funny. Here's how we *will* do it. When you come to give me your oath as King's Champion, say this."

He gave her a parchment on which her oath was written. It read very like the one she'd taken as a knight. At the end, in scarlet ink, were lines, which she read aloud. "'Sire, as token of my fealty, I gift you and your heirs with this most awesome artifact—' Jon, do I *really* have to say 'awesome artifact'?" Jonathan nodded, not bothering to hide his amusement. "Wonderful," Alanna muttered as she read further. "'For which I have gone in quest to the most distant corner of our world. Through peril I have borne it, for the glory of Tortall, and for the glory of King Jonathan. Accept, I beg, this symbol of my devotion to realm and crown, the Dominion Jewel.' Jon, this is some kind of a joke!"

Jon shook his head. "Wait till you hear what *I* have to say in reply. I'd better go—the delegation from Tyra is waiting for me. Don't forget to memorize your lines!" With an evil grin he left Alanna to scowl at her revised oath.

She shoved it into her pocket. "I guess I'm too old to put a frog in his bed," she muttered as she headed for the stables. "'Awesome artifact,' indeed!"

eight

Crossroad in Time

The night before the coronation, Alanna stayed with Jonathan as he kept vigil in the Chapel of the Ordeal. While he meditated on the obligations of Kingship, she worried. None of those who'd made his protection their goal were satisfied that the single men pouring into the city in recent weeks had come to enjoy themselves. They'd had no choice—Raoul, Gary, the Lord Provost—but to let the coronation take place, so they had every fighting man in service to the palace on duty and alert. Alanna attended their talks with Jon that afternoon but had nothing to add. The back of her neck prickled constantly, reflecting her uneasiness, but that wasn't solid evidence of trouble. When she and Jonathan reached the chapel, she was pleased to see Raoul had posted a double guard. The night inched by quietly; the only movement she noticed occurred when she or Jonathan changed position.

The iron door of the Chamber shimmered in the candlelight, a vivid reminder of her Ordeal of Knighthood. Here Jon would undergo the Ordeal of Kings. The only advantage she could see to his entering that room a second time was that the Kings' Ordeal was said to be short. For herself, she knew that no inducement could get her to enter that place again.

Suddenly the light shifted. The Dominion Jewel danced in the air in front of her, so real looking she had to touch the pouch at her waist to make sure the Jewel was in there. She stared, wondering if this was a glimpse of the future, or something of the Jewel's making. The false Jewel shimmered and grew, coming closer, until it overwhelmed her eyes. Inside it she saw:

In the center of the Chamber of the Ordeal Roger lay on a block of stone. He got up and held out his arms. "Come, loved one," he whispered.

She had been warned not to speak or scream. Her jaws knotted to keep from yelling her fury. She couldn't move. Closer he came. She bit the inside of her cheek to keep silent—coppery blood flooded her mouth.

She was in his arms and they danced, his face lit with love and with rage, his sapphire eyes insane. "We'll dance until the end of everything, my darling, my pet," he crooned. "Promise me we'll dance forever."

She shook her head, struggling wildly against his grip. She opened her mouth, then clamped it shut.

She was forbidden to scream in the Chamber of the Ordeal!

She was in the chapel once again, her hands

tight over her mouth. Luckily Jonathan was in some kind of trance, unable to notice her antics. Slowly she lowered her hands, trembling. What did today have in store?

∽

When the first rays of sun slid through the high windows of the chapel, the priests came. Jonathan rose to go with them, still in a trance. Gently they conveyed him to the Chamber and ushered him inside. Alanna tugged at her earbobs, trying to think of nothing at all.

When the door swung open, fifteen minutes later, she was the first one there to catch Jon, as he had once caught her. He smiled at her tiredly, murmuring, "Not bad—if you like ordeals."

Alanna bit back a laugh. Gary came up to take Jonathan's other arm; they helped him to his rooms, where he could sleep for a few hours. With a sleepy wave, Alanna parted from Gary and went to the nearby chamber that had been prepared for her. The last thing she saw as she drifted off to sleep was her gold-washed mail, glimmering at her from the rack in the corner.

∽

In his suite of rooms, Alex of Tirragen sharpened his sword. He was dressed in black and wearing breeches—he did not plan to attend the coronation. Testing the edge of his blade, he smiled.

Delia of Eldorne fussed with her hair at the mirror. Unlike Alex, she was in full court regalia, her emerald silk with its stiffened skirts rustling as she put last-minute touches on her appearance.

"Aren't you the least bit nervous?" she asked, adjusting a hair ornament.

"Why should I be?" was the cool reply. "He's thought of everything."

"What if Josiane succeeds?"

Alex chuckled. "Delia, have you no faith in our Champion? We have an appointment today, though she doesn't know it." He held up the sword, his eyes dreamy. "She won't let a madwoman like Josiane prevent her from coming."

Squire Henrim knocked and stepped into the room. "Lord Alexander, I let the men-at-arms into the back corridors near the Hall of Crowns. They're concealed in the storerooms. Captain Chesli says the Eldorne men have taken their places inside the hall, among the crowd." He bowed to Delia, who smiled.

Alex stood, sheathing his sword. "You'll be with the men on the dungeon level. Before you go there, remind *both* captains they are not to act until the signal, which will come after the crown rests on Jonathan's head. *After* the crowning, understand?"

The squire hesitated. "But—surely—he will be bound to the land. He will use Tortall's magic against the Duke—"

"Idiot!" Delia snapped. "Do you think Duke

Roger hasn't planned for that? Don't question your betters!"

Henrim bowed, shamefaced. "Forgive me, Lady Delia."

With a sniff Delia turned back to her mirror.

"Follow your orders exactly," said Alex. "If you fail, you will pay."

"I won't fail!" the squire promised hotly.

"Take the hidden stair, then. Dismissed."

The youth bowed. "Good luck, my lord. And— long live King Roger!"

"Fool," Alex whispered when the door closed. Of them all, he alone knew Roger's real plans. He alone knew that those like Delia who planned to steal Jonathan's throne so *they* could have power were in for a disappointment. He picked up his dagger and tested the edge. "Now—to work."

～

*F*rom her position along the wall near the altar, Alanna watched with pride as the Mithran priest and the Priestess of the Goddess, acting as one, blessed the silver crown and then Jonathan, who knelt before them. She was grateful that her duties didn't call for her participation in this part of the ceremony. After keeping vigil with Jonathan all night, she was sleepy. Somehow repeated yawns did not seem right for such a memorable occasion. Instead, until it was time to present Jonathan for-mally with the Jewel, all she had to do was stay put and look impassive. On her left, Gary and Raoul did the same.

Raoul winked as she covered a yawn. Unlike the King's Champion, the Knight Commander had spent the night in bed, disturbed only by his nerves. She had to admit he may have gotten as little sleep as she had: Jon's safety today was the responsibility of the King's Own.

She let her eyes drift over the crowd that packed the vast hall. Mourning was officially over; nobles and commoners alike bloomed with color. She could see Myles and his companions—Eleni, Thayet, Buri, and Rispah—all wearing their finest. She picked out other familiar faces: Dukes Baird and Gareth, Sirs Douglass, Geoffrey, and Sacherell. Many wept openly, moved by the beauty of the day and the moment.

A halt in the chanting brought the knight's eyes back to the altar, just as the crown was lowered onto Jonathan's head. Immediately it sparked and glowed, the magic of the land reaching down to envelop the new King. People gasped with awe as Jonathan flared with brilliance; they knew the joining of Tortall and King was complete. Smiling, Alanna touched the ember at her throat.

Jonathan was brilliant with the crown's silver glow, his own magic showing through as threads of sparkling blue. She looked down, and felt sick. The floor of the chamber was awash in blood-colored fire.

"Jonathan!" she yelled as the earth moaned and shook.

Sudden pain, combined with the vibration beneath her, knocked Alanna to her knees. For a moment she could only clutch her belly and scream with agony. It receded, then flared again.

In the Hall, chaos reigned. From the vaulted ceiling mortar dust and chips of stone fell, an ominous hint of the destruction that could occur. People screamed in fear as the ground rolled underfoot like a ship at sea. Alanna was deaf and blind to it all.

The pain was grinding: she felt as if every nerve in her body was being pulled out through her skin. *Thom,* she realized, struggling to get up. *Something's happening to Thom, and I can feel it. I have to go to him!*

"Guard the King!" she yelled to Raoul, lurching to her feet. Faithful was at her side as she hurled herself out of a nearby door, running as quickly as gold mail would allow for her brother's quarters. Pain ripped into her again; she bit her lip to fight it and stumbled on, determined to reach her twin.

Strong arms caught Alanna from behind, helping her along. She looked up into George's eyes and fought to smile. He was dressed as one of the King's Own.

"What is it, darlin'?" he asked. They never hesitated in the long strides that took them up the stairs to the second floor.

"Thom," she whispered. "He's being attacked. The earthquake is magic. It's the color—of Thom's Gift, all blood-red—"

"*Blood?* But his is purple, like—"

"Corrupted," she gasped as they flew down the hall that led to Thom's rooms. "Turned blood-color."

"What color would purple and orange make?" George asked as they came to a halt. "Roger's Gift and the Trebond Gift?"

Alanna felt even sicker.

Inside Thom's parlor the air was heavy, almost liquid; the light was greenish yellow. Alanna froze, wary.

"What is it, lass?" George whispered. He was tense, feeling the menace as she did.

She fumbled at her waist, taking the pouch off her belt. "The Jewel!" She pressed it into his hands. "You have to take it to Jon. What was I thinking of, to carry it away from him? George, please!"

The pouch was lost in the thief's large hands. "Alanna, I can't be leavin' you—"

"You have to!" she cried. "I can't use it. Jon can. And I have a feeling he'll need it!"

George hesitated; a second shock made the ground shiver under their feet. It was over as quickly as it began. Grimly, George stuffed the pouch into the front of his tunic. "I'll get it to him, never fear." He kissed Alanna swiftly and hard, then ran for the Hall of Crowns.

～

Myles saw Alanna go, protecting his head as tiles broke free from the arches overhead, shattering in the main aisle. Jonathan flared with white and blue lights; he was invisible in the fires of his Gift and the Crown. The doors leading out of the Hall were jammed with fleeing men and women, as were the great City Doors. Eleni stood, her face deathly pale. "Not the land," she whispered. "Not the earth itself!"

A flutter of movement in the rear of the Hall of Crowns caught Buri's always-watchful eye: a man stripped away his cloak to reveal a noble-man's purple-and-black livery and a short crossbow. He brought the weapon up fast, aiming for Jonathan. Buri yanked a throwing star from her belt and flung it, killing the bowman. "There's an attack!" she yelled to Myles. "Warn the King!"

Myles's seat was on the great aisle. He was halfway to the altar in a second, moving fast for a plump man. At his warning shout, both Gareths and the Provost joined Raoul to form a protective circle around the King. The King's Own broke into squads, one forming an outer circle around the nobles, the others moving into the crowd to attack the enemy. Both circles parted to let Myles through to Jonathan's side.

"Myles!" Jon gasped through the magics that obscured him. "What's going on?"

"Men in Eldorne and Tirragen colors are attacking anyone who can fight back," Myles said grimly. "And they're trying to kill you. Where are the earthquakes coming from?"

Jonathan shook his head. "I don't know. As soon as I get a chance, I'll try to find out. Where's Alanna?"

"Gone," the older man replied. "Something called her away in a hurry. George followed her, and Coram followed George."

"She has the Jewel," the King whispered. "And where is Master Si-cham?"

Myles was wondering the same thing.

❧

*I*n Thom's chambers, Alanna was suddenly weak, as if something *tugged* at her Gift, drawing it away from her. Steeling herself, she closed her mind to whatever was trying to drain her. Forcing herself to move, she searched for her twin.

He was in the bedroom. Bad as the air in the parlor felt, this was worse: a weight pressed on her lungs. She checked Thom's vital signs. His pulse was shallow and fast. He was cool, alarmingly so after weeks of being too hot. When she grabbed the emberstone, Alanna saw only a trace of his Gift, streaming away from him much as her own had tried to do. She reached past the barrier she'd set on her magic, determined to use it to save him, no matter what the consequences.

Thom's eyes flew open. He gripped her hands with the last of his strength. "Don't! I'm—bound to him. He'll drain you through me—"

"Roger?" she whispered. Thom nodded. She spotted her cat. "Faithful, go for—"

"No time!" Thom snapped. "Listen!" He didn't relax his bruising grip. "His Gift—attached to sorcerer resurrecting him." She put her ear close to his lips to hear. "It got—stronger—as he did." Thom smiled. "*Never* as strong as mine."

She wiped away tears, growling, "Who *cares* if your Gift's bigger!"

"He can only—drain—one at a time. You—you're bound to me. You have some—my Gift—some of his, too. He needs—more, to finish—what he began. *Don't let him get it.* Don't use—Gift. Leeching spells—" He gasped. "He'll take—*all*. Leave nothing." Thom tried to laugh; the result sounded like hoarse barking. "He didn't—get—all mine. *You* have part—" Sinking back, he pulled her with him. His voice was barely audible, his hands cold. "Love you. Always have. Always will."

"No," she rasped, but he couldn't hear.

"Never—know how—he did it…"

He was gone.

∾

Near the staircase leading to the ground floor, George found Coram. "I saw her go, and ye after her," Alanna's oldest friend gasped, catching his wind. "I figured ye'd need help."

George showed him the Jewel. "She forgot she had this. I'm to carry it to Jon."

"What of her?"

"With Thom."

Coram hesitated. "I'd best reach her. Unless—"

"I'll keep the Jewel safe," George reassured him. "It's not that far to the Hall."

"It's far enough." Claw and five of his men materialized from the gallery behind George. "My friends said you'd come this way." He stretched out a hand and beckoned. "Give me the swag now, before I get your blood all over it." He glanced at Coram. "This isn't your fight. Clear out."

Coram hefted his broadsword, his face grim. "She'll never forgive me if I run out on ye now," he told George.

George tucked the Jewel into his belt-purse as he unsheathed his daggers. "Rispah, or the lady knight?" he grinned. Claw's men fanned out, forming a half circle with George and Coram at its center with the stairs at their backs.

"Both," replied Coram. He leaped forward to engage a ruffian, crying, "For the Lioness!"

∾

*P*andemonium ruled in the Hall of Crowns. Other men-at-arms tore off cloaks to reveal purple-and-black or green-and-white liveries. They were heavily armed and had specific targets: the men of the King's Own, any nobleman fighting back, Jonathan and his guards. Their opponents were high-born and wealthy men with flimsy dress swords, unarmed common-born men using anything that could serve as a weapon, even some ladies and children. Many others tried to flee, adding to the confusion.

Buri could see a knot of noblewomen, including the imperious Duchess of Naxen, imposing order in their vicinity. More men-at-arms poured in through the drapery-hidden entry behind the altar, taking the men around Jon by surprise. Raoul yelled a command and ran forward with the guards in the outer circle to engage the new attackers. Buri couldn't see Liam, Coram, or Alanna. Beside her, Rispah had palmed a large dagger and was advancing on an unsuspecting enemy archer.

The K'miri girl was torn. Her first duty was to protect Thayet, but she was also a warrior, trained to act in situations like this.

Thayet solved her problem. "Give me your sword. We have to do something."

Buri glanced at Eleni as she obeyed Thayet. The older woman moved into a pillar's shadow, unraveling the intricate embroidery on her sleeve. She broke off a long thread and smiled at Buri and Thayet. "Don't worry about me." Fixing her eyes on a group of archers near the altar, she began to tie knots in the thread, her lips moving silently.

Buri wrestled a long-bladed pike from a rack of weapons on the walls. Lowering it to an attack position, she launched herself at a clump of men in

Eldorne colors. The first one she engaged backed away from her charge: he stumbled. Buri lunged for the kill and lurched as the ground leaped and rolled in a third quake.

∾

*T*hree men in Tirragen colors raced up the stairs to aid Claw as George and Coram dispatched two enemies. Claw himself stayed back, screeching orders and awaiting his chance. George lost a dagger in a throw, killing a Tirragen guard; Coram killed a rogue and wounded another. The men around them shifted, seeking better positions, and George took the offered chance. He lunged at Claw.

The one-eyed man swore and lashed out with his knives, panicked at dealing with George himself. The thief rearmed his left hand with an extra blade, making Claw sweat: he didn't have the eye or the nerve to fight two-handed. Frantic, he slashed and cut wide-armed, leaving holes in his guard that George deliberately ignored. The bigger man toyed with Claw, spinning him around, raking his flailing arms, taunting. One of Claw's lucky cuts caught George on a cheekbone, another on his chest.

A Tirragen guard faltered. Coram slew him with a murderous slash and fell back, gasping for breath. For the moment he was safe: the two remaining enemies—one Tirragen, one rogue— focused their attention on the Rogue and his rival.

When he saw no one else would interfere, George settled into a fighter's crouch. Beckoning to Claw, he said grimly, "It's us now. The succession must be settled. Fight, Ralon, or Claw—if you've the belly."

His single eye rolling wildly, Claw looked for a way to escape; there was none. He'd always known he couldn't beat the Rogue on his terms. He tried to for several minutes, throwing his cunning into the battle. He kicked and hit, trying to be unpredictable, but George had been weaned on such tricks.

For a moment they locked knives, pressed together body-to-body. Then Claw dropped, George's blade hilt-deep in his chest.

～

*A*lanna didn't know how long she sat, holding Thom's cold hand. She was certain somehow this was all her fault. How was she supposed to live without her other half?

Faithful got her attention finally by latching onto her leg with claws and teeth, kicking ferociously until the pain roused her.

"What are you *doing*?" she screeched.

Wake up, King's Champion! was the angry reply. *You have no time for this—he's going to rip the earth open!*

Alanna knew she couldn't escape her responsibilities, although they'd never meant less to her.

Gently the grieving knight kissed her twin. She walked out of the bedroom, drying her face on her handkerchief as fresh tears ran. "Where's Si-cham?"

As if in answer, the old man staggered in, clutching a bloody right arm. Alanna grabbed a towel and swiftly bandaged the priest before he lost more blood, fighting brief nausea. Si-cham's right hand was gone. Without the rough tourniquet he wore already, he would be dead.

"Don't use your Gift—" he warned as she worked. "Brandy."

Alanna handed him a bottle and watched as he gulped its contents. Rage was replacing her grief. She wanted to act; nursing the old man was not the action she craved.

Si-cham put the bottle down. "I am a fool." His voice was stronger. "Never challenged in all these years, thinking I could not be bested. It's not enough *I* pay for my folly. You will, too." Gripping the table with his left hand, he met Alanna's cold eyes. "Open your mind."

She stepped back. "Why?"

"There's no time to explain. You waste what time we have! If you don't know all, you risk disaster. Do you doubt me?" he whispered. "I made a mistake. Because I didn't make two we are alive. *You* cannot make even one."

She closed her eyes and let him in. A hundred bits of knowledge struck her at once: *Gate of Idramm—a Gate for magic, to drain it into the Gate's*

*master...My hand! He uses it to steal my Gift...
Jonathan Gift-Bazhir/desert magic-Tortall/land crown
Jewel! He alone can bind the earth...Follow the secret
way. (Image of a deserted stair to the ruined temple in
the catacombs.) Not all Roger's power stored in
Thom—some with Alanna...Stay out of Gate-trap
(image of white whirls and loops) leeching spells...
Give King all he needs—send King Alanna/Thom-
Roger's power to hold the land!*

He didn't ask: she never would have let him do
it if he had. He sent Alanna's Gift to Jonathan, using
it as a bridge to link minds with the new King. For
an awful moment Alanna was three—herself,
Si-cham, Jonathan. The blood-colored fire of
Roger's Gift beat down on the priest's defenses,
seeking a way to enter and take the magic forming
around Jon. Suddenly the last of Alanna's magic
was gone, the link broken. Si-cham broke the link
so fast that Alanna was thrown into a faint as the
fourth earth shock began.

～

The nobles encircling Jonathan fought off
another large group of attackers that had come
through the door behind the altar. Myles was taking
a second's breather when he saw Jon lift his hands.
Purple fire swirled around the King's arms, clinging
like a skin. The light of the crown that bathed him
darkened, drinking in the amethyst Gift. A third
fire flowed over Jon's head and back like a hooded

cloak. Myles shuddered at its brownish-red color—
the color of dried blood.

He'd singled out his next opponent when the
ground yawed and bucked under their feet—the
fourth quake. The shock lasted a full minute, ending as abruptly as it began. Huge chunks of plaster
and stone broke free from the arches and roof,
crushing several people on the floor. The enemy
soldiers were frightened but disciplined enough to
hold their places. Their ferocity increased—the
quicker they slew the King, the quicker they could
escape this deathtrap.

ᴥ

Sweating, George turned away from Claw's body.
Five men wearing Eldorne green-and-white had
come up the stairs while Coram and the others
watched his fight. Now Coram retreated to the wall
of the gallery; George went to his side, grabbing a
sword from a dead man as he did. Five more soldiers in Tirragen purple-and-black ran up along
the gallery to block any chance of escape.

"Someone must've—smuggled 'em into the
palace," Coram gasped, cutting down a Tirragen
fighter. "And brought 'em—into the city wearin'—
civilian clothes."

George hurled a dagger to kill a man at the rear,
keeping two more at bay with his sword. At least
twelve others closed them in, and no help was in
sight. *I promised my lass I'd get her Jewel to Jon,* he

told himself grimly. *Thief I may be, but I've never broken my sworn word.*

Coram swore and faltered.

"Lad?"

"A scratch," the man-at-arms gasped, pressing his free hand to his side.

For a moment they thought the earth was shaking, but it was only a sound—a feral roar—echoing down the gallery. Coram grinned. "Finally!" he gasped, before attacking his present assailant with renewed energy.

Liam Ironarm threw himself into the battle with a ferocity that made even George speechless. There was no following the Dragon's movements as he lashed out with fists and feet, striking down any man who opposed him. There was no question of any of the men attacking George and Coram landing a blow on the Shang fighter: six enemies broke and ran.

Liam hurled himself at the last of them, his foot catching the running man just above his shoulders. He went down.

Ironarm returned to George and Coram as the thief tied a rough bandage over the wound in Coram's side. The man-at-arms grinned at Liam, dark eyes glittering in his sweat-soaked face.

"Ye're late, Dragon."

Liam smiled grimly. "I was delayed. Where's Alanna?"

"Back there," George said tightly. By now he

wondered where she had gone. "I have to get to the Hall of Crowns." Reaching in his purse, he brought up the Jewel.

For a moment Liam stared in the direction George had indicated, clearly wanting to find Alanna. Then he sighed. "The Jewel's the important thing. Let's go."

Coram didn't even speak. He had a feeling his knight-mistress was no longer in Thom's rooms, and that he couldn't follow her down the path she walked now. Together the three men set out at a trot for the Hall of Crowns, George supporting Coram.

∿

*A*lanna came around slowly. Her skull pounded with the force of her rage when she remembered Si-cham had stripped her of her Gift, loading it all into Jonathan. She did not like the Mithran's high-handed way of ordering her life, and she planned to tell him so. Rolling onto her stomach, she pushed herself onto all fours. She felt sick and empty—far worse than when Thom "borrowed" her Gift to bring Roger back to life.

Faithful's yowl and Si-cham's scream alerted her to danger: the old man struggled with someone at the door. Alanna grabbed a chair, dragging herself to her feet.

A double-headed axe chopped down, biting deep into Si-cham's collarbone. He dropped.

Josiane stood in the doorway, spattered with his blood, trying to work her axe free.

"Why didn't you blast me, old fool?" she panted.

Alanna knew the answer, although she refused to tell the Princess: if Si-cham had taken that chance, he'd have been open to Roger's leeching spell. He'd broken the link to Alanna and Jon for the same reason; Roger would have taken his Gift unless he concentrated on his own defense. Now Si-cham was dead. He and his Gift were forever out of Roger's grasp.

Josiane freed her blade and stepped over the old man's body, smiling. "He told me you'd be here," she explained. "He said he didn't think I could take you, but I was welcome to try. You aren't doing well, are you?" She inched forward, ready to pounce. Maneuvering for room, Alanna tripped over a foot stool. Josiane darted forward, her axe high.

They'd forgotten Faithful. Screeching, he flew into Josiane's face, clinging as she howled and dropped the axe.

Stop Roger! the cat ordered as Josiane gripped his small body. The Princess hurled him down and stepped with all her might. With Faithful's agonized cry, strength poured into his mistress. She crouched and lunged, drawing Lightning as she moved. With a single, brutal slash she cut Josiane down. Her new strength pounded in her ears as she shoved the dying woman aside to pick up Faithful.

Time to go home, he cried, and was gone. Gently she placed him on a table.

Her fingers shook as she unbuckled her sword belt, letting it and the sheath drop. With Lightning gripped in her hand, she walked out the door, heading for her last conversation with Duke Roger of Conté.

∽

Coram, George, and Liam arrived in the Hall of Crowns as the fifth quake began. This time the fighting halted as everyone waited to see if the roof would come down. The stone floor of the chamber rolled and shuddered like the deck of a seafaring ship, throwing more than one person to the ground.

The crowds were gone, most escaping through the City Doors: only the combatants remained, each involved in his or her own separate battle for survival. Duke Gareth, Gary, and Myles were all that was left of the circle guarding Jonathan. Raoul and several of the King's Own fought desperately to stem the flow of Tirragen and Eldorne men coming from the chambers behind the Hall. The Provost and more royal men-at-arms contained a rush of enemies from the main aisle.

Liam quickly appraised the situation and grabbed a pike, going to Raoul's aid, where the danger of a breakthrough was worst. Coram joined the men around Jon, steadying himself for a long morning. Buri, streaked with dirt and sweat, saluted him with a grin before she and Thayet attacked a cluster of archers. He saw Rispah guarding Eleni, just as he saw several groups of enemies struggling against the invisible ropes George's mother had bound them with. George thrust the Jewel into Jonathan's hands and turned to become part of Jon's protective circle.

The King closed his eyes and reached out with his mind, gripping the Jewel tightly. He called all his magics—his own Gift, the Bazhir desert sorcery, the power of the kings and the land of Tortall that was bound into the crown, the magic of the Dominion Jewel—and he threw them over the length and breadth of Tortall, feeling the Earth's pain as if his own body were being shattered. Like an ancient tree sending out its myriad roots, he bound each crack and fault with sorcery, gripped the whole to him—and *held*.

The crown, dedicated to the realm for centuries, blazed. The Jewel shone even brighter than the crown, and the battles raged in the corridors of the palace. Jonathan was part of all of it, his vision reaching everywhere. Being the Voice of the Tribes had prepared him for such a confusing moment, when someone else might have been driven mad by the consciousness of each person, animal, tree, and stone in the realm. Jonathan was able to encompass it, to set the greater part of it aside, with a bit of his awareness to guard it. His chief vision focused on a small, copper-and-gold figure traveling through the bowels of the castle.

∾

*T*he ground floor, the level below Thom's quarters, consisted of public rooms: the Hall of Crowns, salons, libraries, ballrooms, the banquet room. Alanna bypassed it on one of a hundred staircases without hesitation, her mind and will fixed on the catacombs. Next was the level where everyday business took place: healers, tailors, laundrywomen, scribes, armorers, quartermasters, and mapmakers all worked here. Today this level was empty; Alanna's feet made the only sound. Next was stores: endless rooms filled with every imaginable supply. This level, too, was silent.

The dungeons and guardrooms were the third level below ground. She heard fighting, but the way to Roger that Si-cham had shown her was a safe distance away from it. Here, the shock that Jonathan had contained found her. She waited after its halt, expecting another: it never came, but the ground shivered continuously, shifting slightly from time to time. Pieces of the ceiling hailed down; the staircase began to exhibit tiny cracks and to lose small pieces.

Jon's stopped the big quakes, the Mother-shakers, she thought, *but how long can the palace—or any building—take this constant stress?*

Down Alanna went, her eyes blazing in her

tight face. She halted once, to wipe sweaty palms on her shirt. Then she gripped Lightning afresh and moved on.

The length of the stairs increased as she descended; they were broken up by landings, with a guardroom off each landing. Since the stair she followed was little used, the guardrooms were shut. Now, approaching the catacombs on the fourth level, she found one blazing with light. She halted a few steps above it, considering her options.

Perhaps the occupant knew she wanted no delays: Alex of Tirragen, silver mail glittering, stepped out onto the landing. His unsheathed sword rested in one black-gauntleted hand. "Just you? I'd've thought you'd bring others."

"I'm in a hurry." Her eyes sparkled dangerously. "Get out of my way, before he tears the palace down around our ears."

Shapes moved on the stair below the landing— two big men-at-arms in Tirragen purple-and-black. "Yer lordship—" one rumbled nervously.

"She's panicking," Alex snapped, his eyes not leaving Alanna. "Hold your positions!" He indicated the lit room with his blade. "Step inside, lady knight. There's more space."

She hesitated, looking from Alex to his men. She wanted to scream with rage, or blast them with her Gift...

She walked inside. The furniture had been shoved into a second chamber; branches of candles lit the main room. "Aren't you going to have your friends watch?"

"The only witness I need is right here." He touched his temple with a gloved finger. "You can stretch first, if you like."

"And lose more time? No."

Alex tried a few lazy passes with his own sword, taunting her. "I've waited for this chance."

Exasperated, she snapped, "You're crazy, to want to play 'best squire' at a moment like this."

Alex moved into place. Both swung their weapons up to "guard." "Think what you like."

He attacked savagely, his calm face a violent contrast to his rapidly spinning and slashing blade. Alanna blocked repeatedly, hiding her dismay: after the draining of her Gift, she was a touch slower than she needed to be against an opponent with whom a touch of slowness made all the difference. She fought with her brain, carefully maintaining her defense, watching for Alex to make an error out of his need. She circled, Lightning flowing to stop Alex's blade each time he thrust or cut inward—high, low, either side. She caught his eyes shifting away from her shoulders; like a novice he was plainly searching for an opening. She smiled grimly.

"No one ever wins fighting defensively," Alex snarled.

"*I'm* not the one obsessed with winning," she gasped, her voice cracking.

Alex faltered. Alanna whipped her blade into a reverse crescent; he blocked jarringly, almost too late. She clenched her teeth and swung immediately into a crescent: as Alex's sword rose to stop Lightning, Alanna whipped down into a vertical butterfly too fast to watch, scoring lightly across Alex's middle to bite into his shoulder. The grate of sword on mail made her wince, and she swore for letting her preoccupation with Roger make her forget her opponent's armor. She lunged back to get away from his counter-cut. They were back to circling as the fanatic gleam deepened in Alex's eyes.

Alanna scrubbed her free hand dry, then gripped Lightning's jewel-studded hilt with both hands. Now it was her turn to attack in a series of harsh, downward-chopping blows meant to cleave Alex from crown to sole. He blocked, retreating, until he lunged forward to lock swords body-to-body. As she strained under his downward pressure, Alex snarled and kicked her in the stomach. Alanna yelled and went down, rolling to keep out of his way as he sliced at her. The gold mail across her shoulders grated, and she clenched her teeth against the bruising pain of the impact. Ignoring it, she flipped to an upright stance: Alex lunged in and she countered blindly, Lightning extracting another screech of metal from his armor.

He retreated. She lunged. They exchanged a flurry of blows and blocks, neither gaining an advantage. From the corner of her eye she saw his men-at-arms had disobeyed his order to keep their positions to watch.

A breath too late she saw the complex pass he'd begun. Lightning flew out of her grip into a corner—behind Alex. He leveled his swordpoint at her throat, smiling tightly. "Say farewell, *Lioness*."

She edged back. "An honorable opponent would let me get my sword and continue."

He shook his head. "I learned what *I* need to know. You were good, I admit that. But I knew *I* was—"

She moved in a burst of speed, the little she'd kept back. She leaned away from his sword; her left foot curled up and in, then thrust out, slamming into his belly. Alex crashed into the wall. He got up and threw himself at her with a yell of fury.

Liam had taught her only a few kicks and blows, making her practice incessantly. She could not beat a Shang warrior of many years, but her own speed and the endless repetitions caused what she knew to carry the weight of a fully trained Shang. As Alex charged she swung out of the way and kicked again, throwing him against the same spot on the wall. He lunged once more, cross-cutting with a speed she could not dodge, slashing across her cheek and her bare right hand. In the split-second opening in the path of his sword she rammed forward, crushing his windpipe with one fist as she struck his nose with the other, thrusting bone splinters deep into his brain.

They were pressed together so tightly she *felt* the life flee his body. She backed away hastily, letting him drop. "Is this what it means to be the best, Alex?"

He would never answer.

She seized his blade and spun, determined to finish the guards—but they had fled.

Alanna retrieved Lightning and set off down again. She hadn't gone far when her body reacted to the killing: she vomited over the stair rail for long moments, heaving dryly. She shook with exhaustion. Her treacherous knees threatened to give at every step; she was scared that the stairs would give way under the constant earth tremors. In spite of everything, she forged on, lightheaded, her jaw set. The remaining distance only *seemed* endless.

She reached bottom at the rear of the catacombs. Had she chosen to go the proper way, she would have entered several hundred yards from her present spot, at the foot of the gently sloping ramps leading from the palace temples to the tombs. Roald and Lianne's burial place, newly plastered and decorated, was somewhere near that entrance. Alanna had emerged by tombs three and four hundred years old. Someone had thoughtfully lit the torches. She followed the vision Si-cham gave her, ignoring her growing terror.

The tombs ended, opening onto a great stone floor. In its center, a large, circular design—apparently of white sand—was drawn, its many curls and loops and whirls dizzying to see. On its edge, near her, was a splash of still-wet blood. *Si-cham's, I bet,* Alanna thought as she gulped back a surge of bile. This was the variant on the Gate of Idramm normally used to summon elementals, a spell to drain off the Gift of anyone unfortunate enough to step onto it. This was also the spot where Si-cham lost his hand.

Behind the Gate was an abandoned structure. Legend said it was a temple. Roger lounged there against a fallen pillar, arms crossed over his chest. The air around him was filled with bloody fire that glittered evilly on his black silk robe.

He smiled. "I knew you wouldn't disappoint me. You took longer than I had anticipated."

Alanna prodded one curl of the Gate with her sword, to find the sand of the design was melted into the rock. White heat flashed up Lightning's edge; she yelped, pulling the blade away. He was scrutinizing her. Suddenly she knew why. The knight spread her hands with her old, reckless grin. "Didn't you know, Roger? I'm Giftless. There's nothing for your Gate to take from me."

His eyes narrowed. "How did that—ah. Si-cham. Now I understand."

"That's why your earthquake spell hasn't succeeded," she taunted. "Jon's stopping you. He's got the Jewel, the crown, my Gift—even magic I bore for Thom. Which means he's stopping you with some of your *own* Gift."

He shrugged. "So that's why I didn't have enough to bring this comedy to an early finish. It doesn't matter."

"It *does* matter," she snapped. "There are no more chances for you, Roger. You've bought an ugly death on Traitor's Hill. When it's over, I *personally* will scatter your ashes on the wind!"

"You think I left any of this to chance, dear one? I had a long time to plan. You see, I wasn't *quite* dead when they buried me." She opened her mouth to deny it, but he shook his head. "If we had time, I would explain a powerful working called 'Sorcerer's Sleep.' For *your* purposes, I was dead. For my own——" His face was bleak, terrifying. Then he waved the mood away.

"I planned carefully because *you*, sweet Lioness, too often escape me——you and my kingly cousin. He studied well, better than when I was his teacher. Where he got power that smells of the desert, I suppose I shall never know.

"You saved yourself from my Gate, but you're tired. Come within my reach——" He smiled and picked up a blade lying beside him; it was blood-stained. "I need only lop off a small part of you, as I did Si-cham. That bit will give me a tie to your inner self, and thus a clear road to Jonathan and the sorcery he wields." Alanna paled and stumbled back a step.

Roger put down the knife to walk to the rim of the Gate. "You've grown so prudent, it may be you won't allow me that easy a way. Tell me, then—how long can Jonathan last?"

"Forever!" Alanna threw it at him like a challenge.

"Perhaps." He stepped onto the Gate as the energy whipping through the design tugged at his robe. Silver glittered against black; the Gate's design was duplicated on his clothes. "If Jonathan musters no other sorcery against me—and all those who might make a difference are accounted for—I need only to wait." He came forward until he stood at the Gate's center. "The Earth has her own means of dealing with unbearable pressure. She sheds it, redistributes it, expends it in small tremors. When she can do nothing else, she convulses—and continues to do so, until the pressure is gone. Even the gods cannot stop such an earthquake. Jonathan holds the land, but the pressure of my spell remains. How long, do you think, until that inescapable convulsion begins?"

Alanna felt cold and alone. "You'll be just as dead," she croaked.

His smile was frightening. "Indeed, I hope so."

She gripped her sword, measuring her strength against his. "Why'd you tell me any of this?"

"Because, lady knight, you will share it with me. Did you think I would end it without you?" He chuckled. "I'll tell you a secret. Years ago, when I was your age, just finding the limits of my power, I took up jewelry making. To each thing I made,

I attached a bit of my Gift, to mark it as mine. Necklaces, rings—sword hilts. I even forged swords, to create a masterpiece of a weapon. Why you had to corrupt my design is beyond me."

"It was warped."

"You *would* think so." He reached out, red fire eddying around his fingers. Voice soft, he said, "*With silver and stone I made thee; With Gift and blood I bound thee; With my name I call thee!*"

Lightning jumped, straining toward Roger. If she had still carried his original sword, instead of melding it with Lightning for a whole blade, she never could have kept hold of it. As it was, enough of the crystal blade and its hilt remained to wrench her arms as Alanna gripped it. Her cold eyes met his.

"It will come to me eventually," he said. "And you will follow."

All her muscles knotted; the scars on her palms broke and bled. She dug in her heels and held. *What can I do?* she thought, despairing. *Can't I make even one decision he hasn't anticipated? What does he think I'll do?*

The cold part of herself that stood aloof from everything whispered, *He expects you to fight. So— stop fighting.*

With a teeth-baring effort, Alanna levered the sword back and let go. The effect was like loosing a bolt from a crossbow. Released from her pull, the sword *shrieked* as it flew, making her clap her hands over tortured ears. Roger didn't break his calling spell. He didn't even seem to know what she'd done until Lightning buried itself in his chest.

Roger grabbed the hilt. Amazingly, he laughed. He laughed until his dying lungs ran out of air. The silver design on his robes dripped and ran to the floor. His eyes closed, and he fell. Flames sprouted from the Gate into the stone, devouring the body of Roger of Conté.

∾

*B*uri found her there. With the help of the King's Own, she brought a fainting Alanna to the surface on a stretcher. Revived by the warmer air at the ground level, Alanna got Buri to help her walk to the Hall of Crowns. She was sickened by the bodies in evidence everywhere: clearly the assault had been heavier than anyone had expected. Men of the Palace Guard admitted them to the Hall with deep bows, and Buri waited silently as Alanna took in the scene before her.

Between quake and uprising, the Hall was in ruins. The City Doors hung from their hinges; the stone risers had buckled and collapsed in sections. Pieces of roof and arches had fallen, dragging banners and garlands down to litter the floor in a mockery of a holiday. Survivors hunted in the rubble, freeing the trapped and pulling out the dead. These were placed on the main aisle for burial. Only later would the bodies in Tirragen or Eldorne colors be separated, to be burned on Traitor's Hill.

The Provost limped over, brushing heavy silver hair back from a sweat-streaked face. "Not as bad as it looks," he said in his terse way. "More of them dead than us. They weren't expectin' much opposition." His ice-blue eyes caught Alanna's and held them. "You take care of your end of things?"

She grinned wolfishly. He grinned back. Buri was interested to note more than a slight resemblance between them at that moment. "Indeed I did."

The Provost put a gentle hand on her shoulder. "Good." Pausing, he added, "Your...friend. Cooper. He did well today." Favoring a wounded leg, he returned to help the searchers.

Eleni, looking worn and old, bandaged her bruised and wounded son. Seeing Alanna, George winked and blew her a kiss. When his mother scolded him for moving, he silenced her with a hug. Thayet, seeing the direction of his look, waved tiredly. She sat with her head on a noblewoman's shoulder, a shattered sword on her lap. Her new friend was as exhausted and battered as she.

Rispah fussed over Coram nearby. She also kept a sharp eye on Delia, who was bound and gagged with strips of what looked like someone's petticoat. Noting Alanna's look, Rispah grinned. "My lady here thought she'd knife his Majesty while the fightin' was thickest and the menfolk all occupied," she explained. "She didn't know I figured her game."

Gary, sporting bandages of his own, kissed Alanna swiftly. "Father had a heart attack," he said quietly. "He'll be all right, thanks to Duke Baird. They're at the infirmary now—Baird and Father and Myles. Myles fought two of them, single-handed." Gary smiled tiredly. "They were huge. I don't know what possessed him. But he killed one, and George finished the other."

"As a mercy to the poor man," George explained as he joined them. "After Myles hurt him so." He cupped Alanna's face, his grave hazel eyes searching out her own. He nodded, liking what he saw, and kissed her gently. "I'd watch out for Myles—he's that fierce when he's angry. Didn't even want to go and get his wounds stitched. Lucky Duke Baird insisted. We can't have Myles terrorizin' the prisoners." Softly he added, "He's fine, lass."

"The ladies saved us all," Gary went on. He indicated Thayet, Eleni, Buri, and Rispah. "They kept the archers from killing his Majesty. We're proud of them—of you." He glanced at Alanna and looked away again, his eyes troubled. "Jon—the King—told us what you did, in the catacombs. He saw it all, somehow."

Alanna faced the altar. Jonathan sat at its base, leaning against the stone. His face was drawn. She was shocked to see white threads in his hair where none had been that morning. The Jewel was in his lap. He stirred; Geoffrey of Meron gave him a cup of water. The altar itself had been cleared to make room for the body of Liam Ironarm.

Did I know? she asked herself. *Did I suspect?* There was no way to tell. She climbed the altar steps to look at the Dragon alone.

Eight arrows were piled beside him; his knuckles and wounds were neatly bandaged. Her eyes burned, but she was cried out. Helplessly she plucked at his sleeve, wishing she could bring him back. Crying would have helped.

"He and George saved my life—they saved us all." Jonathan dragged himself up to lean on the altar. "You'd just gotten to Roger when Tirragen soldiers attacked me in force. Myles was down by them, Duke Baird, Raoul, Duke Gareth. They're all right. I guess Raoul will have a limp to show for it. Coram and Gary were drawn away. I was—helpless." He grimaced.

"You did more than enough." Her broken voice was hardly audible.

"But I couldn't do anything else. George and Liam kept me from being...interrupted." Alanna shuddered, knowing the land would have shaken itself to pieces if Jon's concentration had broken. "Two archers got clear. Liam took the arrows meant for me. He didn't even falter, until the last." Jonathan's eyes met hers. "It isn't much consolation, I know, but—they'll sing about the Dragon's last fight for centuries." After a moment he added, "I'm sorry."

She tried to walk away; her weakened knees faltered. George caught her instantly.

"It was the death he wanted," the King said. "We'll honor him, always."

Alanna nodded dumbly. Jon reached for her: there was a flash, and a tiny ball of reddish-purple fire leaped from his fingers to her own bloody ones. Gently he took her hand and kissed it. "We did it, King's Champion. Tortall is safe."

Epilogue

*H*eralds went out to explain to the people what had happened on Coronation Day. There would be no weeks of celebration that year. Tortall needed time to mourn, repair, and rebuild. Instead the new King planned a festival to mark the first year of his reign, on the anniversary of Coronation Day. Afterward he would travel through his kingdom, the first such royal journey since his grandfather's day.

Those found guilty by the Courts of Law of taking part in the rebellion lost their lands and wealth; they and their families were sent into exile. For Delia, the only living ringleader, the Courts decreed life imprisonment. The sentences for all should have been death—the laws on treason were strict—but Jonathan would not begin his rule with executions. He granted more pardons in the first week of his official reign than had King Roald in all of his.

A week after the funerals, the King found his

Champion in the catacombs, seated on a bench and gazing at the blackened Gate of Idramm. Lightning stood there, thrust into the center of the design. The blade was streaked with soot, the jewels of its hilt cracked and blackened. Jonathan gripped the sword, trying to free it without success.

"It's all right," Alanna told him. "I don't want it. There are other swords, and I like Lightning right where it is."

Jon released the weapon and looked at his filthy hands. "Good."

"I'm just thinking. Will you please get away from the Gate? You make me nervous."

The King shrugged and came to sit beside her. "What's on your mind?"

She hesitated a moment before saying, "Would you...mind, if I went to the Bloody Hawk for a while? I just need time to think, and I'd like a rest." She smiled. "I've had a busy year."

"Take all the time you want," Jon assured her. "I know where to find you if there's need."

∾

*A*lanna to George Cooper, Baron of Pirate's Swoop, written in late July:

> *...so Jon has put you to work finding the last of the coronation rebels. I'm not surprised. It is very quiet here. Tell Myles I have enough sleep at last. I miss you...*

She entered into the daily routine of the tribe, hunting lions with the young men and hearing the legends of the Bazhir from the shamans. She took her turn at sentry duty, enjoying the quiet and the clearness of the stars. Shortly after her arrival, Alanna saw a new constellation at the foot of the cluster called "The Goddess." She never found out who named it, but everywhere she traveled in later years she always heard it called "The Cat."

Young people came from all over to meet the Woman Who Rides Like a Man. Most were youths, but an occasional girl visited as well. Many of the boys were headed north, to join the King's Own. The girls planned to try their own fortunes, most of them as fighters.

∽

In the second week of October, Thayet and Buri came to the Bloody Hawk escorted by a squad of the King's Own. Alanna was glad to see them, now that the edge had worn off her grief for Thom, Liam, and Faithful. It wasn't long before Alanna began to wonder if Thayet had come to talk about a particular subject. Whatever it was, she couldn't bring herself to discuss it for days. Instead she talked about the school she'd begun with the help of Myles, Eleni, Gary, and George; or the Midwinter weddings for Myles and Coram; and Alanna's doings. She met Alanna's friends in the tribe and tried her hand at weaving.

Buri joined the girls who shocked the elders by studying warrior arts. When she showed them K'miri trick riding, she drew the young men, uniting the two groups in their eagerness to learn.

"I'm glad we came," Thayet told Alanna a week after her arrival. They sat in front of Alanna's tent after the evening meal. From the central fire they could hear Buri teaching her friends a rude song about city dwellers. "She misses the excitement of the road," the Princess added. "She's a lot like you that way."

Alanna massaged her palms with a wry smile. "If that's so, she'll find other things to challenge her. She won't be able to help it." She paused, then decided to see what was up. "You aren't here because you wanted to give Buri a holiday, Thayet. And it's a long ride just to say 'hello.'"

The Princess looked away. "Jonathan…admires the Bazhir. He let me read their history. He thinks the K'mir, the Doi, and the Bazhir may be descended from one race. Though the Bazhir are more cousins than in the direct line—"

"*Thayet.*" Alanna sighed.

The other woman knotted her handkerchief. "He wanted me to know everything about you, and about it being over. He said I should have the story straight." Her voice was soft. "But I have to wonder, because you and he are so close, still—"

Alanna took the handkerchief away before her friend could damage it. "We always *were* close, long before we were lovers. I imagine we'll always *be* close, but not in the same way. We're friends. And I'm his Champion."

"But everyone seems to think— When you come back—"

"*Everyone?*" Alanna wanted to know. "I think someone doesn't think that at all, or he wouldn't spend so much time with you."

Thayet whispered, "If I hadn't come to Tortall—"

Alanna drew a design in the sand. "Nonsense. I wanted you to be safe; we all did. And I knew you'd make a better Queen than I would."

"*What?*" yelped the Princess.

"Jonathan needs someone who will treat him like a person, not just a King," Alanna explained. "I can't. I'm his vassal, for all I'm his friend. You were born and reared to be royalty. It doesn't frighten you. You won't let him turn into a prig. You won't let him be smug." She hesitated, then said, "I was hoping by now you'd like him."

"But you're my *friend*!" Thayet wailed. "I can't take your man!"

Alanna hugged her. "He isn't *my* man. He's yours, if you love him and he loves you. I want you both to be happy. I'd prefer you were happy with each other."

Thayet sniffed and wiped her eyes. "I probably look like a hag."

Alanna grinned. "Don't fish for compliments. It isn't becoming."

A watery chuckle was her answer. "I was so *happy* at not having to go through a marriage of state."

"Well, that was before you met Jon, so that's all right."

Now that she didn't have to worry about upsetting her friend, Thayet wanted to hear about Jonathan when he was younger. When that subject was exhausted, she told Alanna of the changes they hoped to make in Tortall. Buri arrived. When Thayet stopped for breath, the K'mir said, "Glad it's not me she's talking to, for a change. People in love are boring." Thayet made a face at her companion.

Much later, as she and Alanna lay in their bedrolls, Thayet whispered, "Alanna? Is there someone for you?"

Alanna blinked, suddenly watery-eyed. "I don't know."

"He'd be very unconventional, I know." Thayet sighed. "Most men—"

"Would panic if they thought of marrying a lady knight," Alanna finished. "Someone like that would bore me silly. I've been very lucky with men." She fingered the ember at her throat, wondering where George was.

"Then you'll be lucky again."

The next morning Alanna was performing her Shang exercises when she heard a sentry's warning whistle. It was answered by two others, and then a whistle sounded to mean "No danger." She picked up her sword, wanting to check anyway, when a woman behind her said, "It's me they're whistling about."

Alanna spun and stepped back into a fighting stance. The wiry female, now in front of her, raised her hands to show they were empty. Her tightly curled hair was more grey than chestnut; her eyes were pale in a tan, weathered face. On her gloves was the Shang globe surmounted by a bristling cat. "The reflexes are all right," the Wildcat said, her voice light and dry. "Do you expect an attack even now?"

Alanna lowered her sword. "I've had an interesting year."

"Hunh." Liam's master examined her carefully. "So you were his last pupil. He thought you could be one of us, for all that you're too old." Alanna looked away, afraid she might cry. "Come up on the ridge with me. I'm just passing through. You can see me off."

"You've come a way to 'just pass through,'" Alanna said, her emotions under control again. She followed the Wildcat up to a ridge that commanded a view of the southern road. The older woman stopped to stare across the desert, lines deepening at the corners of her eyes. "I want to tell you I'm sorry—about Liam. I wish I could have prevented it."

The Wildcat waved her explanation away. "You have to understand Shang, Lady Knight. We all know we risk early death. And he guessed, or suspected. He wrote me from Corus, the day before he was killed. If he got lucky, I was to forget it. If he didn't, I was to give you this."

She put a folded and sealed parchment into Alanna's hands. Alanna saw the older woman's eyes brim with tears. The Wildcat gave her a tiny smile. "I love him more'n my own sons. It's good to know he used his death well."

Opening the parchment with hands that shook, Alanna read:

Kitten, Knowing you, you think it's your fault I got killed when I did. You're thinking, if you hadn't dragged me along...Forget it. Remember the Doi woman, Mi-chi, saying I knew my fate? Years ago a Doi told me I'd know when it was the Black God's time for me. I think this is it. If I'm wrong, and I live, the Wildcat will burn this letter anyway, so you won't find out that I wrote this.

Don't blame yourself. When could you ever tell me what to do? I chose my life. I accepted Dragon rank, knowing no Dragon has lived to be forty. As it is, I'm the oldest Dragon in almost a hundred years.

The truth is we never saw death the same (like some other things), so I didn't talk about it with you. All you think of death is ending. To me, it's how a person goes. Dying for important things—that's better than living safe.

I often visited Tortall, though we never

met there. The last two times—the first before
I found you, and the second when we sailed
into Port Caynn—I felt a change. Like the
land when spring is coming. Bazhir talking to
northerners, not fighting them. Commoners
and nobles planning the future. Even you, my
kitten, your great disguise—it's part of something new that centers around your Jonathan.
If I can protect this beginning, I will have died
a Dragon. You should grow old, and testy
(testier), and raise lions and lionesses with a
man who loves all of you. Even your Gift, and
your independence, and your stubbornness.

Practice the kicks off your left side—I
don't care if they tire you out more than the
right-side kicks.

Remember to rub that balm I gave you
into the scars on your hands.

The Wildcat had gone while she read. Glad to
be alone, Alanna sat and wept, letting the Dragon
go at last.

Thayet and Buri left a few days later. Alanna
started to think about her own trip north, before
the roads turned bad with winter rain and snow.
Since she was trying to weave a blanket for George's
Midwinter present, she decided to set out when it
was done. She was working alone in her tent one
afternoon when a shadow blocked the light on her
work. George Cooper, cloak and riding boots covered with dust, entered the tent.

Alanna put down her shuttle. She could feel her heart drumming, and it took an effort to say lightly, "I was sort of hoping you'd come before this."

He sat beside her, examining the cloth on the loom. "I'd hoped to come before this, too," he admitted. "Truth to tell, givin' up the Rogue and turnin' respectable—it takes gettin' used to. Some days I get out of bed not knowin' who I am. Jonathan kept me busy, like I wrote you. Too, the castle down at old Pirate's Swoop had to be fixed up proper before I brought—" He stopped. "Jon's announced he's to marry Thayet," he said abruptly. "The Bazhir will have told you."

"It's one of the advantages to having a King who's also the Voice." His face would be easier to read if his back wasn't to the light!

"Thayet says you gave your blessin.'"

"I did." She curled her hands around her elbows to hide their trembling.

"You're not sorry for it? Had you wanted, you'd be Queen."

"I didn't want it."

He reached out to toy with the emberstone. "What *do* you want, Alanna?"

She caught his hand and met his eyes, smiling. "I want to be yours. If you're still interested."

His fingers tightened on hers. "Why?"

Alanna looked down. "I love you."

He made her look at him. "Enough to wed with me? Enough to give up roamin' and settle down and be lady of Pirate's Swoop?" She looked at him quizzically, and he blushed. "Well, to roam with me along." Alanna nodded. George took a breath. "Enough to bear my—our—little ones?"

She blushed. "I'd like to have you to myself for a year or two. After that, we'll have all the children we want." Her voice cracked as she added, "I'll be proud to."

Rising, George pulled Alanna into his arms. "So I finally tamed myself a Lioness," he whispered when they broke their kiss.

Alanna laughed. "I wouldn't call it *tamed*, laddy-me-love. The lady of Pirate's Swoop shouldn't be *tame.*"

George grinned. "Particularly not when she's King's Champion, to boot. *That's* all right, then." He picked her up for another kiss. When he finally put her down, he took her hand and drew her out of the tent. "Come on, Lioness. We can tell your tribe we're betrothed."

*It's been ten long years since the proclamation
that girls might attempt a page's training.
At last, someone has stepped forward . . .
Meet Keladry of Midelan,
the next girl knight of Tortall
and heroine of Tamora Pierce's
newest quartet from Random House:*

Protector of the Small.

---

*Turn the page
for an exciting preview of book 1:*
FIRST TEST.

Alanna the Lioness, the King's Champion, could hardly contain her glee. Baron Piers of Mindelan had written to King Jonathan to say that his daughter wished to be a page. Alanna fought to sit still as she watched Wyldon of Cavall, the royal training master, read the baron's letter. Seated across his desk from them, the king watched the training master as sharply as his Champion did. Lord Wyldon was known for his dislike of female warriors.

It had been ten long years since the proclamation that girls might attempt a page's training. Alanna had nearly given up hope that such a girl—or the kind of family that would allow her to do so—existed in Tortall, but at last she had come forward. Keladry of Mindelan would not have to hide her sex for eight years as Alanna had done. Keladry would prove to the world that girls could be knights. And she would not be friendless. Alanna had plans to help Keladry through the first few years. It never occurred to the Champion that anyone might object.

Alanna half turned to see Wyldon better. Surely he'd read the letter at least twice! From this side the puffy scars from his battle to save the younger princes and princess were starkly visible; Wyldon's right arm was in a sling yet from that fight. Alanna rubbed fingers that itched with the urge to apply healing magic. Wyldon had the idea that suffering pain made a warrior stronger. He would not thank her if she tried to heal him now.

Goddess bless, she thought tiredly. How will

I ever get on with him if I'm to help this girl Keladry?

Wyldon was not flexible: he'd proved that to the entire court over and over. If he were any stiffer, Alanna thought wryly, I'd paint a design on him and use him for a shield. He's got no sense of humor and he rejects change just because it's change.

Still, she had to admit that his teaching worked. During the Immortals War of the spring and early summer, when legendary creatures had joined with the realm's human enemies to take the kingdom, the squires and pages had been forced into battle. They had done well, thanks to their training by Wyldon and the teachers he had picked.

At last Lord Wyldon returned the letter to King Jonathan, who placed it on his desk. "The baron and the baroness of Mindelan are faithful servants of the crown," the king remarked. "We would not have this treaty with the Yamani Islands were it not for them. You will have read that their daughter received some warrior training at the Yamani court, so it would appear that Keladry has an aptitude."

Lord Wyldon resettled his arm in its sling. "I did not agree to this, Your Majesty."

Alanna was about to say that he didn't have to agree when she saw the king give the tiniest shake of the head. Clenching her jaws, she kept her remark to herself as King Jonathan raised his eyebrows.

"Your predecessor agreed," he reminded Wyldon. "And you, my lord, implied agreement when you accepted the post of training master."

"That is a lawyer's reply, sire," Wyldon replied stiffly, a slight flush rising in his clean-shaven cheeks.

"Then here is a king's: we desire this girl to train as a page."

And that is that, Alanna thought, satisfied. She might be the kind of knight who would argue with her king, at least in private, but Wyldon would never let himself do so.

The training master absently rubbed the arm in its linen sling. At last he bowed in his chair. "May we compromise, sire?"

Alanna stiffened. She hated that word! "Com—" she began to say.

The king silenced her with a look. "What do you want, my lord?"

"In all honesty," said the training master, thinking aloud, "I had thought that our noble parents loved their daughters too much to place them in so hard a life."

"Not everyone is afraid to do anything new," Alanna replied sharply.

"Lioness," said the king, his voice dangerously quiet. Alanna clenched her fists. What was going on? Was Jonathan inclined to give way to the man who'd saved his children?

Wyldon's eyes met hers squarely. "Your bias is known, Lady Alanna." To the king he said, "Surely the girl's parents cannot be aware of the difficulties she will encounter."

"Baron Piers and Lady Ilane are not fools," replied King Jonathan. "They have given us three good, worthy knights already."

Lord Wyldon gave a reluctant nod. Anders, Inness, and Conal of Mindelan were credits to their training. The realm would feel the loss of Anders—whose war wounds could never heal entirely—from the active duty rolls. It would take years to replace those who were killed or maimed in the Immortals War.

"Sire, please, think this through," Wyldon said. "We need the realm's sons. Girls are fragile, more emotional, easier to frighten. They are not as strong in their arms and shoulders as men. They tire easily. This girl would get any warriors who serve with her killed on some dark night."

Alanna started to get up. This time King Jonathan walked out from behind his desk. Standing beside his Champion, he gripped one of her shoulders, keeping her in her chair.

"But I will be fair," Wyldon continued. His brown eyes were hard. "Let her be on probation for a year. By the end of the summer field camp, if she has not convinced me of her ability to keep up, she must go home."

"Who judges her fitness?" inquired the king.

Wyldon's lips tightened. "Who but the training master, sire? I have the most experience in evaluating the young for their roles as future knights."

Alanna turned to stare at the king. "No boy

has ever undergone a probationary period!" she cried.

Wyldon raised his good shoulder in a shrug. "Perhaps they should. For now, I will not tender my resignation over this, provided I judge whether this girl stays or goes in one year's time."

The king weighed the request. Alanna fidgeted. She knew Lord Wyldon meant his threat, and the crown needed him. Too many great nobles, dismayed by the changes in Tortall since Jonathan's coronation, felt that Wyldon was their voice at court. If he resigned, the king and queen would find it hard to get support for their future changes.

At last King Jonathan said, "Though we do not always agree, my lord, you know I respect you because you are fair and honorable. I would hate to see that fairness, that honor, tainted in any way. Keladry of Mindelan shall have a year's probation."

Lord Wyldon nodded, then inspected the nails on his good hand. "There is one other matter," he remarked slowly. He looked at Alanna. "Do you plan to involve yourself in the girl's training? It will not do."

Alanna bristled. "What is that supposed to mean?"

"You wish to help the girl, understandably." Wyldon spoke as though the mild words made his teeth hurt. "But you rarely deal with the lads, my lady. If you help the girl, it will be said that you eased her path in some special way. There are rumors that your successes are due to your magical Gift."

"By the Goddess," snapped Alanna, crimson with fury. If the king had not forbidden her to challenge men on personal grounds years before, she would have taken Wyldon out to the dueling court and made him regret his words.

"Alanna, for heaven's sake, you know the gossip," King Jonathan said. "Stop acting as if you'd never heard it before." He looked at Wyldon. "And you suggest…"

"Lady Alanna must keep from all contact with the girl," Wyldon replied firmly. "Even a moment's conversation will give rise to suspicion."

"All contact?" cried Alanna. "But she'll be the only girl among over twenty boys! She'll have questions—I could help—" She realized what she had said and fell silent.

King Jonathan gently patted her shoulder. "Is there no other way?" he asked.

Wyldon shook his head. "I fear not, sire. The Mindelan girl will be the cause of trouble as it is, without the Lioness hovering over her."

The king thought it over. At last he sighed. "Lord Wyldon has the right of it. You must stay away from Keladry of Mindelan, Alanna."

"But Jonathan—sire—" she pleaded, not believing he would do this.

"That is an order, lady knight. If you cannot accept that, say as much now, and I will find you work elsewhere."

She stared at him for a long moment, lips

tight. At last she got to her feet. "Don't tax your-self. I'll find knight's work myself," she told him. "As far from Corus as possible." She stalked out of the room, slamming the door in her wake.

The men stared at the door. Each of them was trying to remember if Alanna the Lioness had ever spoken to Jonathan in that tone before.

* * *

Baron Piers and Lady Ilane of Mindelan watched Keladry read the reply from the training master. A Tortallan who did not know them well might have thought the man and woman felt nothing, and that their ten-year-old daughter was only concerned, not upset. That was far from true. The family had spent the last six years living in the Yamani Islands, where displays of deep emotion were regarded as shameful. To get the Yamanis to respect them, they had all learned to hide their feelings. Home in Mindelan again, they still acted as Yamanis, hiding uneasiness and even distress behind still faces.

Kel struggled to reread the letter, afraid to say a word. If she did, her shaking voice would give her away. Instead she waited as she tried to control the anger and sense of betrayal that filled her.

"It is not the reply we expected," Baron Piers said at last. He was a short, stocky man. Keladry had his build, delicate nose, and dreamy, long-lashed hazel eyes. Her brown hair was several shades lighter than his. When Kel did not reply he continued, "His declaration of ten years ago was that girls could become pages. Nothing was said of probation then."

"Keladry?" asked her mother. "You can say what you feel. We are no longer among the Yamanis." She was a thin, elegant woman, taller than her husband by nearly a head, with hair that had gone white very early in life and a deep, musical voice. All Keladry had from her was height. At the age of ten the girl was already five feet tall and still growing.

It took Kel a moment to register what her mother had said. She tried a smile. "But, Mama, I don't want to get into bad habits, in case I go back with you." She looked at Lord Wyldon's letter again. She had expected to be a page when her parents returned to the Yamani Islands in eighteen months. From the tone of this letter, perhaps she ought not to count on that.

"It isn't right," she said quietly, even fiercely. "No boys have probation. I'm supposed to be treated the same."

"Don't give your answer yet," Baron Piers said quickly. "Take the letter with you. Think about what it says. You're not hasty, Kel—this is a bad time to start."

"Reflect as if you have all of time, even when time is short," added her mother in Yamani. "Be as stone."

Kel bowed Yamani-style, palms flat on her thighs. Then she went to find someplace quiet to think.

First she went to her room beside the nursery.

That wasn't a good choice. Two of her brothers' young families lived at Mindelan. With the children and their nursemaids next door, there was enough noise to drown out trumpets. No one had seen her creep into the room, but her oldest nephew saw her leaving it. Nothing would do for him but that she give him a piggyback ride around the large room. After that, all of the older children wanted rides of their own. Once that was done, the nursemaids helped Kel to escape.

She tried to hole up by the fountain in the castle garden, but her sisters-in-law were there, sewing and gossiping with their maids. The kitchen garden was her next choice, but two servants were there gathering vegetables. She stared longingly at her favorite childhood spot, the highest tower in the castle, and felt a surge of anger. Before they had gone to the islands her brother Conal had teasingly held her over the edge of the tower balcony. Until that time she had visited the top of that tower at least once a day. Now the thought of it made her shudder.

There were hundreds of places she might use around the castle, but they were all indoors. She needed to be outside. She was trying to think of a place when she remembered the broad, shallow Domin River, which ran through the woods. No one would be there. She could sit by the water and think in peace.

"Miss?" called a voice as she strode through the inner gate in the castle wall. "Where might you be going?"

Kel turned to face the man-at-arms who had called to her. "I don't know."

The man held out a small horn. "If you're not going to the village, you need one of these." He spoke carefully. The baron and his family had been home only for three months, and the people were still not sure what to make of these strange, Yamani-like nobles. "They told you the rule, surely. Any time you go outside the castle or village, you take a horn. You never know when one of them monsters, centaurs or giants or whatever, will show its face."

Kel frowned. The legendary creatures that had returned to their world five years before had an unnerving way of showing up when they were least expected. For every one that was harmless or willing to get on with humans, there were fistfuls that weren't. Bands of men-at-arms now roamed throughout the fiefdom, searching for hostile visitors and listening for the horn call, which meant someone was in trouble.

I'm not going very far, she wanted to argue, but the Yamanis had taught her to obey a soldier's commands. She accepted the horn with a quiet thank-you and slung it over one shoulder. Checking that Lord Wyldon's letter was tucked securely in the front of her shirt, she left the road that led from the castle gate and headed through their orchards. Once past the cultivated trees she entered the woods, following a trail down to the water.

By the time she could see a glint of silver

through the trees she had worked up a mild sweat. The day was warm and the walk was longer than she had thought it would be. When a rock worked its way into her shoe, she sat on a log to get it out.

"It's not right," she muttered to herself, undoing the laces that held the leather around her ankle. "You're a page for four years. That's how it's been done for centuries. Now they're going to change it?" When she up-ended the shoe and shook it, nothing fell out. She stuffed a hand inside, feeling around for the stone. "And just because I'm a girl? They ought to treat me the same. All I want is the same chance as the boys. No more, no less. That's right, isn't it?" She winced as a sharp edge nipped one of her fingers. Working more carefully, she wiggled the bit of rock out of a fold in the leather. "Probation is not fair, and knighthood training has to be fair."

The stone was out; her mind was made up. If they couldn't treat her the same as they would the boys, then she wasn't going to settle for a half portion. She would have to become a warrior some other way.

Kel sighed and put her shoe back on. The problem was that now she would have to wait. The Queen's Riders took volunteers when they were fifteen or older. The queen's ladies, those who were expected to ride, handle a bow, and deal with trouble at Queen Thayet's side, went to her in their fifteenth year as well. And who was to say Kel wouldn't be living in the Yamani Islands by then?

One thing she knew: convent school, the normal destination for noble girls her age, was not a choice. Kel had no interest whatever in ladylike arts, and even less interest in the skills needed to attract a husband or manage a castle. Even if she did, who would have her? Once she'd overheard her sisters-in-law comment that no man would be interested in a girl who was built along the lines of a cow.

She'd made the mistake of repeating that comment to her mother, when Kel's plan to be a page had first come up. Her mother had gone white with fury and had put her daughters-in-law to mending several years' worth of old linens. It had taken a great deal of persuasion for Kel to convince her mother that her quest for knighthood did not mean she wanted to settle for second best, knowing she would never marry. Getting Ilane of Mindelan to agree to her being a page had been a negotiation every bit as complicated as what her father had done to get the Yamanis to sign the treaty.

And see the good that did me, Kel thought with disgust. Lord Wyldon offers me second best anyway, and I won't take it. I could have saved my breath talking Mama around.

She was ready to get to her feet when the sound of bodies crashing through the brush made her look up. Gruff voices reached her ear.

"Hurry up!" a boy growled from near the river. "Do you want us t'get caught?"

"The Cow's at home," replied a second boy's

voice. "She stays there all morning."

Kel stood, listening. If they were on the look-out for her, then they were up to something bad. In just three months she had taught the local boys she was someone to respect. Kel grabbed a sturdy fallen branch and ran toward the voices. Racing into open ground between the trees and river, she saw three village boys. They were about to throw a wriggling cloth sack into the Domin.

Her mouth settled into a tight, angry line; her hazel eyes glittered. "Put that down!" she cried.

TAMORA PIERCE captured the imagination of readers everywhere with *Alanna: The First Adventure*. Since then she has written seventeen books: two completed quartets set in the fantasy realm of Tortall: The Song of the Lioness, The Immortals, as well as the first three books of the Protector of the Small quartet. She has also written the Circle of Magic books and the first two books of what will be The Circle Opens. Ms. Pierce's fast-paced, suspenseful writing and strong, believable heroines have won her much praise; *Emperor Mage* was a 1996 ALA Best Book for Young Adults and *The Realms of the Gods* was named an "outstanding fantasy novel" by VOYA in 1996.

An avid reader herself, Ms. Pierce graduated from the University of Pennsylvania. She has worked at a variety of jobs and written everything from novels to radio plays. She lives in New York City with her husband, also a writer, and their three cats, two birds, and various rescued wildlife.

Visit Tamora Pierce's Web site
for more information at:

www.sff.net/people/tamora.pierce